The Destiny of Salmon

a novel by

Mitch Evich

Dedication

This book is dedicated to Joseph DeRoche (1938-2013)—poet, mentor, editor, and friend. Unlike some editors, who want to take ownership of an author's manuscript, Joe's intent was largely passive, in a good way. He grasped that I largely knew what I was doing. His role, basically, was to restrain me from my own excess. A key suggestion that Joe made about *The Destiny of Salmon* was that I open the narrative with the fishing boat leaving Bellingham, en route to southeastern Alaska. Originally, I'd filled in the book's back story—a couple of chapters on dry land to introduce the characters.

Joe's suggestions were always commonsensical. He was expert at curbing young writers of the sin of overwriting. He had grown up in coastal Maine, and one reason he liked my novel was that my fictional depiction of Mike Kristiansen reminded Joe of his own father. Joe took his Catholicism seriously—he was an ordained Franciscan priest, but never led a congregation. His poetry was formal and disciplined, but also infused with musicality and humor. I recall going to one of his poetry readings, attended by a large gathering of undergraduates, and he held his young audience in rapt attention.

I finished a draft of my novel in the summer of 1989, in less than a year, and asked Joe to read it. A couple of months later I received a letter from him, commenting: "I've worked with a number of writers, in and out of the University, but without exception you're the one that works the hardest with structure, and has the keenest sense of how to put something together, tear it down, and build it back up. And you're also the one who has the clearest dedication to what I think of as serious writing that I expect to see." In a lighter vein, he declared, "And if you stop writing, you should be shot by a firing squad of disappointed readers."

At that point, I was ecstatic. But within six months, I was in the doldrums. Throughout the eighties, the publishing industry was in flux. Largely gone were the days when publishers would take risks with young novelists on a regular basis. And the number of small presses was dwindling. For a brief period, I was brimming with optimism. I'd met Russell Banks, a novelist I venerated. Banks put me in touch with his agent, and I was asked to submit a few sample chapters of my fiction. Soon the agent agreed to read the entire manuscript. Then I waited for a reply. By then, summer was long gone, and we were in what Germans call the *Totenmonat*—November, the month of death. In this dreary atmosphere, I learned that Russell Banks' agent had declined to represent my novel.

It was at this point that I started thinking of myself as a "struggling writer." I'd met my wife, Paula, in a graduate seminar, but I didn't see her again for about another year, in a chance encounter. We both knew how to live with little money. When our first child arrived, in the early nineties, our challenges compounded. We'd been working as adjunct lecturers, and the pay was exceedingly low. I found myself in adjunct-instructor hell, and, some days, I taught courses at both Northeastern and Boston Universities. The colleges were about a mile apart, and I would hoof it to each campus. Throughout that period, and over the following two decades when I held full-time jobs as an editor and reporter, I continued to write, often both before and after work, producing my novel *The Clandestine Novelist* and a book of essays, *A Geography of Peril*, in addition to a number of short stories.

By the late nineties, and through today, self-publishing has become ridiculously easy—often tempting writers to publish well before their work is ready to be read. Well, in my case, I have been waiting to publish this novel for almost 30 years: I am ready to give birth.

Chapter 1

The water was calm the morning we left Bellingham, and the *Ambition* didn't roll at all. The sun came up, first just a sliver of orange above the crests of the Cascades, then a flame too hot to look at. Dad took off his mackinaw and pulled from his shirt pocket a pair of wire-rimmed sunglasses, wiped them with his sleeve, and put them on. Then he reversed his cap, picked up the log book, and jotted something down. "We're on our way, Pete," he said with a grin.

I was pretty glad to be getting started myself, although you wouldn't have known it from the look I gave Dad.

"Don't be such a poor sport. We're on our way to the land of the midnight sun."

We sat on a wooden bench atop the cabin. The sunlight made the water glitter, and in the mountains purple shadows had spread over fields of snow. "The sun won't really be up at midnight, will it?"

"Not where we are," Dad replied. "But it'll stay up real late. Give us more time to fish."

"Yeah. And less to sleep."

"Aw, come on, Pete, don't be such a wimp." Dad nudged me in the shoulder. "We'll get a few hours in. That's all you need when you're on the fish."

"I don't know about you," I said, putting up a forearm to fend off the glare, "but I kinda like having time to sleep."

"I do, too, Peter. But we'll have time to catch up." He glanced toward the sandy brown bluff of Point Roberts, near the Canadian border, one of the places we normally fished.

"Now look at all this," he said, gesturing around at the bluff, the hills full of fir trees, and the huge white cone of Mount Baker. "Could you ask for a better day to be leaving town?" He turned and breathed deeply through his nose. "And can you smell that? George must be cooking something good. Find out when the heck we're gonna eat."

I headed toward the ladder at the rear of the cabin but George was already on his way up, carrying the first of two heavy ceramic plates filled with scrambled eggs and fried potatoes and slices of honeydew. After that he passed up mugs of coffee. I set the hot mugs down quickly, and brought the food to Dad. Pretty soon George joined us, in his beige hunting jacket with furry white lapels. Just an hour or two earlier, at the dock in Bellingham, he'd said goodbye to Debbie, his wife. It looked funny when he hugged her, she being so pregnant. And George himself wasn't the slimmest guy in the world.

"This calls for a toast," he said now, holding out his mug. "To Alaska!"

"To Alaska." Dad's voice was quieter. Then we all clinked mugs.

"To the *Ambition*!" George said. "To the salmon, and to their beautiful silver hides."

Dad said, "God bless the salmon," and George said, "God bless money," and Dad said, "God bless forty cents a pound." George rubbed his big hands together. "Damn it, we're gonna do good! God bless this country."

"I wouldn't go that far," Dad replied.

"Then God bless this voyage. May it be safe and profitable. And not necessarily in that order."

Dad frowned. "But isn't that bad luck?"

"I don't know," George said. "Should I knock on wood?"

"You could whistle."

"And whistle up a storm?"

Dad set down his fork. "That's what my grandfather believed."

"They didn't have radar," George pointed out. Again he raised his mug. "To radar! To the fathometer! To that sleek young Caterpillar engine!"

Dad glanced at George and grinned. "I think we should have gotten a virgin to piss on the net. That's what the old Yugoslavs did."

"That's gross," I said.

"Oh I don't know," George said. "I think it would be quite a ceremony."

I looked down at my plate and frowned, sniffing the grease and onion smell of the potatoes. I speared the last of the potatoes with my fork, swallowed, and headed down the ladder. I slid open the door at the rear of the cabin and slipped inside. The galley was hot from the oil stove, full of the frying smell. Wade Norton sat nearest to me, wearing his maroon varsity sweatshirt with cut-off sleeves. He was shoveling in chunks of ketchup-drenched scrambled eggs. Closer to the stove Gordon Booker had lit his pipe and was reading *Time* magazine, his thick dark hair wound in a ponytail.

Wade put down his fork, his cheeks still bulging. "Your dad gonna take the wheel all the way to Alaska?"

"How should I know?"

"Come on, man," Wade smirked. "It's only seventy-two hours."

"I think he'll sleep some of the time."

"He'd better. He's got to get his rest, so he can catch us lots of fish."

I fiddled with the buckle on my belt, then glanced at my watch. "I think he knows that."

"Yeah, I guess he would." Wade smiled. "Your Dad has to catch a whole shitload this summer, doesn't he?"

Gordon looked up from his magazine. He was a biology teacher at my high school, and probably used to handling guys like Wade. Wade once said Gordon was a homo, because of his hair. I had been less than thrilled when Dad told me he'd hired Wade, my least favorite classmate, for the summer.

"That's rule number one on a fishing boat," Gordon told Wade. "You're not supposed to say bad things about the skipper."

"Can't I say what I think? It's a free country, isn't it?"

"Sure it is. But this is a fishing boat, not a democracy. If you don't like things, you quit. You don't bitch. You just quit."

"Who said I was bitching?"

"No one did." Gordon took a drag on his pipe. Wade glared at him. I glared at Wade, and he glared back at me. Then I asked him to get out of my way. I tried to say it in a tough voice, but instead I sounded as if I were asking him for a favor. Wade smiled and said, "Of course I'll get out of your way."

I climbed the ladder to the cabin-top. It felt good to be back outside, the wind blowing lightly from the northwest, down the wide throat of Georgia Strait. I liked the way the water stretched in front of us, a path to lead us from all our problems. I crossed the flying bridge and tapped Dad on the shoulder. "If you get tired," I said, "I'll take the wheel as soon as I finish the dishes."

"Thanks, but I feel fine. I'll be good for most of the day."

"Will you sleep tonight?"

"I'll sleep great."

"I'm going to take a nap after doing the dishes, then."

"Sure. Go ahead and sleep." He was staring at a navigation chart.

"Dad?" I said. "Couldn't you have found some other way to pay back Wade's dad?"

Dad's old boat, the *Stavenger*, had been leaking a lot the summer before, and Wade's father did the work real cheap when he took the boat up on the ways. Dad said, "Mr. Norton's probably the best shipwright in town. Wade's a small price for that."

I said, "For you, maybe," and went back down to the galley to wash dishes. Gordon was still reading. Dad hadn't been crazy about hiring him, either. It was only because our regular skiffman had quit to go fish with his uncle in Bristol Bay. That was the trouble with crewmen, Dad had said. You couldn't always depend on them. Except for George, who had fished with Dad for years.

When I was done, I went to my bunk in the fo'c'sle. The cadence of the engine made it easy to fall asleep. It sounded almost exactly like the *Stavenger*. Dad's grandfather had built the boat sometime around the end of World War I, and Dad never would have sold it if he hadn't decided to go to Alaska. The *Stavenger* was sixty-four feet long, longer than the law allowed for fishing up north, and the *Ambition* was only fifty-two. Mom wasn't happy when she'd heard what Dad wanted to do, but by then they were separated.

When I woke up, Dad was still at the wheel, with George and Gordon. Dad spread a chart on the bench, and counted the miles to Campbell River, the closest town. Then he rubbed his jaw and shook his head and told me to go get Wade and take a look at the bilge. "See how high the water's come up against the shaft boards. And be careful. That shaft's gonna be spinning full speed."

When I asked what was wrong, Dad said, "That's what I want you to find out." I headed back down the ladder, called for Wade to come out of the galley, and together we lifted the hatch boards and climbed into the hold. We wedged our fingers in at the sides of the plywood that covered the shaft alley and pried it open. The floorboards were slimed with oil and it was hard keeping my boots in one place. The next thing I knew I was flat on my ass, and water was flying everywhere. It stained the walls of the fish hold and speckled Wade's face and arms. "What the hell?" I heard him yell. But there wasn't time to stand there listening. I climbed out of the hold and went to tell Dad. He told me to hold the wheel while he and George checked things out.

When Dad returned, he had an expression that meant everything was fine. At least that's what he wanted it to mean. He wiped his hands, still coated in grease and bilge water, on the thighs of his jeans. "Leaking a little worse than I figured," he finally said. "Just means we'll have to pump out a little more often."

"You sure?"

"Sure as I can be," he said, and shrugged. After a moment I said, "I hope you're right," and he shrugged again.

He stayed on top the cabin until it was dark. Even then, Gordon and I had to talk him into turning over the wheel. As soon as Dad was gone Gordon lit his pipe and took a long, slow drag.

Then he said, "I think we're heading into unexplored territory." His pipe bowl glowed like a miniature torch.

"You mean you're not sure where we're going?" I asked, realizing, more clearly than before, that I sure didn't.

"I mean with your father finally going to bed." Gordon sucked again on the pipe. The smoke smelled like red rope-licorice. "I call it first-time-in-Alaska syndrome. Guys like your dad never want to give up the wheel."

I stared into the dark, trying to make out the fuzzy shoreline. You could just barely see it beneath the half-moon above the mainland. I looked down at the water. It extended a few yards in front of us, and then there was blackness. Next to Gordon a shaft of light swept round the radar screen, each time illuminating a pale gray outline of the shore, and dots for each boat ahead of us. We were the small bright point in the center.

"Wade thinks he doesn't know what he's doing."

Gordon grinned. "Every crew has someone like Wade. I think it's necessary—from a social point of view. The rest of the guys need someone to vent their frustration on."

"Better him than me."

"You're damn right it is." Gordon leaned back, one hand still on the wheel. "The first year I fished, up in Kodiak, I had hair a lot longer than it is now. So you can imagine what the crew thought of *me*. They probably figured I was some sort of hybrid, a pale-skinned Native American."

"But you stuck it out."

"Kind of hard to quit once you're out fishing. Besides, the money was good. Guys will put up with a real bastard of a skipper so long as he's making them money."

Again I thought of Wade, and of Mom, and of a fisherman named Bud Peters, who looked at Dad strangely when Dad told him he was going north.

"I'm still afraid we're gonna do lousy."

Gordon took another drag on his pipe, then set it down and rubbed one of his eyebrows. Sometimes he made me nervous the way he talked, like everything was a riddle I had to figure out on my own. He was a good teacher, though. I still felt bad about the times I fell asleep in his class.

"That's the first thing a person ought to know about fishing," he told me. "That in the end you can't really control how you do."

Off our port were the lights of Campbell River, dense along the shoreline, scattered higher on the hill. Sour smoke from the pulp mills drifted across the water, and cars flowed along the waterfront like magnified blood cells. I thought about how nice it would be to pull into the harbor and sleep, to forget about everything until the next day. It was a lot easier in the daytime to know where you were going.

But we went past the city and headed for Seymour Narrows, the tiny channel that led into Johnstone Strait. Dad came back on top as soon as we started to get close. I poured him a cup of lukewarm coffee and he drank it very quickly, then he took back the wheel. Gordon motioned toward the rocky wall at the far side of the narrows. "A lot of boats have sunk here over the years."

"I know that," Dad replied.

"How?" I asked.

"Crazy tides, Pete," Gordon said. "Tricky as hell."

"My father used to tell me about boats being driven backwards by the current," Dad said. "Damn, I wish right now I had a better chart."

"Stay out of the middle," Gordon said, "and you'll be fine."

Dad nodded.

"I'll help take it through if you want."

"That's OK." Dad gazed straight ahead. "Flash the spotlight, Pete. I don't really want to hit a log right now."

The spotlight sat mounted on the rim of the flying bridge. I rotated it back and forth, but I still couldn't see much. Just handling the damn thing made me nervous. It was as if I was now responsible for whatever happened next.

We came around a bend in the narrow and the tide caught us and swept us along at almost double speed. The boat squirmed like a fumbled football, leaning far to starboard, so all at once we had to grasp the railing. Dad's coffee mug flew off the counter and he said "fuck!" and grabbed the wheel and cranked it hard to port. Then we came back the other way so it seemed like we lay almost sideways against the black water and something in my stomach rose into my throat and almost into my mouth.

"Shine the spotlight, Peter! I can't see where the hell I'm going!"

The tide boiled in huge pools. A tiny fir tree floated by, drawn into my circle of light, and then was sucked beneath the surface.

"Are we stuck?" I shouted, but Dad replied, "We're fine, Peter." Now his voice sounded calm, maybe too calm.

He twisted the wheel back to starboard and the boat popped upright, and we glided forward, just as before. Gordon bent over to pick up his pipe. "Gotta be careful of those eddies," he said.

"So I see." Dad gripped the wheel with both hands. He grabbed a napkin off the dashboard and wiped his forehead.

"You want to go down and rest?" I asked.

"Not much point in that now. Gordon, why don't you go sleep and I'll wake you and George in a few hours."

Gordon picked up his jacket and his pipe and headed down the ladder. Dad told me to go check the bilge, so I followed Gordon into the galley, found a flashlight, and climbed into the fish hold. The water seemed almost as high as when Wade and I had looked at it. I hoisted myself back out of the hold, grabbed the steel pump handle from the side of the cabin and jammed it into the slot at the base of the pump.

I took the deck bucket out of the john and flung it over the side to get some water to prime the pump. The bucket skimmed along the water's surface and I wrapped its slim yellow line around my wrist. Just then I felt a jerk, the kind a sport fisherman must feel when he hooks a big one. The bucket had gone all the way under, dragging me against the bulwarks, my sneakers skidding along the deck. "Damn it!" I said. I braced one knee against the side and pulled as hard as I could. When I finally wrestled the bucket back on board, half the water sloshed out and soaked my socks and shoes.

"Son of a bitch!"

I wish I had a joint, I told myself. Because it would calm me down. But it would be a hassle to get the weed out of the locker beneath my bunk. And Dad wouldn't like it. Not after the promise I'd made. I said I wouldn't touch the weed all summer long, unless things got really bad. And they aren't that bad. Not as bad as they've been.

I thought of a story Dad had told me about when he was a kid, how he and Ed McGregor hiked up some creek shit-faced, and clubbed a couple spawning salmon with baseball bats. He said they thought it was pretty funny while they were doing it. But afterwards they felt kind of sick. It occurred to me now that Dad would have smoked pot, too, if it had been around back then.

I poured the water into the bilge pump, to prime it. Nothing happened at first, so I pumped a little harder. The pump made a loud sucking noise and spit out an oily wad of grease and seaweed and God knows what. It smelled like a sewer and made a mess of the deck. But at least now the water was flooding out. I pumped with quick, short strokes, first one hundred, then three hundred, then six hundred, until my wrists ached and I had trouble keeping count. When the pump finally gasped for air, I hurried up the ladder to tell Dad. "Eleven hundred strokes," I said.

"That's worse than before." He tried to laugh. "Guess I won't be sleeping much tonight."

"But you've got to."

"At some point I do."

I clenched and unclenched my fists, and massaged my forearms. "You gonna be able to fix this thing?"

"Jesus, Pete, it's not like we have much choice."

"But how much will it cost?" I asked, and as soon as I did, I wished I hadn't. I didn't like thinking about money any more than Dad did. Especially the money he owed the bank.

"We'll talk about that stuff after the season," Dad said. "Not now.

"But it kind of scares me, too," he said, quietly. He lowered his head and rubbed his neck. "But only a little. If we don't talk about it, maybe it will go away."

The shoreline was harder to see now, the channel a lot wider, and Dad was moving us toward the middle. He was gnawing on the fingernail of his thumb. I sighed and stared at the half-moon, now almost directly overhead. I couldn't tell if he was serious or not. That's what Mom said—that Dad wanted to wish away all the problems in the world. Not that Mom was one to talk.

After a minute Dad looked up too. "Can you see the constellations?"

"I can see the Big Dipper."

"That's too easy. How about Taurus?"

I tried to find something that looked like a bull.

"No, look," Dad said. "Those stars right there are its horns. And farther back, that's its tail."

"So where are its balls?"

"I don't know, Pete. You tell me."

I looked harder, but still the bull failed to take shape. I wondered if maybe the people who named those things had better imaginations than us. They probably had a lot more time to just sit around and stare into the sky. But Dad said we'd have some time for that, too, at least during the first couple weeks. I asked when we'd reach the ocean and he said early the next afternoon, and that it would blow a bit northwesterly.

All the years we'd fished in Puget Sound, we'd never really been out in the open. Once in a while it got a little rough in the Strait of Georgia, and then the *Stavenger* would roll from side to side and sometimes a plate or a bowl of salad would slide off the galley table and crash against the floor. One time I even started feeling a little sick, thanks to this really fatty bacon George had fried for breakfast.

Dad said things might be a lot different in a smaller boat like the *Ambition*. "But I wouldn't worry too much about it," he told me now. "Cause we'll find out soon enough.

"Oh, and Pete? Could you make me another cup of that instant coffee? Then wake George and go to bed."

So I mixed the coffee and brought it to Dad and then I climbed into the fo'c'sle and shook George by the shoulder. He blinked and rolled over, face down on his mattress. I shook him again and his hand jerked up and almost hit me in the face. He mumbled that he was sorry, lowered himself onto the floor, stuck one of his big arms through a sleeve of his shirt and bent down to pull on his boots.

I got into my bunk, took off my socks and shoes, stacked them in a corner where I wouldn't hit them with my legs, slipped out of my jeans, and pulled the sleeping bag all the way over my head. No one can touch me in here, I thought. I am a caterpillar and this is my cocoon. In the morning I will climb out as a butterfly. But not a butterfly. Something stronger and less delicate. Something that doesn't get all crumpled looking the first time it rains.

By the next day the boat was rolling from side to side, but it was a nice, easy motion, like a carnival ride at a slower than normal speed. Gordon held the wheel on top of the cabin, with George to one side of him, the navigation charts stacked in his lap. Dad sat straight up, his arms folded, his head down and his eyes closed. I looked at him and whispered, "Why doesn't he go down to his bunk?"

"Says he can't sleep down there," George said.

Dad jerked up his head, blinked, looked around, and asked where we were. "It'll still be a few hours before we hit the ocean," Gordon told him. "You want to try to sleep?"

"What the hell. Just make sure you pump out every hour." He got to his feet and climbed slowly down the ladder.

"It's about time," I said. "I thought he was gonna sit up here the whole trip."

"That's just Mike," George said. He stood up all of a sudden and pointed. Ten yards off the bow something was thrashing around in a crisscrossing motion. Gordon and I stood up, too.

"Look at that!" George said. "A baby Killer Whale!"

"It's a porpoise," Gordon insisted, but George said, "The hell it is. And look—there's three more!"

Now they glided right alongside us, sometimes cutting in front of the boat, corkscrewing so that their pale bellies glowed beneath the green water. They had the same black-and-white orca markings on their backs as a killer whale, even a shiny, black dorsal fin.

"Trust me, George," Gordon repeated, "they're porpoises."

"I bet they're having fun," I said.

Gordon's head stayed steady, following them. "Either that or they're warning us of something."

George snorted. "Is that what they taught you in biology school?"

"That's what I learned up in Kodiak, before the *Katharine K* sank."

We all leaned over the railing on the flying bridge. I felt Wade's hand on my shoulder, his tobacco-juice breath hot on my neck. "What's the big thrill?" he asked.

"Porpoises." Gordon pointed to where two dorsal fins had broken the surface, a pair of smooth black backs rising from the water.

"Cool. Makes me wish I had my pellet gun."

"And I bet you like to blow away seals, too," Gordon said.

Wade shook his head. "I was only kidding. Unless a seal is trying to steal your salmon. Then you've gotta do something—at least scare them away."

"Don't they have a right to the salmon, too?" I asked.

"Jesus, Peter, what kind of a fisherman are you?"

I'd never fired a gun, even though Dad sometimes invited me on his hunting trips. Dad admitted that he went along mainly to be with his friends, and sometimes he came home tired, or maybe a little drunk, complaining how he'd wasted a whole day. But I didn't mention this to Wade. I didn't want to deal with it.

"Good fishermen play by the rules," Gordon said to Wade, "and blasting away seals usually isn't among them. Fishing can be a terrible thing, in its own right, when you think about what we do. But it can be beautiful, too."

"It's a way to make money."

"Maybe for you," George said, "but Gordon's right. We kill fish so we can live."

"That's corny. You guys just think about things too much."

"Evidently," Gordon replied, "that's not a problem for you."

Wade pulled out a can of Skoal, twisted loose the tin cap, squeezed out a pinch of the damp brown stuff inside, and slipped the container back into the thigh pocket of his jeans. Then he spat into an empty pop can. "When we gonna get to the ocean?"

"Any hour now." Gordon was measuring something on the chart. "Better strap yourself in. It's going to be rolling quite a lot."

Wade said, "I kind of like it when it rolls."

George and Gordon looked at each other and laughed. "You may not like this," George said.

Two hours later Dad was out of his bunk and we were leaving the protection of Vancouver Island. Dad made a security call to two boats a couple hours ahead of us. They said the weather was fine—a big swell but nothing dangerous. "Sounds good to us," Dad said into the microphone. He hung the microphone on its hook. "Here we go," he said.

George served baloney sandwiches with lettuce and mayonnaise, Fritos, cookies, and pop. I ate mine too quickly. Then we were out in the ocean and I could see the breakers crash against the rocks at the base of the lighthouse on the mainland. We were taking the waves head on now, riding through them as if they were short, quick dips in a roller coaster. All five of us stood on the flying bridge, gripping the railing. We kept dipping into the trough and slamming against the water, our faces wet from the spray.

It was fun at first. But then I wished I hadn't eaten the sandwich and that George hadn't put so much mayonnaise on mine. It was nothing that a couple Rolaids shouldn't have cured. But I ate two of the chalky tablets and then four and the indigestion kept getting worse. Dad locked both hands around the wheel and looked at me. "How you doing, Pete?"

"Just fine," I said.

"What about you, Wade?"

"I shouldn't have eaten so damned many cookies."

Gordon smirked. Wade gave him a dirty look.

"I think I'll go down and try to read," I said.

"Don't, Pete," Dad said. "It's not a good idea."

"I think it might help. You know, get my mind off things."

I got through two paragraphs of an article in *Sports Illustrated* and then the nausea got worse and then it was so bad that I wished I could throw up right away and get it over with. But it wasn't as easy as that. I climbed back on top the cabin and gripped the railing. I leaned over the side of the flying bridge and tried to suck in the fresh air. Instead I got a whiff of diesel fumes from the fuel tanks. Now when I looked ahead, every wall of water seemed taller, more frightening. I lowered my head and breathed hard and deep, but it didn't really help. A tingly feeling numbed my feet and hands, and the taste of baloney was rising in my throat.

Wade wasn't doing any better. His face had lost some of its color, and he was staring straight ahead. His eyes narrowed and he clenched his teeth.

"How we all doin'?" Dad asked.

"I'm OK," I said.

"I'm doing fine," said Wade.

"Hold it," Gordon said. "I'll get something for you." He staggered across the top of the cabin to the ladder at the rear. Twice he had to stop and clench onto the railing at the side.

"Be careful!" Dad shouted.

Gordon came back with a rectangular box full of pills and a bottle of water. The pills were inside little pockets of plastic with tinfoil on the back.

"What are they?" I asked.

"Dramamine. Motion-sickness pills."

"I don't *do* drugs," Wade said.

I said, "Give them to me," and tore open two of the plastic pockets and washed down the pills with the water.

"They'll start to work in about twenty minutes," Gordon said. "Until then, just hang on." He swallowed two of the pills himself.

"How long until we get back inside?" I asked.

"About two hours," Dad said. "You gonna be OK?"

"I don't know." I lowered my head again and wondered if maybe it would happen now, in front of everyone. But after a while my mouth went dry and I began to feel drowsy and unconcerned. The snap was out of it. The Dramamine had taken the edge off things. I sat back and watched us bounce against the trough. I was just watching now. I wasn't taking part. I was watching us on TV. I could change channels if I wanted.

"How you doin', Pete?" It was Gordon.

"I'm fine. What about you?"

Gordon grinned back. "I'm doing fine, too."

But Wade was losing the battle. His face was paler now. His teeth cut into his lips. "Fuck it!" he said. He stepped quickly toward the ladder and climbed down onto the deck. Then he clutched the rigging and leaned over the bulwarks.

"Careful, damn it!" Dad shouted.

"That's what he gets for trying to be a tough guy." Gordon was laughing. I laughed along with him. The Dramamine made it easy to laugh.

"Don't rub it in," George said. "He's just a stupid kid."

"The boy's gotta learn someday."

George shook his head. "He can learn without you teaching him."

Back inside Fitz Hugh Sound, Dad tried to go to bed. But the boat was leaking too much for that now. By midnight he was sending someone to pump out every half-hour. I asked if he thought maybe we were going to sink, and he asked if maybe it was time for me to go to bed. I remembered Mom saying that if Dad had any sense, he wouldn't have gotten another wooden boat, not after all the problems with the *Stavenger*.

"Good for her," Dad said when I reminded him. "But I don't think there's much she can do about it right now."

I looked back at the foamy white wake trailing us in the dark. "But what about you? When are you gonna go to bed?"

"When I damn well feel like it."

In the morning Dad was asleep in his bunk near the galley. He had on all his clothes, including his jacket, and he lay on his back with one leg dangling over the edge. It was as if he could jump out of bed and take the wheel before he woke up.

The forest along the shore looked different now. The Douglas firs had given way to something tougher and more bristly. The hills were steeper, with slopes that curved the wrong way, as if they'd been scooped out by giant spoons. A waterfall poured from the top of a cliff. Gordon said this was the North Country, that the scenery would get better the farther north we went.

We kept going for the rest of that day. Dad said we'd limp into Ketchikan one way or another, that I just ought to relax. But it wasn't easy. I read some more of my magazine, I watched the miles creep by on the navigation charts, I tried to calculate at what time we'd finally reach town. Then I went to bed. You could do that, if you tried hard enough. You could sleep and forget where you were, even if you were bouncing around in the open ocean.

But then Wade was pushing the heel of his hand against my head, telling me to hurry up and take his place at the wheel. It was drizzling now, so I put on long underwear and a heavy gray sweater and boots and raingear over that. Then I climbed onto the flying bridge. The air was thick with rain, and Dad needed the radar, even though the sky was already pale. I asked him if maybe we should steer from down below, but he said he didn't want to, he couldn't see things from there, we'd just have to keep ourselves warm as best we could. I boiled water on the stove and made instant coffee and held my hands over the burner and stayed inside a little longer than needed.

We entered a channel with a long Italian name I couldn't pronounce, and finally we saw the faint glow of Ketchikan. "Maybe I should go kiss the earth as soon as we tie up," Dad said, his eyebrows wet from the rain. "You know, like Christopher Columbus."

"Maybe you could claim it for Bellingham."

"Or maybe I could just take a nice warm shower. And you can go call your mother."

I wasn't sure I wanted to. It was easier not to think about it, now that we were apart. I knew damn well that was part of the reason I was up here, to get away from Mom. But I'd wanted to get away from Dad, too. Maybe I would have run away, if I'd had some place to go. Or maybe Dad and I were running away together.

I thought about Christmas Eve, when Mom and Dad's marriage was falling apart. The three of us had gathered around the little fir tree Dad had chopped down and Mom had decorated, smiling and pretending nothing was wrong. We weren't very good at it. Dad had bought Mom the skimpiest negligee I'd ever seen, a little pink lacy thing that was almost transparent and barely high enough to cover the tits of an eighth-grader. I cringed when I saw it, because I don't care how well you know your parents, you just can't imagine them having intercourse. I got the feeling that Mom couldn't imagine it either, because she gave Dad a look that said, It was a nice thought, I guess, but really, Mike—won't you ever grow up? And Dad read the expression as clear as I did, and sighed and said he'd be glad to take it back if it didn't fit.

Then Mom gave Dad a pair of binoculars for the boat, which Dad genuinely appreciated, because I'd broken one of the lenses of the old pair the summer before, fooling around gazing through the damn thing backwards. It was a nice moment, seeing Dad's smile when he tore open the wrapping paper and realized the binoculars were of the Marine Electronics brand, the best in the business. But then Mom said, "I guess you can't say I don't do anything to help out the boat" and I cringed again, because I knew what was coming next.

"You help out lots, honey," Dad said. He was busy reading the back of the box.

"But not as much as I could."

"Whatdidya say?"

Mom sat on the living room carpet with her arms around her knees. A glass of wine was on the bookcase. "Nothing," she replied. She was leaning back and staring at the ceiling. "Nothing we want to talk about on Christmas Eve."

"It must be pretty bad, then," Dad said. He was still reading.

"You're right, Mike," and now Mom's voice was kind of shaky.

Dad set down the binoculars, crossed over to where Mom was, and sat down alongside her. "What is it?"

"Nothing I want to discuss with Peter here."

I got up, muttered "Jesus!" grabbed my coat and headed for the door. Dad said, "Where the hell are *you* going?"

"I'm going for a walk. I don't want to be here when you and Mom start swearing at each other."

"You're not going anywhere. Sit back down."

I did as I was told.

"Let him go," Mom said.

"Oh hell," I said, "Go ahead and fight. See if I give a fuck."

Mom started to cry. Then she said, "You know what I am? A lousy wife and a lousy mother and my son smokes marijuana all the time, and my husband—it's as if I don't even know him. I don't even know what he does for a living."

Dad looked very confused.

"Why can't I be like Ruth Wilson, or Joan Zerenkich? They *like* being married—they like being married to fishermen."

"Ruth Wilson is a domineering bitch," Dad said. "And Joan, to use Peter's term, is an airhead."

"Dad's right," I said. "Mrs. Zerenkich is even ditzier than her daughter. I'd hate to have a mother like that."

"That's sweet of you, Peter." She dabbed at her eyes with the negligee. "But those women, they work on the boats, they're interested in what their husbands are doing."

Dad looked up hopefully. "You want to work on the *Stavenger*, honey? You could be the cook."

Then Mom was shouting at Dad, and I wondered why I hadn't left when I had the chance. "I don't even like boats! That's the problem. I wish you were—I wish you were an architect or an accountant, or even an insurance salesman! I'm sick and tired of being your wife!"

Dad tried to comfort Mom, but it was like trying to comfort an untamed animal. Every time he put his arms around her, Mom twisted away from him and cried even harder.

That was enough for me. I put my coat back on, went to my room, reached inside my desk and brought out my pipe and a little baggie of weed. Then I slipped out the back door. In a few minutes I was nice and stoned.

It was a cloudy night, but warm for December. I walked through the streets of south Bellingham, empty now except for me. I liked being alone. I stared at the red and green Christmas lights on the office buildings until the colors blurred together. I stared at them for a long time. Then I thought: I'll leave. I'll hitchhike on Interstate 5, all the way to California, and pick grapes for a living. It was an awesome plan. I couldn't wait to get going. But it got colder out and began to rain, and the buzz was wearing off, and I was getting hungry as hell. So I turned around and walked home.

Dad was asleep on the couch when I got there, and I thought, At least Mom won't drag us all to church in the morning. I went to the refrigerator and made myself a sandwich of corned beef with Swiss cheese and lots of hot mustard, and I drank a big glass of milk. Then I went to bed and listened to Pink Floyd's *Dark Side of the Moon* until I fell asleep. When I woke up, Dad was gone. Mom said they'd talked for a long time and that there was nothing more to say. She said that maybe she and Dad would be back together in a couple months, but I told her I thought that was a crock of shit. Then Mom started to cry again, and said, Peter, do you have to use such filthy language, and I said, Yes, because you and Dad deserve it. Then she slapped me across the face, and I started to cry, too.

In a couple months Mom was seeing some hot-shot businessman, and Dad—well, Dad had plans of his own. I wasn't crazy about going with him, but the more I thought about it, the more I saw I didn't have much choice. I couldn't bear hanging around Mom and her new boyfriend. His name was Richard Reynolds, and Mom had met him the year before, when she first started working for his real estate company. The newspaper said Mr. Reynolds owned half of Whatcom County. He wore dark slacks and sport coats and ankle-high leather boots that zipped up at the side. And he talked about building this enormous waterfront resort that would draw people with money from Japan and all over the world.

Now I pulled the hood of my rain jacket tighter over my head, and stared at my wrinkly hands. The rain was dripping off the bill of Dad's cap. I asked him, "How long will it take to get that leak fixed?"

"Maybe a day, maybe only half a day if we're lucky. We just gotta make sure we make that first opening."

"What if we don't?"

"Then we're screwed." Dad forced another smile, and wiped his face on the inside of his shirt.

"But I wouldn't worry about it. You got to keep assuming things will work out for the best."

"Don't they always?" I said, gazing toward the haze of lights, the rolls of mist hanging halfway up the gray hills.

Dad shrugged, then cut back the engine and peered through the binoculars toward the harbor. "It helps to think so, Peter," he finally replied.

Chapter 2

We tied up near the shipyard, and Dad and I walked around to where the office was. The door was locked, so I peered through the window. Inside were a couple of folding metal chairs, and desks cluttered with envelopes, engine-part catalogues, and sheets of the crinkly yellow paper you get with a car-repair bill. On one wall hung a smudged calendar picture of a redhead in an orange bikini, cradling in her arms what looked like the chrome tailpipe of a motorcycle. The floor looked oily and needed to be swept. A cardboard sign taped to the door said "8 to 5, Mon-Sat." It was only 6 a.m. Dad muttered something and went back to the boat.

I followed a path through brown weeds and blotches of wet sand stained with oil, past scraps of plywood and heaps of rusted metal, until I came out on the other side of the shipyard. All of Ketchikan seemed built along a single road that skirted the waterfront, penned in by hills. Huge patches of forest were missing, and near the road, cranes had carved an enormous hole out of rock. Houses clung to the slopes as if they'd been dropped there.

I started back toward where Gordon said a cannery would let me shower. Beer cans and wine bottles littered the side of the road, and I passed what must have been last night's vomit, diluted by rain. Every several minutes a seaplane roared overhead. Trucks whizzed by and splashed mud. I was all set to give one guy the finger, until I saw a hunting rifle mounted in the back. Another pick-up shot past, even faster than the others, but came to a hard stop, and then back toward me in reverse.

Inside sat a muscular Indian, wearing jeans, cowboy boots, and a dark-brown leather jacket. He looked about the age of Dad, with big cheekbones and hair wound in a braid. He asked me if I needed a ride somewhere, but I shook my head and told him I was just going down to the cannery.

"But that's a half-mile away. Come on. Get in. You'll get run over, walking that close to the road."

I climbed in and locked the door behind me. The Indian held out his hand. "Robert Frank," he said. After I told him my name he asked if I was off one of the boats.

"Must be its first year up here," he replied, when I told him that Dad ran the *Ambition*. I watched the orange needle on the speedometer. At 40 miles per hour I buckled shut my seatbelt. "You work on a boat?" I asked.

"Not this year I don't. I got a job at the cannery." He pointed at his cap and smiled. A patch stitched onto the crown said Sea-Pac Fisheries. "I'm management. At least that's what the real management tells me. Instead of slicing and dicing the heads off fish, I stand around and watch others do it."

"You think you'll make more there than you could fishing?" I asked.

"This year, you bet. I'm on salary—a guaranteed income."

"But the humpy run is supposed to be real good."

"That's what all the biologists are predicting," Robert Frank replied with a shrug. "But it's a funny thing about scientists. I never know when to believe 'em. And not just because I'm an Indian and all the scientists are white. It's because they're wrong half the time. You ever watch the weather on TV? Some guy in a suit talking about a high-pressure system that's going to bring sun for the next three days. So you go out fishing and it rains and blows like hell."

"But just because the biologists are predicting a good year—that doesn't mean it will be bad, does it?"

"I don't know. A few humpies normally start to show in the creeks around town by now. I haven't seen a goddamned thing."

Robert Frank put on the brakes and eased the truck into neutral. He pointed to a long, narrow shed with walls of corrugated metal, and told me that the men's showers were on the other side. I thanked him and climbed out of the cab.

"I hope your father has good luck this summer," he told me. "We could all use a little good luck."

He waved goodbye, a short jerk of his hand, and drove off. I watched the mud kick up from his wheels and then I walked to the showers. I wished I'd brought a pair of thongs. Pools of water collected in spots where the cement floor sagged, and the pale blue paint on the walls was cracked and peeling. The shower curtain was slimy and the window didn't open. Inside the stall, strands of somebody's hair clung to a bar of soap.

But at least the water was hot. I turned the handle until I could barely stand it, until my skin turned red and the steam rushed through my nose. I stayed under until I almost forgot where I was. Then I wrapped my towel around my waist, tip-toed through the pools on the floor, and wiped the mist from the mirror.

On the left side of my nose were three small zits, which I squeezed one by one. I studied my upper lip to see if anything resembling hair had taken root. Dad, in the three days since we left Bellingham, had a nice start on a beard. I slid a stick of lime-scented Mennen beneath my arms, slipped on a fresh pair of boxer shorts, cleaned my ears with Q-tips, and used the blade of my knife to scrape the black gunk from my fingernails. I combed my hair straight back and then flopped it over the top, so that when it dried I might look like Ric Ocasek of The Cars.

But my hair never got the chance to dry because it was raining a lot harder now and the rain was driven by the wind. Even the hood of my rain jacket wasn't much help. I was pretty well soaked by the time I got back to the boat.

By then it was almost 8 a.m., and Dad was ready to head back to the shipyard. When we got there the office door was still locked, but I thought I heard someone moving around inside. Dad pounded on the door's rectangular window and said, "There better be."

The door opened. Standing there was a man in a brown cardigan over his mechanic's jumpsuit. He motioned us in, his hand scrawny and splotched with brown. "Raining like hell today, isn't it?" he said.

"Yes," Dad replied, his hair dripping. "It is."

The office wasn't much warmer than outdoors, and I wondered if Dad was as cold as I was. By now I had to piss again, and I stood with my legs tight together, hoping we'd get out of here quickly. "That's one thing nice about Ketchikan," the man said. "Droughts ain't never a problem. You from Washington?"

"Yeah. And we got a leak that's pretty bad. Can you get me up on the ways?"

"That depends. Got one boat up there now, as you might've noticed. How's tomorrow morning sound?"

"Not that good. But I can't afford to be picky."

"Fishermen never can. If they could, I'd probably never make any money." The man chuckled, and gazed back out the window. His teeth, I noticed, were stained a dull shade of brown.

Dad's expression stayed the same. "So you'll get us up there first thing tomorrow morning?"

"Before the cock crows twice."

The man's name was Phil Stockman. He told Dad about all the fish we'd catch this summer, how we'd be up to our asses in humpies before we knew it. Dad said that was what everyone was saying.

"That's funny," I said without really thinking, "'cause I just talked to a guy who thinks the run's going to be a failure."

Mr. Stockman stared at me, his brown teeth lit up by the overhead light. "*Who?*"

"Some guy who works for the cannery." When Mr. Stockman kept staring, I added, "I think his name was Frank. His last name."

Mr. Stockman put his hand on Dad's shoulder as if they'd known each other for years. "That must be *Robert* Frank. Not the most reliable fellow in the world, if you know what I mean."

"Peter," Dad said, "what did this Mr. Frank have to say?"

I hesitated, looking for a door that might lead to a toilet. "Not much, actually. Just that there should already be fish in the creeks around here."

"That's ridiculous," Mr. Stockman said. "The fish won't start showing for a couple more weeks."

Dad didn't look so sure. He said something about making the Hidden Falls opener, and Mr. Stockman began another private session of laughter. "Boy, ain't that a crapshoot—one hundred fishing boats crammed into what's really just a goddamned lake. It doesn't surprise me that someone gets shot at once in a while."

"Do you have a bathroom?" I asked.

"Round back," Mr. Stockman said with a jerk of his thumb. He handed me a large key attached to a triangular block of scrapwood with "john" written on it in thick black ink, and started telling Dad about how big the dog salmon were at Hidden Falls. I walked through the rain, which was lighter now but just as steady, and found the door with a hand-painted sign that also said "john." I stuck the key in the lock and jiggled it long enough to consider drawing down my zipper and letting it fly on one of those heaps of oily sand and weeds. But finally the bolt slid free and the door creaked open and it felt so good to piss that I hardly even noticed the smell.

This toilet had the old kind of seat, black and open at one end, and someone really needed to scrub the bowl. Mom would never have gotten near it. Hers was baby blue with a dark-blue shaggy seat cover and the water was blue, too, as if going to the bathroom was a beautiful experience. But you couldn't fault someone for wanting things to look nice and to smell nice—Mom was used to having nice things. Her father, before he moved to California, owned a big house overlooking Chuckanut Bay with a courtyard in the middle. He'd been a surgeon at St. Joseph's, a really important one, at least from what Mom said. He'd wanted Mom to attend the University of Washington, and she would have, she said, "if things had worked out the way I'd planned."

The night before we left Bellingham she had cooked a special dinner for me, a chicken recipe her mother sometimes made, with lots of mushrooms and tomatoes and vinegar and chopped peppers. Afterwards we drank red wine together and Mom turned on an oldies station she liked to listen to whenever she'd had enough to drink. The Platters were singing about being together again at twilight time. Mom said, "Dance with me," and I said, "You gotta be kidding," but she drew the curtains so no one else would see, and then we loped around the living room, arms circling one another's waists. She kept telling me what a good dancer I was, even though it was hard enough to keep from stepping on her feet. But it was nice, seeing how much fun she was having, as if she was a teenager herself. In bed that night I listened to The Cars with my stereo headphones and tried to decide if I was doing the right thing, going with Dad. But it was too late for that. In the morning Mom drove me to the harbor and hugged me for a long time when we said goodbye. Then she hugged Dad very quickly and walked back to her car. A few minutes later we pulled out of the harbor and left.

Now I decided to go call her. I washed my hands under the hot water in the sink, wiped them on my jeans, locked the door behind me and brought the key back to Mr. Stockman. Dad was already gone. So I walked along the main road toward a grocery store with a phone booth outside. Mom said "hello" in a way that made me think she'd just woken up. I wondered if Mr. Reynolds was in bed with her, making the whole room smell like cologne, his hairy body wrapped around hers.

"Peter, is everything all right?"

"If something happened, you think I'd be able to call you about it?"

"Don't be smart. You sound different."

"It must be the phone," I said. "The static makes it hard to hear."

"Honey, you really ought to speak more clearly."

"I *am*. It's this goddamned phone."

"Just because you're in Alaska doesn't mean you have to swear."

I sighed and watched drips of rain run down the glass walls of the booth. A semi-truck hauling a bed of timber roared by, and for a moment I couldn't hear anything at all. That was the trouble with telephones. You could never say what you meant.

Mom was asking about the trip.

"It was great." I said it real quickly.

"You sound tired."

"I was up most of the night. Pumping out the boat."

"Oh dear. Is it leaking bad?"

"It's nothing to worry about, I don't think." I glanced at my wristwatch. "How are things?"

"Business is a little slow this week, although a lot of Californians have been in the office. Do you know what people call them now? Californicators." Mom laughed. "Which isn't very nice. Although if this keeps up, Chuckanut Drive is going to start looking like a suburb of Los Angeles."

"I meant Mr. Reynolds."

"I haven't seen him since you left, Peter."

There was something ridiculous about having your mother going out on dates—I was asking her the questions she should have been asking me. "Listen," I said, "I need to change out of these wet clothes. And I'm real sleepy. Do you mind if I go?"

She said that would be fine, and warned me to be careful not to catch cold. But she sounded disappointed. We said goodbye, and I walked back toward the boat. I had nothing against Mr. Reynolds personally—he was a nice-looking man who always did his best to make me feel welcome. Sometimes he took me for rides in his turbo-charged Porsche and he promised to teach me golf. One time Dad stopped by without phoning, to pick up some tools, and Mr. Reynolds was sitting right there on the couch. They shook hands and said polite, adult things to each other, but to me they looked like two dogs sniffing each other's butts.

Dad was asleep when I got back to the boat, but woke up as soon as I came in. He thanked me for phoning and asked how Mom was, and I said she was fine, as far as I could tell. Then I asked him why he didn't bother to call her himself. He said he would, if he felt it would do any good, but that half the times they talked they just made each other madder.

For the rest of that day, Dad napped for an hour or two and then paced around the boat, or around the docks, looking at his watch, checking the tide-tables, the navigation charts, or the oil level in the engine. In the evening George said he should forget about everything and go out to one of the bars, but Dad said no, since nowadays he hardly drank at all, and he sure as hell wasn't going to start at a time like this. So George asked the rest of us if we wanted to go instead, and I was glad for the chance to get away from the boat and from Dad.

The bar was on the main road about a half-mile from the dock, near a steep hill with a tunnel through the middle of it. The place looked like something in a circus that might be taken apart and moved. At the door a guy with a Fu Manchu moustache and cowboy boots didn't bother to check IDs. We walked right in and sat down at an empty table with chairs that didn't quite sit flat on four legs.

A stripper was bumping around the stage with a red scarf between her legs, while the stereo played Steve Miller's "Abracadabra." George said something to a waitress in a snug blue blouse and she came back with four gin and tonics on a round metal tray. George gave her a twenty and plucked the slice of lime from his drink, biting into it as if it were sweet, leaving only the green rind. He tried not to make a face, but his eyes scrunched into slits, and his mouth twisted into a frown. "Didn't think I could do it, did you?"

"An accomplishment to be proud of," Gordon replied. He had on an olive-green beret, tilted to one side. "But I thought this was all behind you, now that you're about to become a parent."

George talked a lot about becoming a father, although sometimes it sounded like he wished the whole thing could be postponed. Dad said he liked the way George never let things bother him. But this was different.

"Hey, a man's gotta grow up some time," George said with a laugh. "But tell me where it says 'when'? And I got at least another month."

Gordon shook his head and George frowned. "And don't give me any of this too-old crap, Gordon. I bet you're almost as old as me."

"I'm thirty."

"Close enough." George paused, glancing at the stripper on the stage. "Now, Mr. Expert, answer me this: how come every goddamned woman in these bars is overweight?"

"For Christ's sake, George, if you were young and slim and beautiful, would you be in a place like this?"

"But I *am* young and slim and beautiful."

Wade had been staring into his drink, as if something were swimming around in it. Now he looked at George. "You're just really drunk," he said.

"Look who's talking. At least I've drunk enough so I deserve to be drunk."

"Hey," Wade said, "I've had just as much as you."

Gordon said, "Is that something to be proud of?"

Wade looked back down at his ice cubes. He muttered something none of us could hear, while I twisted in my chair to get a better look at the stripper. She made me think of an old painting, a pink-skinned woman lying naked on a fancy velvet couch. She finally got her bra off so all she had left were her flamingo-pink panties. Then those were gone, flung onto her pile of clothes. She wiggled around with her back to the audience, and a few of the fishermen shouted her name. But most of them acted like they'd seen it all before.

The crowd was mostly white guys, with a few Indians. Looking around I caught a big whiff of cigarette smoke mixed with the smell of Gordon's pipe. Everywhere else was the sweaty scent of too many people in a small place. Then I spotted a man in a brown leather jacket sitting by himself, reading a newspaper and sipping a beer. It was the guy who had given me a ride to the cannery.

I waved but he didn't recognize me. I went to his table and tapped him on the shoulder and asked him to join us. He didn't seem crazy about the idea. But finally he came and sat down next to me, and I introduced him to the rest of the crew. George looked at him funny when I said his name. "You the one saying the run's gonna be a failure?"

Robert Frank took a drink from his glass mug. Then he looked at George. "Could be. I couldn't say for sure. After all, I'm not a scientist."

Wade said, "What the hell kind of answer is that? Everybody knows the run's going to be great."

"I like your confidence, son. You fished up here before?"

"No," Wade said. "I haven't."

"First year, it's always gonna be a great run. You wouldn't have come if it wasn't."

"I came to make money," Wade said, real slowly. "Not to listen to strangers tell me the season's gonna be a bust."

"Listen to what you want, son. Just don't let yourself get too disappointed if you're wrong."

"Don't call me 'son.'"

"Don't be a jack-ass," Gordon said.

"You stay out of this!"

"Whoa!" Robert Frank said. "Young white man getting hot beneath the collar."

"Go to hell!" Wade said.

"Go back to the boat," Gordon said. "George, take Wade back."

George was slumped back in his chair, smiling, eyes half-closed. "Aw, come on, Gordon, just let him argue. It's probably harmless. Besides, I'm in no position to get anyone back to the boat, including myself."

"Oh the hell with it," Robert Frank said. "I was planning on going home early tonight anyway. You watch your mouth, son. Before long you're gonna meet up with some local who's not as patient as I am."

Then he looked at me. "I wish your father the best this summer."

"Thanks," I replied, not knowing what else to say. Robert Frank swallowed the rest of his beer, left some money at his table, put on his jacket, folded up his newspaper, and walked out the door. Wade said, "Bad as the fuckin' Lummies."

The Lummies lived on a jut of land on the north side of Bellingham Bay. Most of the shoreline was owned by whites, and their houses were spacious and the yards were big. But if you went inland a bit there were little tarpaper roofs and sheets of plastic instead of windows, and trailers parked in dusty lots. There were rusting cars half hidden by blackberry bushes.

Gordon leaned across the table until he and Wade were only about a foot apart. "You ever hear of the word 'racism?'"

"You ever heard of minding your own goddamned business?"

"And let you get the crap kicked out of you?"

"I could have held my own."

"Boy, you're really enlightened, aren't you?"

"It's probably just like Puget Sound," Wade said. "Goddamned Indians are given every break in the world."

"I don't think so," Gordon said. "And don't forget, there were reasons why Judge Boldt decided it was necessary to give them a bigger share of the salmon."

George sat up and stared across the table. He looked like someone woken from a nap. "What reasons were those, Gordon?"

"The way we took their fishing grounds away. After all those treaties had been signed."

"We didn't take *anything* away," George said. "Mike's Dad, Mike's grandfather, they fished for years right alongside the Indians. The Indians, they just couldn't compete."

I looked down at what was left of my drink, sniffed mostly gin, and figured I better not.

"But they couldn't compete because the whites had all the money," I heard Gordon say. "The Indians never had a chance."

"That ain't our fault," George replied. "Jesus, Gordon, did they teach you this in college? Why the hell do you think we're up here right now, instead of down in the Sound? Because thanks to the Indians, we don't get enough time to fish."

"True and not true." Gordon paused. "We'd be here anyways, I think. For the adventure, if nothing else."

George's face turned red. "You think Mike Kristiansen is up here for *adventure*? Jesus, Mike doesn't have a fucking choice! The best fisherman in Bellingham, and he couldn't make enough to support his fuckin' family!"

"That's not true," I said. "Dad was doing OK."

"But Peter," George went on, "why do you think your mother took that job? Because Mike insisted she take it, because the way things were he couldn't keep up on the payments on the house. And how do you think that made your Dad feel, having to ask your mother to help support *him*?"

"But my mom wanted to work. She told me. She likes work."

"But look what happened. She met that Reynolds yo-yo and kaboom! Mike's marriage blew apart."

"Things were falling apart for a long time," I said.

"Let me get this straight." Gordon ran his fingers through his beard and looked toward the ceiling. "You're trying to blame Mike's separation from his wife on the Boldt decision?"

"No, of course not. It's just that, well, hell, it complicated everything. You know I got a kid on the way, and I gotta figure out a way to pay for it. Now if they'd just let us fish, like they used to, you know, three, four days a week—"

"If you guys had kept fishing three or four days every week," Gordon said, "there wouldn't be any salmon left!"

Wade looked up from the table. "At least the Indians wouldn't get 'em."

"Shut up, Wade," George said. And then, "No, Gordon, that's not what I want. There just had to be a better way of doing things."

"Probably," Gordon said with a yawn. "But whatever it was, they didn't do it, and here we all are. No point wondering what might have been."

"What if Robert Frank is right?" I said.

"He's fuckin' wrong, Peter," Wade told me. "Can't you see that?"

"But what if he's right?"

Gordon set down his pipe and touched the tip of his beard. "There's gonna be a whole lot of pissed-off fishermen. And a lot of financial problems, too. A skipper buys a new boat, or makes improvements, well, he rolls the dice, he takes a few chances. And in this case, the salmon, they're the dice. And sometimes things roll your way, Peter, and sometimes they don't."

George said, "They've been rolling against us fishermen too fuckin' long already!" He pounded his big fist against the table, the ice cubes rattling in his glass.

I stood up to go to the can. I stood up too fast. The whole room was spinning. Another stripper had taken the stage, younger and prettier than the first one, and "Honky-tonk Woman" roared from the speakers. She'd already peeled off a sweater, and was fingering the hooks on her rose-colored bra. The fishermen pounded the tables. "Lynette!" one of them shouted. "God bless you and your boobs, Lynette!"

"Probably time to get moving," Gordon said. "The skipper will be mad as hell if we roll in at some ungodly hour. And I think we've seen enough for one night."

I glanced back at the stage. Lynette had her hands cupped around her tits, massaging the nipples, making them glow beneath the hot ceiling lights. She looked down at what she was doing, almost bashfully, as if she was somebody's older sister. Then she gave us all a quick little dirty smile.

Outside George was slumped against the wall with his eyes closed, and Wade stood there frowning, his arms folded across his chest. Gordon motioned for us to get started, and we walked quietly back to the boat. From the cabin I could hear Dad snoring, and we had to be careful not to wake him.

Chapter 3

The leak turned out to be simple to fix, and by mid-afternoon the next day we were ready to head for Hidden Falls. Dad said the problem had something to do with the rudder or the propeller, where they bolted onto the stern. He explained what Mr. Stockman had done to fix it, but none of it made much sense to me. Mr. Stockman watched as we pulled away from the dock, and wished us all the best. "Just don't let anyone push you around up there," he said, and Dad nodded and waved.

We traveled all that evening and night, and for most of the next day. Just after dawn we passed the town of Petersburg, at the head of Wrangell Narrows, and that was the last town we saw. The mountains rose almost from sea level now, and even the tops of smaller hills were covered with snow. A glacier wound down a valley and poured into Frederick Sound like a tire-tracked road of ice. Close to shore you could smell the pine trees.

Now and then bald eagles circled above us, gliding like airplanes. Sometimes they swept straight down, wings held back, bodies made small, eyes focused on the flash of a leaping fish. A quarter-mile away I saw the broad black tail of a humpback whale, and then a puff of steam. I went to grab my Pentax, to have something to show Mom, but the picture would have been stupid, a speck of black against the water.

The rain had stopped, although it was still overcast, and not very warm. Dad had gone down for another nap, and Gordon and I were at the wheel. A yellow-and-blue touring ferry was lumbering toward us with dozens of people perched on its observation deck, staring at us through cameras and binoculars.

"Look, Peter," Gordon said, "we're a tourist attraction. Let's swing in a little to give these folks their money's worth."

He nudged the wheel to port, and we began to veer toward the ferry. Through binoculars I could see people pointing, a woman tugging on her fat husband's sleeve. Little kids jumped up and down against the guard rail, and a young couple stopped right in the middle of whatever it was they'd been doing. Gordon said, "Wave to them. Let 'em know we're all just friendly Joes."

I stood up, raised my arm over my head, and waved it back and forth. A whole chorus of arms fluttered back at me, and through binoculars I saw big, cheesy smiles. "Jesus," I said. "They sure are excited to see us."

"It's probably the most exciting thing that's happened this whole trip," Gordon replied. "It's not every day they get to say hello to a real fisherman."

"You think we're worth staring at?"

"Maybe not, but put yourself in their shoes. They've probably come from the East Coast, or California, to see if everything they've heard about Alaska is true. And now they see this quaint little fishing boat, with quaint fishermen on board. Of course it might never dawn on them that I'm actually a schoolteacher, that you're a student, that this is something I do to get away from exactly the kind of life most of them live.

"No, they see you and me up here, standing atop the flying bridge, and think 'Now goddammit, there's a couple of young men who have control over their lives. They're not working in nine-to-five jobs, cursing the boss under their breath, doing something they hate. Nope. Those young men, they're free. They're as free as cowboys on the open range.' We're stereotypes, Peter. We're what everyone would want to be."

"But that's just a lot of crap," I said.

"Maybe to us. But not to them. And it is sort of true, for me. That's why I'm up here, to get away from everything. Hell, I don't need the money. Now your Dad—oops, hold on, Peter!"

The wake from the ferry rolled toward us and Gordon spun the wheel hard to port, trying to hit the big wave head on. But it struck us at a quarter-angle, and everything pitched way over to one side. I had to clutch onto the side railing.

"Shit," Gordon said. "That's gonna wake the skipper."

At least he was the one holding the wheel—I was just a bystander. I even thought about picking up the binoculars again and gazing toward the mainland, pretending to scan the water for fish. Instead I sat there looking down at my shoes.

Dad appeared less than a minute later. "Jesus, Gordon. What the hell's going on?"

"Dumb mistake. I got too close to the ferry."

Dad rubbed the knotty muscles in his neck. "But we're way out in the middle of Chatham Strait. You should have given it at least a quarter-mile."

"I know it was stupid. But I wanted Peter to wave to the passengers. As a joke."

Now Dad's eyes bore down like a drill press. "You think this is some kind of pleasure craft?"

Gordon lowered his head, as if Dad were his dad, instead of mine. "I can assure you it won't happen again, Mike. You want to go back down and rest?"

Dad said he'd rested long enough, and sat down. Gordon didn't say much after that. No one did. But pretty soon we could see the fishing boats clustered in the bay just beyond Hidden Falls. To the south more of them milled around near where a huge waterfall spilled from halfway up a hill. The boats looked tiny down below, as if they might get caught in the torrent and sink.

"Aw, fuck," Dad said. "Everyone and their brother."

Now when we entered the little bay, just beyond the creek that the fish went up to spawn, we could see the salmon soaring free of the water with missile-like thrusts. The dog salmon here weren't like humpies, which came in from the ocean in the millions. Most of these fish would be caught in the first couple sets. Every few seconds another broke the surface, sometimes two or three at once. Two eagles circled lazily above us, eyeing the salmon the same way we were.

Everyone else was watching, too. The bay couldn't have been more than a mile long, maybe a half-mile wide. Yet fishing boats were everywhere: big steel jobs that looked like warships, sleek fiberglass models, older wooden ones like ours. The boats circled in and out, moving right up to the orange netting at the mouth of the creek. Some boats had found a good spot and were sitting on it with their anchor cables jutting from their bows.

"Goin' to be tricky as hell to get the net in the water," Dad said. "Guys will be corking each other forwards and backwards."

Gordon said, "It looks like a lot of them are going to try it farther down the strait. Did you see where the marker was? We could get in line if you want."

"And take turns?"

"If we line up now, we might get third set."

Dad frowned. "That'll be at least an hour. Things might be cleaned out by then. And I'm not crazy about sitting on my ass."

"You want to try it right here?"

"I don't know. I'm not sure we have much choice."

"You know," Gordon said, "we're not exactly the most seasoned crew in the world—we might have a heck of a time just getting the gear back on board."

Fishing with a power block was a lot different than using a mechanical drum, like we'd had on the *Stavenger*. All it took was one guy to operate the drum, but with the block, three of us stood on the stern, guiding and piling the net as it came down. Drums weren't allowed in Alaska, Dad had said, because they made the boats more likely to flip over on their sides. We'd made a couple practice sets with the block in Bellingham Bay, but we weren't very good. Wade had kept bumping into me and saying it was my fault. Maybe he was right.

"We'll go over everything this evening," Dad said. "Hell, all we really need is one good set."

But a lot could go wrong in a single set. It seemed way too easy to fall overboard, especially when the seine pile started getting high and steep and you were standing on top of it. Or the net might get tangled around the propeller of the skiff or the rudder of the boat. A hydraulic line might blow, spewing slippery oil across the deck. Or someone might forget to tie a line, and maybe half your fish would escape. That was my main goal as a fisherman—not to screw up. But that was a bad attitude. Dad liked to say that nothing goes wrong unless you let it.

That evening he had us out on the stern, checking the bunt end of the net, the part the fish get trapped in. It was warmer than usual, but still damp from the rain. Mosquitoes swirled around us, pricking our faces and the backs of our hands. George hacked through a clump of rotted lashings and slashed at the bugs with the blade of his knife.

"It's revenge of the food chain," Gordon explained, sitting cross-legged on the net pile, patching a tear in the bunt with a needle of heavy twine. "The salmon feed off little fish, we feed off the salmon, the mosquitoes feed off us."

"Gordon," Dad said, "do you know what to do if we can't get the whole net in the water?"

Gordon looked up from beneath the brown hood of his sweatshirt. "Not much I can do from the skiff. Except drift and hope you can dump the whole thing."

"Just make sure the net doesn't get wrapped around the wheel. Now, George, you and Peter and Wade, you're going to have to work real fast. We probably won't tow at all. Get everything hooked up as quick as you can."

George turned toward me and Wade, flashing his knife. "You hear that? No screwing around."

"I'll do *my* job," Wade said. "Don't you worry about me."

"Spoken like a true team player," Gordon said.

"Hey, I'm serious. I ain't gonna cost us any money. What about you, Pete? You're not going to freeze in the clutch, are you?"

"If I fuck up," I said, "you'll be the first to know."

The snow in the hills was still pink from the sun when we went to bed. Gordon was reading a book called *Zen and the Art of Motorcycle Maintenance*. George lay flat on his back, his eyes closed and his hands folded across his belly. Wade was sharpening his knife on a whetstone.

Gordon snapped off the single lightbulb at the head of the fo'c'sle, but it didn't get much darker, thanks to the overhead hatch. I couldn't sleep, thinking about screwing up. Thank you, Wade, for that. I imagined the net spilling into the water, and me forgetting to hook up the end of it, so the whole thing floated away,

Dad screaming, Wade glaring at me kind of smugly, George looking like he'd just had money snatched from his hands.

This is what it must be like to be an athlete, I thought, the night before a big game. But I'd been an athlete, and it wasn't like this. Or was it? I couldn't remember. I was a pretty good baseball pitcher in middle school, had what the coach said could grow into a wicked curve. I was left-handed, which helped. And wild. That was the toughest thing for a hitter, the coach said, a wild lefthander with a wicked curve. After eighth grade I got bored and quit. Maybe because I was afraid of hitting someone with my fastball. I couldn't remember. I fell asleep and dreamt about home. But Dad woke me up before it was over.

It was three o'clock. Fishing didn't start until six, but we had to be out there, bobbing around for position. Dad liked a spot over by a little island at the south end of the bay. One of the steel boats called the *Anna Rose* had the same idea. Fish jumped two or three at a time, but it was hard to tell which one of us was going to get them, or even whether we'd be able to set our net. The sun came over the hills on the other side of Chatham Strait, turning the water bright red, as if the whole bay might burst into flames. "I don't know what this fellow on the *Anna Rose* is thinking," Dad said, his breath forming little puffs of steam in the cold air, "but we were here first. It's our set."

Gordon grabbed the binoculars. "I hope he knows that. He's bigger than us."

The *Anna Rose* wasn't much longer, it couldn't be, according to the law. But it was a lot wider, and it was painted mostly black. We couldn't even see the skipper, hidden inside the wheelhouse. Dad tried calling him on the radio, but he didn't respond.

At 5:30 Dad sent Gordon down to start the engine of the skiff. It coughed white smoke and roared to a start. Gordon hooked up his skiff-radio and slapped on his headphones. Dad said something into the microphone and Gordon waved his arm. Then Dad climbed back on top the cabin. "Whatever happens with the *Anna Rose*, don't give up your position. We're gonna take that set no matter what."

Gordon nodded.

"Even if we have to cork him?" I asked.

Dad said, "I hope that won't be necessary."

To cork someone, you set your net right in front of theirs. Dad said only assholes corked people. But that was in Puget Sound. Things might be different up here.

"If you cork him," Gordon said, "do it all the way. Don't let him have a thing."

By five minutes to six we were ready to go. Gordon sat in the skiff, headphones on, staring at Dad up on the cabin. George studied the rope that would cut loose the skiff and send the net spilling into the water. Two men in orange jackets from the state Fish and Game Department circled the bay in a powerboat, speaking through a megaphone. Every few minutes they announced how much time we had before everything started.

My throat felt dry as sandpaper now. The *Anna Rose* was still sharking around, not letting us on to what it would do. Dad glanced in a half-circle, first to the other boat, then to us down on deck, then to where he wanted to set the net.

Wade looked like he wanted to wrestle someone. "Those bastards better not try it. Because if they do—"

"Just do your job," George said. "Let Mike do the worrying."

Then it was 5:59 and the men in the powerboat were counting off the final seconds. One of them had a flare gun raised above his head.

I looked back at the *Anna Rose.* It was jumping the gun. A puff of white bellowed out of its smokestack, and the engine got louder, with a faster cadence, the boat picking up speed and surging toward us.

Dad wheeled around like a startled artillery gunner. Then he thrust the clutch into gear, glanced back at the other boat, and cranked the wheel hard to port. With his free hand, he signaled George to cut loose the skiff and get into position for the set.

The *Anna Rose* tried to race inside of us, to set their net and seal us off, and for a moment I thought we might collide. But Dad was too quick. Our seine was already spilling into the water, and the *Anna Rose* had nowhere to go. The skipper stood outside the wheelhouse, screaming and flinging out his hands, but Dad stared straight ahead.

The whole bay was filled with boats and equipment now. The skiff engines spewed white smoke and cork-lines floated everywhere. It was hard to tell what belonged to who. We dumped all our net and then Wade and I hustled to get everything hooked up to bring it back on board. Wade raised his fists above his head.

"We corked the son-of-a-bitch! Good for your old man! We corked 'em royal!"

"It wasn't like he had much choice," I spat out between hard, heavy breaths. "I thought that guy was gonna run us over, the way he came charging our way."

"But that's the way you gotta be!" Wade shouted back. "You can't be Mr. Nice Guy. People will step all over you, stomp you into dust. You gotta take whatever you can get. And boy, did your dad take it!"

There was no point in towing like normal because, with the *Anna Rose* so close, we didn't have room to get the seine into its half-circle. In the skiff Gordon closed shut the net only a minute or two after it all went into the water, and now George was calling for Wade and me to start bringing it through the power block. Soon we were piling the net on board, me on the corks, Wade bunching together the web and the lead line, George using the winch to draw in the manila rope that sealed shut the bottom.

"We gotta hustle!" George shouted, pointing to the *Anna Rose*. Its crew was bringing their net back on board, with the skiff still hooked to the end. "They're trying to take this set before we can. I gotta run the block a little faster. You guys gotta keep up."

But we were already stacking as fast as we could. Seawater streamed down from the power block, drumming against the hood of my rain jacket, dripping off the bill of my cap, chilling my fingers and wrists. Every minute or two a red jellyfish came through the block, splattering us with its poison, making the backs of my hands itch and burn. A speck of the acid lodged in the corner of my eye, and for the next few minutes I saw everything through a blurry squint.

Wade kept bumping into me, as if he were blinded, too. I told him to watch out, and he said, "*You* watch out!"

The circle of corks kept shrinking until the ring was smaller than a backyard swimming pool, and now we could see the dog salmon cutting back and forth in groups of five or six, their blue-green spines flashing just below the surface. Wade was smiling, without the bitter part. I smiled, too. It was more fish than I had ever seen. They began to dart in all directions. We had done it. We really had. We had set our net in the right place. Fishing up here must be easy, I thought, if you could catch this many the first time you tried.

But we still had to get them on board. Dad was at the controls, hoisting the big bag out of the water, the salmon pounding against each other, sending out a spray of jellyfish and slime, making the boat tremble and shake. The bag came to rest atop the bulwarks, causing us to lean way over on our side. "Goddammit!" Dad said, but then he wrenched a little harder on the power block and the whole thing thumped down on deck. The fish made a frantic flapping noise. Dad was shouting, motioning, helping us open the hatch covers so we could dump the fish into the hold. Then I hurried back onto the stern to hook up the skiff. Gordon had on a big smile, his thumb jutting into the air.

"Get ready!" Dad shouted.

The *Anna Rose* was getting ready, too. They were coming our way. But something was wrong. It didn't register at first. Everything happened too fast. I couldn't figure out why they hadn't turned. I caught sight of the skipper, dark-skinned with a moustache and large bald head, leaning out the window of the wheelhouse. He looked like a villain in a cartoon. His fist was clenched, and he was screaming something, but the words didn't make sense.

"Let her go!" Dad yelled. "*Let that sonofabitch go!*"

But it was too late. None of us could move. George stood with his mouth open, hands at his side like a kid amazed by the strength of an adult, staring at the broad steel keel of the *Anna Rose*.

"Oh my Lord God," he murmured.

"Brace yourself!" Gordon yelled.

At the last instant the *Anna Rose* slowed down. But the boat kept coasting forward. The keel slammed into our hull a few feet from the bow. The wooden planking groaned in pain. Dad looked like he'd taken a bullet through his gut.

Now we're *really* going to sink, I thought, as my legs went out from under me and I slammed against the deck, the sun blinding me, the sky making me imagine I were somewhere else.

Chapter 4

I knew the shore was close and the water calm, that I'd swim like mad if I had to. But I didn't want to get up. Clouds drifted overhead, and a breeze cooled my face. I smelled the seawater, and the fish slime, and I could hear the fish still flopping around. Silver salmon-scales clung to the insides of the bulwarks, and a pink jellyfish the size of a frisbee sat a few feet from my head.

But still I didn't move. I'd do it when I had to, when the water came rushing in. Someone would let me know if we were going to sink. I saw Wade on his knees, his arms around the guardrail, like a wrestler riding an opponent. George had fallen on the net pile, and now was climbing to his feet. Gordon stood near him, glancing around. He looked to be eight feet tall.

"I'm terribly sorry! I'm terribly sorry!" a voice was saying.

"Are they going to sink?" another voice wanted to know. "Geez, Dad, maybe we should call the Coast Guard."

"Shut up, Tommy." Then he said, "Get out of my way." And then, "Sir. It was all a mistake. You must believe me."

"A lot of fucking good that does us right now!" It was Dad. Then: "Peter, get off your butt and get into the fo'c'sle, find out what the hell's going on!"

Gordon was already on his way into the galley. Good for him, I thought. Someone should be doing something. Someone should be taking charge. But he can handle it. I'll just lie here a couple minutes. No one will notice.

"You OK?" Dad shouted. "You didn't hit your head, did you?"

Slowly I got to my feet. I felt woozy. But nothing else was wrong, at least not with my body.

"You see," said the first voice, which belonged to the bald-headed skipper of the *Anna Rose*, "I was racing you for the set, and damned if the steering didn't jam. Amazing, isn't it, with a boat as new as mine?"

The *Anna Rose* drifted about twenty feet away. The skipper stared at Dad, as if waiting for him to admit that yes, it was amazing. But Dad was looking at Gordon.

"We're not leaking—at least not badly," Gordon said. "But the ribs in the bow took quite a blow."

Dad nodded and headed into the fo'c'sle himself. By the time he came back out, the Fish and Game powerboat was heading toward us, its engine whining and its bow lifting above the water. Both men crouched in the stern, the collars on their orange jackets turned up and their heads hunched down.

The powerboat bumped against our hull and one of the men steadied a hand against the railing. He was young, with very short hair and a poor excuse for a moustache.

"You need help?"

Dad shrugged and said, "We can manage," as if all we had was a flat tire.

"You taking on water?"

"Would I be talking to you if we were?"

"Say again?" and, when Dad didn't reply, "May I look around?"

Dad said, "Suit yourself," and the man climbed on board and studied the damaged planking, while his partner sat in the stern of the powerboat with his arms folded. The first man pulled a notepad from his hip pocket and wrote something down. "We'll have to file a report on this," he said. "But only after I talk to the other skipper. You're not going to mind sitting here a few minutes, are you?"

"Don't ask me," Dad said. "You're the one in charge."

The man looked up from his writing.

Dad said, "Just do what you have to do and get it over with. So I can get us back to Petersburg and get this thing fixed."

The man tapped his pen against the notepad. Dad put his hands to his forehead, and ran his fingers along his face and through his beard. Then he looked across the bay. The dog salmon were still jumping, and a single eagle drifted overhead. I could hear the grind of machinery as the *Anna Rose* crewmen piled the nets on board, the steady thump of the diesel engines, and sometimes a "fuck!" or a "damn!"

"Do what you have to," Dad repeated. "Just do it quick."

"You gonna sue that guy?" I asked an hour later, as we started back toward Petersburg. Dad was hunched over the wheel, heading straight into the sun. The light reflected sharply off the water, and both of us had on shades. He took his off, rubbed his eyes, and shook his head. "I sure as hell ought to. If I had any brains. But Jesus, what a pain in the ass. God only knows how the legal system moves up here. Besides, that fellow sounded like a pretty good liar."

"But didn't you see the look in his eyes?"

"Sure I did. But that's not enough to make him pay. I'd need a lawyer who can lie just as good as he can."

"You gonna get one?"

Dad shrugged, and put the sunglasses back on. "You make it sound as simple as taking on fuel and groceries. First we gotta get this boat back in action. Then I'll worry about how to pay for it."

We reached Petersburg late that night, unloaded the dog salmon the following morning, and had the *Ambition* hauled back on land. But by Friday the shipwright still didn't know when he'd be done. So Dad and I sat on top the cabin and watched the other purse seiners creep out of Wrangell Narrows and disappear into Frederick Sound, on their way to the next opener. "I hope they do good," Dad said, "but not too good."

After that I went to the only movie in town, called *Butcher, Baker, Nightmare Maker*. The younger kids squealed at the gore, but I just felt sleepy. I stepped back into the afternoon glare and thought about what to do next. I'd been to all the bakeries in town, and I'd drunk all the milkshakes I could stand. I'd swum laps at the public pool until my skin smelled always of chlorine. I'd read forty pages of a book by Jack London called *The Sea Wolf,* and I'd read magazines, dirty ones that George kept hidden beneath his pillow, with pictures of women with breasts like cows. I'd followed every nice ass I'd seen, glancing at the girls from the corners of my eyes, checking out their tits. I didn't care what they thought, because no one knew me here. But it got boring, not being known.

Finally I walked back to the boat and took out the weed from the locker beneath my bunk. So much for promises. Did that make me a stoner? I didn't want to think about it. At least Dr. Cline, the counselor they sent me to after the school had found the dope in my locker, couldn't blame it this time on peer pressure. There wasn't a peer of mine anywhere near me, except Wade, and he didn't count.

I followed a long, steep trail that led to an overlook above town. The path was slick with mud and I had to keep brushing away the spider webs. I was breathing pretty hard by the time I got to the top. From up there Frederick Sound looked frozen solid, little bits of sea foam curling at its edges. Now and then an eagle swooped overhead, and I might have been able to get some good pictures if I'd had my camera. Instead I rolled a joint and smoked it slowly, then another after that. I didn't feel good about it, but I didn't feel bad, either. Just nice and relaxed. I lay in the grass, the tall blades tickling my ears. I knew I should call Mom, but I didn't want to. Maybe it was my fault, I said to myself, what happened, between her and Dad, but I couldn't help it. We don't choose our families. And they don't choose us. God I must be fucked up.

I tried to think about other things.

Clair Reed. She likes getting high. She liked getting high with me. I think she did. She has a smile that goes right through you. I like the way her hair is so short, almost like a boy's. Not exactly. More like she's pretending to be a boy. I should have kissed her, that time she gave me a ride. I know she wanted it. Maybe I could have gone up her shirt. She would have liked that a lot. I started getting hard. It pressed against my zipper, like a dog that won't go away. I didn't have much choice, all alone. I did it real quick. You're disgusting, I told myself. You're the most disgusting person who ever lived.

It turned out I hadn't brought as much pot as I'd figured. I smoked the rest of it two days later behind an old tool shed at the other end of town. I walked around afterwards with nothing much to do.

The day after that the other boats started coming back. We were off the ways now, tied up at the float on the other side of the harbor. A purse seiner from Bellingham called the *Navigator* edged alongside us, and a crewman in a hooded sweatshirt flung me a bristly rope, which I looped around the cleat on our bow. Someone else climbed aboard our stern, hooked up another line, and two more guys pulled the *Navigator* snug against us. A man I recognized as the skipper, named Stan, climbed over the bulwarks, his rubber boots squeaking against the deck and his reddish hair hanging in bunches beneath his cap. "Peter," he said, stretching out his hand, "your dad around?"

I reached out, surprised that he remembered my name, and felt the grip of his big fist.

"I think he's up at the shipyard paying his bill."

"No matter." Stan's face was sunburnt, giving his pale cheeks a strong red tint. "Just thought I'd stop by to chew the beef. I heard you guys took quite a shot last week. Everything OK?"

I jammed my hands in my pockets, and stared at my shoes. "We're still floating."

Stan spat into the water. "Well, I can see that. But I bet your dad was mad as hell about missing this last opener."

"He wasn't real happy."

"Not that you missed a whole lot." Stan rubbed his face and winced. "If it keeps up like this, you're going to see a real ex-o-dust for down south in no time."

"You think so?" I asked, a little too enthusiastically.

"Well, hell, the predictions are pretty good for Puget Sound. They're good for up here, too, but geez, a guy would think a few of those damn humpies would start to show."

"But it's still early, isn't it?"

"I'm just being an alarmist," Stan said. "The fish will get here, I think. But it sure would be nice to be down south."

"But you guys had a good season up here last year, didn't you?"

"Some guys did. Not everyone. Better than the Sound, 'cause that was a disaster. But it won't always be like that, especially not this year. I'll tell your dad what I'm talking about, if he drops by tonight. One of our kids caught a halibut up near Hidden Falls, and we got a shitload of shrimp. And lots of beer."

Stan grinned and peeled off his baseball cap. "Some whiskey and tequila, too... Damn! I keep forgetting Mike doesn't drink the hard stuff anymore. But that don't matter. Tell him to get his ass over here just the same."

That evening the *Navigator*'s wide wooden deck looked like a backyard patio, the air pleasantly scented from the barbecue coals. Stan was wearing a chef's apron with a picture on front of a salmon leaping after a lure. He had a thick flank of halibut rested on a cutting board next to a plastic bread-bag filled with shrimp, and alongside that was a row of liquor bottles and two styrofoam coolers packed with ice and beer and cans of pop. From a portable cassette player a tape was playing that sounded like Willie Nelson.

"My good friends Mike and George," Stan said. "How the hell are you?" He reached for Dad's hand and slapped George on the back. "You guys are still the news of the week, after your face-off with the *Anna Rose*. Damn. What a story!"

"Yeah," Dad said. "Lucky us."

George said, "But I hope everyone knows it was *us* that got the fish."

"That's what's so heroic," Stan said. "Here we got this little wooden Bellingham boat, run by a guy who's never fished up here before, going head-to-head with one of the monster steel boats from Ketchikan, and then corking the hell out of him!"

Dad frowned. "I didn't cork him. I had the set the whole way."

"Aw come on, Mike. It makes a better story. This feisty little Bellingham guy, taking one of the big boys head on. Like David vs. Goliath, the Jets vs. the Colts, Washington crossing the Delaware. You've got balls, Mike. Up here a fisherman needs balls."

"A fisherman needs more than balls. You got anything to drink, other than whiskey and tequila?"

"Rum. Gin. We got all sorts of things."

"Beer?"

Stan grabbed a Rainier from a cooler and tossed it to Dad. Then he offered him a seat in a lawn chair. Dad sat down and yanked off the pull tab. "Maybe it would have been better if we'd gone straight to the bottom. Not that the insurance money would have been much at all."

"No," Stan replied, "that would have been tragic. But that the boat's all right—that you've been able to fix it, that you've lived to fish another day—that's heroic in my book."

"We haven't fixed it yet. Not totally."

"You will. If I know you, you'll be back out in no time."

"Sounds like we haven't missed a whole lot," George said. "I heard things weren't worth a shit up there."

"It's like I was telling Peter," Stan said. "I almost wish I was back home with my wife."

I thought of Dad being home, with Mom and Mr. Reynolds. Dad had been living in a basement apartment with a column of mold advancing up one wall and a big wet spot on the bathroom ceiling. Mom visited once and was disgusted.

"Geez, I must be going soft in the head," Stan went on. "All spring all I wanted was to get away from her and the little brats. I used to lie in bed Saturday mornings, kind of hung over, just wanting to take it real slow and real easy, thinking that's what a man deserved. But then I'd hear Tony and Erica racing around the house, shrieking at the top of their lungs, the voice of some weird cartoon character blasting from the TV, and think, 'My God, they're possessed by the fucking Devil.' And all I wanted to do is get my ass up to Ketchikan. But here we are, only a couple weeks into the season, and I'm sitting around homesick—like a big, fat weanie!"

George nodded. "Goddammit, I know the feeling! My wife, she's pregnant, with our first. It drove me nuts. I guess I'm not the best man in the world when it comes to meeting my wife's needs."

Someone smirked.

"Not *those* kind of needs, smart ass. How could I know what she wanted, when she started moaning about something at two in the morning, saying she was hungry or cold, or God knows what? You try it sometime, it's tough as hell. But now I feel like, Jesus Christ, I'm up here, screwing around, and she's about to have a baby. Our baby. And I'm up here."

"We're getting old and soft, George, and we're still young men. Think of it!"

Stan and George looked at each other and laughed. Dad stared across the water, toward the steep green hills on the other side of Wrangell Narrows. His beer can had buckled in his grip. He reached up with his other hand and rubbed the back of his neck and yawned. "Stan, you want to flip me another one?"

"Sure, Mike."

Dad ripped loose the tab, took a drink, and set down the can on the deck. "We heard some weird stuff down in Ketchikan the other week. How the biologists were way off base, that the run's not going to be worth a damn. Scuttlebut is scuttlebut, but it still makes you think."

"I'll tell you what," Stan said. "If that's true—which I don't think it is—then the only thing to do is get yourself outside, and fish the coast. I've been up here a good ten seasons, off and on, and especially back four–five years ago, the humpy runs were piss poor. The way to cover yourself is to get out in the ocean, scratch away on the sockeye, and on the dogs and silvers. Two years ago, out at Noyes Island, damn, we had close to a thousand sockeye in one day."

"A fine, fine day it was," said a squatty-looking guy with a yellow Caterpillar Engines cap and a raspy voice. He took a puff on a cigar, blew out the heavy smoke, and folded his arms. "As fine a day as a day ever gets."

"You're absolutely right, Scottie." Then, to Dad, "The kind of day us guys live for."

"Sure, Stan, but you've got to get the right kind of weather. You can't go out there and fish if the wind's howling forty miles an hour, and you got twelve-foot seas."

"It would be tougher for you guys, no doubt about it. The *Navigator* is a good sea boat, the best I've ever had. We roll around a lot, but we've never been in danger, I don't think. You could do it, too. You'd just have to be a little more careful."

"But first we have to get some days to fish."

"That's the problem. If the humpy fishing is lousy, then they might just shut us down for a couple weeks. Then you'll really see guys racing for Point Roberts. A fast boat can make it from Ketchikan in sixty-four hours. Just think, Mike. Nice, warm summery weather, no pink jellyfish drumming on your head, no twelve-hour runs back to port. You could go sleep with your wife, when you weren't fishing. It's life at the country club, compared to this."

"I don't know about that. I haven't had much of a chance up here yet."

"Don't worry, partner. You'll get your shot."

The casette came to an end, and the voices got quieter. Stan got up and tended to the shrimp on the barbecue grill. Someone else was rolling chunks of halibut in a creamy batter and dropping them into a saucepan filled with simmering oil. Pink sunlight slanted through the half-empty bottles of liquor. I grabbed a plastic cup, plunked in a couple ice cubes, added some whiskey and then some Coke. It was about four parts whiskey, but I tried not to make a face. Then I ate a whole lot of shrimp and halibut, and poured in the whiskey again.

I sat back in my lawn chair, feeling the cool metal armrests against my palms, listening to Waylon Jennings, thinking that if you'd had a couple drinks and lots of food, maybe country/western wasn't the worst thing in the world. It wasn't as bad as Mom's oldies station. And I liked the way the alcohol numbed everything out, even the cold. It seemed kind of strange, sitting out here drinking and not breaking the law. The only thing missing was a little weed to top things off.

I wondered if Gordon had some. You had to figure he did, a guy like him. But I couldn't imagine asking. It was not one of the things you normally asked. Of course he wasn't my teacher anymore—now we were equals, in a way. But I knew I shouldn't be smoking the stuff all the time, anyway. Then I asked myself if that had ever stopped me before. It was 10 p.m. now. The sky was dark blue, and the air had the crisp, cold feeling of Bellingham in March or April. I didn't feel as numb anymore. I decided this would be as good a time as any to call Mom back. I'd been meaning to for several days. It was Monday evening and Mom was probably home alone, so long as she wasn't at Mr. Reynolds'. I told Dad I was going back to the *Ambition* and headed back up the dock, hid behind a bush and took a long piss. Then I walked through the cannery bunkhouses, toward a pay phone. Someone was playing

The Cars. It was the *Candy-O* album, the one with the redhead with the big boobs on the cover. Then I smelled the smoke, like burning leaves and twigs. I strained my nostrils to make sure I hadn't made a mistake. But I'd recognize that scent anywhere.

I put off making the phone call. Instead I knocked on the door to the bunkhouse. Right away I wished I hadn't. I imagined some thick-neck types telling me to get lost. Or a couple of greasers in a poorly lit room with matches and needles and syringes scattered across the floor. What I finally heard was a girl's voice, kind of suspicious sounding.

"What do you want?"

And then another girl, between giggles. "Ceci, don't be so paranoid. Gawd, who do you think it is? The police?"

"Then *you* get it," the first voice said. "I think we should pretend no one's here."

"Geez, you're dumb," the second voice replied, getting louder and closer. "I mean, *really*. Don't you think that whoever it is can hear us?"

The door swung open.

"Hi," I said.

The girl with the second voice stared at me. She was tall, with a black t-shirt that said "The Ramones" in gold letters and a pink beret holding her hair straight back, so you could see the roots. She looked pretty old.

"Yeah? What?"

I stood there like someone who can't remember where he lives. Both girls were staring at me. Finally I decided to tell the truth.

"I thought maybe I smelled some pot."

"Well, we don't have any," the first girl said. She studied me more closely. "Are you some sort of spy for the cannery? You know, we could lose our jobs if you said we were smoking weed."

"I'm not with the cannery. I'm a fisherman. I didn't mean to barge in." I turned away.

"Wait," the other girl said. "Come back here."

I stepped inside.

"And close the door. Did it really smell that bad?" She was using the edge of a postcard to sweep ashes off her nightstand onto a sheet of notebook paper. She crinkled up the paper and threw it into a dark-green metal wastebasket.

"It smelled pretty strong, when I was walking past. But I have a pretty good nose for that sort of thing."

"I *told* you," she said to the first girl. "We're lucky we didn't get the manager down here."

"Ceci's paranoid," Ceci's roomate said. "About everything."

"I am not," Ceci said fiercly. Then, to me, "Are you really a fisherman? Or are you just saying it to impress us?"

I told her that I wasn't the kind of person to make things up. At least not important things.

Ceci sat cross-legged on her bed. She had on a pair of jeans that were baggy at her hips but tight around her ankles, without

80

shoes or socks, and a thin white blouse unbuttoned in the front, over a gray t-shirt. Her hands were wrapped around her toes and she was staring at the ceiling. She said, "My boyfriend was a fisherman."

"Was?"

"He's not my boyfriend anymore."

The roommate scowled and threw back her head. "It was a short-lived affair. Such a tragic end. Ceci just couldn't keep him happy."

"Shut up, Ruth!"

One thing for sure, Ceci was better looking. She wore her hair short, with dark bangs just above her eyebrows, and her eyes were almost green, like a cat's. When she got angry her chin jutted out and her mouth turned into a frown that was almost a smile. You couldn't tell if she meant it or not.

She turned away from Ruth, toward me.

"Do you like fishing?"

"It's all right."

"It must beat working in a cannery."

"You don't like it?"

"I hate it."

"It sucks," Ruth added. She lit a cigarette.

"Then why are you up here?"

Ruth blew out a mouthful of smoke. "Maybe Ceci should tell you." But then, with barely a pause, "You see, she met this guy down in Seattle—that's where we're from—this fisherman guy, the one she used to go out with."

"You don't have to tell him every little detail."

"Anyways," Ruth went on, "Ceci thought it would be great, to come up here and work in the cannery while Kevin was up here fishing. Because we need the money. We start college, at Washington State, in the fall. But the work is terrible. It's gross. The fish smell is horrid. It's worse than a farm. And the workers, most of them, are weirdos. Especially the Japanese. If I were a guy, I'd be on a boat too."

"Well, you're not a guy," Ceci reminded her. Then to me, "Sorry we don't have any pot left, but it's not surprising, the way Ruth tears through the stuff. Do you get high very much?"

"Not really," I said.

"Me neither. It was Ruth's weed. I wouldn't buy it. It's a filthy habit if you ask me."

"What Ceci is trying to say," Ruth cut in, "is that she's perfect."

Ceci had the fierce look in her eyes again. "You ever thought about going for a walk right now? That cigarette smoke is really starting to get on my nerves."

"Oh have it your way, I'll go for a walk. It's a nice night, isn't it?"

I said that it was. Then Ruth left.

"Do you like The Cars?" Ceci asked.

"They're the best," I said right away.

Ceci unfolded her legs and reached toward the portable stereo, to flip over the tape. She had tiny feet, with the nails unpainted, clipped close to her toes.

She sat back on her bed. I sat down on Ruth's. The room was mostly empty, except for the nightstands, an orange backpack, the stereo, and a poster of Jim Morrison. He was naked from the waist up, his arms raised and a gold chain around his neck.

Ceci leaned against the wall, and stared at the overhead light. "Have you ever listened to that 'Shoo Be Doo' song with a good pair of headphones?"

I nodded.

"It's bizarre," she said, still gazing at the light. "To hear all those voices coming at you at once. You might as well be in a time tunnel—everything's so distant and out of place. This guy I know, he told me that everything in the world is disjointed, totally unconnected to everything else. It's sort of depressing, when you think about it. He thinks that we're all alone, even when we're most together. Do you think that's true?"

"Yeah. I guess so. But it's still a good song."

We sat and listened. Ceci stared at the poster. "Do you think Jim Morrison looks like Jesus?"

"He'd need a crown of thorns on his head."

"But look at his expression. Can't you imagine him up on the cross, the blood dripping down? He died right on stage, didn't he?"

"I think so."

"That's sort of the same thing, isn't it?"

"Yeah, sort of."

"Or maybe I'm just talking funny, because of the pot."

"No, that makes a lot of sense."

She smiled and yawned. "I want you to tell me about fishing. But first you have to tell me your name."

"Peter."

"Not just Pete?"

"Pete is OK, too."

"I like 'Peter.' It has more distinction. Are you making a lot of money? That's what everyone says. That fishermen make lots of money."

I told her the whole thing, our big haul at Hidden Falls, and how the *Anna Rose* rammed us. But I changed the details a little, like anyone would in my position. She sounded pretty interested, saying things like "Really?" and "Wow!" and asking all sorts of questions. So I just kept going, and pretty soon we weren't talking about fishing at all. I was telling her about Bellingham, and school, and Mom and Dad. Even about what happened on Christmas Eve.

Ceci said, "My parents split up a long time ago. But you get used to it."

The last song on the tape was fading out, and I was mad at myself for letting the personal stuff slip out. I told her I was sorry if I had bored her.

"That's all right, I like listening to other people's problems." She glanced out the window. "You're pretty young, aren't you?"

"I'm seventeen. Sort of."

She looked at me the same way as when I said I didn't smoke pot very much. She seemed to be studying me.

"I mean I will be, in less than a year." I stopped. There was something weird about the way she was looking at me. "I should probably take off now," I said.

"You're a real darling," she said. Then she crossed over to Ruth's bed, flung her arms around me and kissed me on the cheek.

I reached out and tried to get my mouth over her's, but she put her hands out, with her elbows against her ribs, and held me away from her body. We were like wrestlers struggling for position.

She spoke in almost a whisper.

"You better go, Peter. Ruth will be back any minute. But thanks for coming by. Come back again sometime. OK?"

I told her that I would. Then I let go of her, stepped outside, said goodbye, and walked slowly toward the boat. It was too late for calling Mom. But that didn't matter. Nothing much at all seemed to matter, the way I was feeling now.

Chapter 5

The party was still going on when I got back, only now it seemed louder. Willie Nelson was on the road again, and the voices of the fishermen boomed across the water and competed with his. "You're damn right!" someone shouted. "You're absolutely right!" Next came a chorus of throaty laughter.

Closer up, I caught a smoky whiff of the coals, and the smell of lighter fluid, stale beer, and barbecued fish. Stan had his cap turned backwards, smiling and drinking from a blue plastic cup. It occurred to me that Stan was a wonderful person, that George was, too, that the world was pretty wonderful, most of the time. But that's not how it is, I decided a moment later. It just seems wonderful. To you. Not to someone else. But who cares about anyone else? If I say it's wonderful, it is. At least for now. So there.

I climbed on board the *Ambition* and stepped into the galley. Dad stood in his underwear, teetering on one leg, wrestling with a sock. It was one of those tight brown nylon ones that cling to the hair on your shin. Dad made a little hop as his foot yanked free, and then he stumbled backwards into his bunk, bumping his head against the wall.

"Damn it!"

"You OK?"

"Yeah. Just fine." He felt for the bump with his hand. "What's up, Pete?"

"You look like you had too much to drink."

Dad shrugged. "I had my share."

"You gonna be hung over?"

"I wouldn't rule it out."

"I thought you didn't drink anymore."

"Maybe that's the problem."

"Try lots of water with aspirin," I suggested. "That's supposed to help."

"I bet you'd know." Dad peeled off the second sock, and stuffed it halfway inside its match. Then he tossed the pair into a pillowcase filled with dirty clothes.

"Aren't you supposed to ball the socks together *after* they're washed?" I asked.

"What's the difference?"

"That's how Mom does it."

"If she does it that way," Dad said, pulling off his shirt, "then it must be correct."

"Your way, you just have to separate them later on."

"Since when did you become an expert on laundry?"

"I was only trying to help."

"Your help is appreciated." Dad yawned and scratched under his arm. "Where did you take off to tonight? You hook up on a hot date somewhere?"

"I guess I just wanted to be alone," I said, and I tried to imagine what might have happened, if Ruth hadn't been coming back.

"Well, at least you only got a whiff of Stan's hot air. The rest of us, Jesus, we had to suck it in all night long."

"What was he talking about, fishing in the ocean?"

Dad let out another yawn. His hair was flattened from wearing a cap, making his head seem almost square. A single light bulb stuck out above his bunk, and beneath its glare I could see the little pink patch of scalp, gleaming through the thinning forest of brown. It made me think of the soft spot on the head of a baby.

"That's just Stan, always building things up. Every story he tells makes it sound like it was him who discovered the North Pole."

"Is he serious? About the ocean?"

"It's an idea," Dad said, "but I wouldn't say it's a good one. That's all we need, getting tossed around in big ocean swells. Sure, you catch a few more sockeye, but when it blows too hard you can't fish. Then you sit in some little inlet on the pick, not making a cent. My dad fished up north, False Pass, in the Aleutians, when I was a kid. They used to take a real beating. We don't need it. At least I don't."

Dad slid open a drawer beneath his bunk, grabbed a fresh undershirt, and slipped it on. "Besides, Pete, the ocean is for bigger boats. If the humpies show like they're supposed to, we'll come out fine no matter where we are."

"But what if they don't?"

"It's too late at night for talkin' about that. Because I'm going to bed."

As he reached for the light, Gordon stepped into the galley, a red knapsack hanging from his shoulder, his long hair still wet, and a towel around his neck. "Too late for what?" he asked.

Dad wrapped a dark Navy-surplus blanket around his shoulders. "For talking about whether the humpies are gonna show."

"Worry no longer, Mike, they're on their way. I talked to a guy off the *St. Marie* tonight. Says they were out at Noyes Island last opening, things were pretty fishy. One guy had a couple thousand."

"I heard that, too. But it's all just scuttlebutt until we see for ourselves."

"Maybe we should go out there and try it," I said, forgetting how I almost threw up on our way through Queen Charlotte Sound. Did being with Ceci make me braver?

"Peter, what the hell did I just tell you?"

"What *did* you tell him?" Gordon asked in a pleasant voice.

"That there's no use getting thumped around in the ocean when you can work inside."

"But it might be a good chance to break us in," Gordon said in that same relaxed tone. "Give us a little combat experience."

"I had enough combat at Hidden Falls," Dad said.

"But it might come in handy, later in the season."

"Might just get the shit kicked out of us, too."

George was climbing from the *Navigator* onto our deck. He stepped inside and sat down. Gordon told him, "Good news from the Western Front. They caught some pinks off Noyes the other day. The little guys are starting to show."

George nodded. "That's what Ken Johnston was saying. Hal-ee-lu-yah is what I say. It's about time."

"Hell," Dad said, "those reports aren't worth piss in a toilet, the ways those guys exaggerate. You gotta divide by two just to get a rough idea of what they really caught."

"Better than hearing they didn't catch a thing," George said.

"I guess so." Dad yawned again. "But I'll feel a lot better when we have a couple thousand on board."

"I will, too." George looked up and clasped his big hands, a frown replacing his smile. "Debbie must be gettin' pretty anxious, sitting at home with that baby kicking around, and no money coming in. But rumor has it we'll get two days next time, which must mean something good is goin' on. You wanna run outside and see what's hitting?"

Dad rested his head against his fists. "I don't think so, George. If the fish are there, they have to come in. We'll get 'em on the inside just as well."

"But if the weather's nice, what would we have to lose?"

Dad looked around, first at George, then at Gordon, then at me, and finally he smiled. "You guys all sound pretty eager. I guess I could maybe be talked into it. But I'll have to give it a lot of thought. If the weather's OK. Hell, we'll see. I'll talk to Stan. Might be kinda pretty out there on a nice day. Maybe see some sea lions flopping around."

He rubbed his hands together. "That's another thing about False Pass. My dad used to tell me about how the sea lions would sit around on the rocks and watch the fishermen plugging away, as if they were laughing, like fishing was all a big joke."

"I suppose it was, to them," Gordon said.

"A pretty expensive joke." Dad snapped out the light. "But now the skipper needs his rest. We'll talk about it more in the morning."

I went to bed too. It sounded strange hearing Dad talk about his own dad, someone I knew only from the black-and-white photo on the bureau in my parents' bedroom. He had a thick gray moustache and serious, watchful eyes, as if he did not quite approve of what he saw. He died of a stroke a couple years after I was born. That made Dad the skipper of the *Stavenger*, as well as a husband and a father, all before he turned twenty-three. The old guys who had fished alongside my grandfather liked to tell me how fast Dad learned to work the reef and the spit and the other spots around Point Roberts, how within a couple seasons he could hold his own against just about anyone. They never said anything about how he was doing with Mom and me.

Still, I envied Dad, because as far as I could tell he'd always known he'd become a fisherman. His father was a fisherman and his grandfather was a fisherman, and maybe all our ancestors in

Norway had been fishermen, too. Good for them, I always figured, if that's what they had wanted to do. Sometimes I felt that it would have been nice for Dad to have had another son, someone who could learn to love fishing as much as he did. Or that I would have been born a girl.

Pretty soon I fell asleep. I dreamt about lying alongside Clair Reed on top of one of those thick huge pads that pole-vaulters land on. No one could see us where we were, and I had somehow gotten all her clothes off. (Or maybe she had taken them off herself.) We were both naked but we weren't touching yet.

You should call Ceci, I reminded myself, once I had woken up. Then I remembered Ceci didn't have a phone and I was glad because I hated talking to girls on the phone. Fact, I hated talking to anyone on the phone, including Mom. But that's what you get for being seven hundred miles away, I decided. And that's what Mom gets for being separated from Dad. Not that she was the only one to blame.

Tuesday went by, and Wednesday, but still I put off doing what I'd promised myself I'd do. On Thursday, Dad told us all to get ready, because we were going to the ocean. The state had given us two days to work, and Dad agreed to trail the *Navigator* down Sumner Strait the next morning to Steamboat Bay, on the inside of Noyes Island. So I had to act quickly. Around nine o'clock Thursday night, I walked up the dock and along the main road back to Ceci's room. But when I knocked on the door it was Ruth who answered.

"Ceci's not around." Then she bowed, sweeping her arm across the entrance. "Although you might as well come on in."

I stepped forward so I was just inside the door. Ruth had on a white sweatshirt, with "WSU" stenciled across the front in red letters, and purple eyeshadow. "Is she gonna be back later on?"

"I suppose. Since she lives here. Unless she ends up spending the night with someone else. Some guy from the cannery—don't worry, it wasn't one of the weird Japanese guys—he has a car and I think he took a bunch of them out to a bar down the beach a couple miles. He asked me to come, and maybe I should have, I don't know." She looked at me as if she wanted my opinion. "But I think he's kind of a creep in a way, although Ceci doesn't, but don't you think she's crazy about him, because she's not. Anyway, I was just kind of tired tonight, and I felt like staying home."

She glanced around the room. Her bed was unmade, the pillow lay on the floor, and a long crack I hadn't noticed ran diagonally up the wall. "If you can call this home, you know what I mean?"

"Yeah, I guess. Listen, we leave early in the morning. For the ocean."

"And?" Her eyes turned on me and I tried to stay calm, to get all the words out the way I had planned.

"Well, I just wanted to stop by, before I took off. I don't know when I'll be back."

"Oh, I get it. Like one of those old war movies. Burt Lancaster and Deborah Kerr in *From Here to Eternity*."

"I never saw it."

"I'm only kidding." She had her arms folded, one hand gripping her elbow. I glanced toward the door.

"I gotta get up real early tomorrow. And since Ceci isn't here..."

"Whatever." Ruth turned her back, grabbed a pack of Winstons off her nightstand, and reached for a plastic red lighter. She cupped her hand over the flame, and then looked back at me over her shoulder. "Peter, you like getting high, don't you?"

"Now and then."

She turned all the way around, hands on her hips, the cigarette held between her teeth so that smoke drifted out the corner of her mouth. "Don't give me this 'now and then' crap, because that's why you came here the other night. You wanted our dope."

"Yeah. Sort of."

"Oh, come on. You were pounding on the door, sniffing us out like a bloodhound."

"I'm trying to quit." Although I'm not very good at it, I felt like adding.

"How admirable." Ruth stared at me. "I think goal-setting is very important to all of us, if we want to reach our reachable reaches as human beings. No, I mean that. I'm not just being sarcastic. I think it's good that you're trying. If I had a problem with the stuff, I'd quit, too."

"It's not a problem with you?"

"Not really. It's fun. Sheer recreation. And it's a wall. Something to cut yourself off from the rest of the world. We all need walls of one kind or another. Don't I sound like a counselor?"

"Kind of."

"Listen, Peter, the reason I say this is because I got a whole lid of this stuff, it's from California, it's pretty good for domestic, but I couldn't smoke it in a million years all by myself. Especially since Ceci is on her Ms. Righteous kick—although that doesn't pertain to alcohol, I should tell you. Anyway, if you want to buy some of it, it's yours." She rubbed out her cigarette on the post of her bed. "I'll sell cheap."

"Let me take a look."

Ruth opened the drawer of her nightstand and pulled out a zip-locked sandwich bag, bulging at the sides. When she unzipped the liner, the aroma rushed out at me.

"Smell it," she said.

"Smells good."

"There's some stems and shit—it's not Acapulco Gold—but it will set you back pretty good if you let it."

Ruth sat down on Ceci's bed next to me, cradling the bag against her chest.

"Check it out."

I reached in and took a pinch between my thumb and forefinger, and rolled it around. It was more green than brown, a little on the under-ripe side, and kind of rough. But it would do

95

the job. Not that I actually needed the stuff, I reminded myself. I just didn't see any point in passing up such a good deal.

"Twenty bucks for a quarter," I offered.

"Sounds good." She smiled, and leaned back against the wall. "Sir, would you like your purchase gift-wrapped?"

"Actually, another one of those zip-locked bags would be great."

She reached back inside the drawer. "And will that be Visa or Master Card?"

I pulled out my wallet and gave Ruth a twenty. She studied the picture on front, folded it up and tossed it into her drawer. Then she said, "You wanna try some of it out?"

"Now?"

"Yeah. I got some papers."

"I gotta get up real early."

"We'll just do a joint, it will help you sleep."

"Maybe some other time. Like I said, I'm trying to quit."

"Aw come on, don't be so sure of yourself, quit some other time." She stared at me again. "Unless you're really serious about it."

I said that I was, although I probably didn't sound all that convincing, considering I'd just bought twenty bucks of the stuff. I put on my jacket and stuck the weed in an inside pocket. Then I zipped shut the jacket and moved toward the door. "Be sure to tell Ceci I stopped by."

"I will. And have fun on your big adventure."

I walked out the door and headed toward the boat. After fifty yards I almost turned around. I would have, if it had been someone other than Ruth. But she made me too nervous. Besides, it was important to stick to my plan. The weed I bought would be for emergency use only, like the bright-orange rubber survival suits we stored on top the cabin.

I climbed into my bunk and fell asleep right away. Then Dad was shaking me by the shoulder, urging me to get up. I found my socks, buttoned my shirt, pulled over a sweatshirt and slipped on my leather slippers with the hard rubber soles. For once it wasn't a struggle to get out of bed. The sky was growing light and a thin fog had settled over the water. I shivered in the cold.

"The other guys can sleep for now," Dad said. "You and me can take it through the narrows."

I cut loose the lines and pushed off the dock with a bumper ball as Dad eased his way out. Everything was damp and slick. Up ahead I saw the *Navigator*, a white blotch almost hidden by the fog. I climbed the ladder back onto the flying bridge.

"Does Stan know where he's going?"

"He makes this trip all the time. We'll stay right on his tail the whole way through."

"Probably not a good morning to run aground."

"Jesus, Pete, do you have to be so optimistic?"

"But it happens. Stan told me."

"Sure it happens. If you're a klutz. But we got a good chart here, the markers are real visible, and we got Stan up ahead. Not a thing in the world to worry about."

"Except hitting a rock."

"Shut up and navigate." Then he smiled. We wound through the channel as if it were an obstacle course. Sometimes the shore came close enough so I could have pegged it with a stone, and once a rocky little island surfaced in our path. But Dad barely said a word. He just glanced at the fathometer now and then, and asked me to match up the red and green lights we passed with the lighthouse markings on the navigation charts. It was like playing a board game.

The sun came over the hills and slowly the fog burned away. I could smell the pine forest along the shore. Two deer in a beachside meadow lifted up their heads and looked at us with puzzled expressions. "Better not wake Wade," Dad said. "He's liable to go after them with his Buck knife."

"At least he'd be off the boat," I pointed out, as the deer darted into the woods.

"Come on, Peter, we need the guy. Be pretty hard for us to fish without him."

"I know. He tells me every chance he gets."

"You guys got to learn to get along," Dad said, "I don't want a fistfight breaking out right in the middle of a set."

"Don't worry, I'm not going to take on Wade. I'd get my butt kicked."

"You never know. You've got the reach on him."

"I'm not into fighting."

"Me, neither. But people are always doing things on boats you wouldn't expect."

"So if I punch Wade, can I do it when he's got his back turned?"

"That would be unsportsmanlike. A fifteen-yard penalty and loss of down." Dad grinned. "Oh hell, do whatever you want."

Late that night we rounded Cape Ulitka and turned into the sheltered channel called Steamboat Bay. At the far end was an old wooden cannery building with a couple of purse seiners tied up at its dock. Most of the boats sat anchored in the bay itself, including a couple of large tendering vessels, the ones that would buy our fish. It was nice and quiet when we arrived. We all went to bed almost as soon as Dad killed the engine.

The following morning we headed back out into the ocean to check out the fishing grounds. The west side of Noyes Island was mostly cliffs and sharp spires of stone, with a few barren red trees. On the inside of a rocky point called Cape Addington birds with long black necks and bat-like wings swooped out of a cave. A little farther down we saw the sea lions slumped on the rocks. Sometimes they bellied over the edge and into the water, but mostly they just lay there, damp lumps of yellow-brown carpet.

Salmon jumped steadily, up and down the shore. Dad held a toothpick between his teeth, and was staring through binoculars.

"Looking pretty darn fishy," he said with a grin. "Maybe there was something to that scuttlebutt after all."

"I'd bet money on it," George replied. "I'd bet my whole goddamned share."

"That's not much, so far. But maybe it will be after Tuesday. Oh hell. We'll find out soon enough. Just so the weather holds." Dad licked the tip of his index finger. "They say there's a low-pressure system somewhere out there over the ocean, heading our way. But maybe it won't get here in time."

He held his finger against the breeze. "God I hope it doesn't," he said.

The next morning the stars shone and you could barely feel the wind. We lifted the anchor and slipped out of Steamboat Bay, heading around Cape Ulitka and back into the ocean. The waves swept in, lifting us up and then sucking us down, but without the snap to it. Boats jogged along the shore, their skippers leaning out of wheelhouse windows and peering through binoculars. Everything was gray and shadowy, too dark to see the fish. Then the sun started to rise, lighting up the low-lying clouds, turning the water pink, making the ocean look almost harmless.

We barely caught a thing the first couple sets, and we wondered what had happened to all the jumpers we saw the day before. Dad reminded us that it was still early. Then at nine in the morning we brought a big bag of humpies over the side, five hundred, maybe six hundred, flapping crazily and spilling into our hold.

It got better after that. Twice the bag of fish was too large to hoist on deck all at once, so Gordon pulled the skiff alongside us and hooked one side of the corkline to his railing. Then George and Wade and I guided the big brailer net in and out of the pool of fish, sometimes scooping a hundred or even two hundred at once. The brailer had an aluminum handle about four feet long and a ring shaped like an enormous basketball hoop. With the weight of the fish inside, it was too heavy to lift ourselves, so Dad hooked the chains at the top of the hoop to a pulley block and hoisted it out with the winch. Wade and I helped guide the bag over the deck, and then George yanked on a cord that opened the hoop net at the bottom and let the fish slide into the hold. It seemed kind of dangerous, the way the brailer handle would start swinging around. But you didn't have much time to think. Not when you were trying to get all those salmon on board.

We worked until dark and then we headed back into Steamboat Bay. We tied up alongside one of the big tenders and put on our yellow raingear and climbed into the fish hold and sunk in until the dead salmon came up to our knees. I pitched the little humpies two or three at a time, clutching them in my sand-coated gloves, flipping them into the hoop net lowered from the tender, bending and pitching until the muscles in my back knotted and sweat dribbled off my chin. But I couldn't scratch it because my gloves were covered with slime. So was my rain jacket. It was pretty gross, when you thought about it. But not when you thought about the money.

By the time I got inside my sleeping bag it was almost midnight, but before I knew it Dad stood pounding on our bunks, as if no time had gone by at all. It was 3 a.m., the sun was ready to rise, and he was telling us to get on up, quick as we could, 'cause we had a whole day to go, another day to go out and catch more fish. We got up, all right, although we might have still been sleeping, the way we stumbled around on deck.

After a while the sun cleared the islands, the salmon started to jump again, and we let the net peel into the water. We worked through the morning and afternoon and evening, dumping the net and then reeling it in, plucking the salmon from wherever they got tangled in the mesh, spilling the rest into the hold, then starting all over again. It got pretty grueling after a while. The wet bars of twine cut into our fingers, and sometimes red jellyfish singed our hands. Some of the acid got inside my boot, soaking through my sock, making my toes itch and burn. But you couldn't really complain when you were catching all those fish.

After dark we headed back into Steamboat Bay and tied up alongside that same big steel tender. Dad put on his mackinaw over his workshirt and replaced his rubber boots with leather slippers, while the rest of us got ready to pitch out the salmon.

George buttoned the metal snaps on his rain jacket. "I guess this means we're back in business, doesn't it?" He looked at me and Wade and grinned. "And what all did I tell you? You can't keep a good man down, that's what. And Mike Kristiansen is as good as they come. He'll get 'em in the end one way or another. Ain't that right, Mike?"

Dad just shrugged and shook his head. "Aw, George, cut the flattery bullshit. We might not even be here if you guys hadn't talked me into it. There isn't any magic to it. Just hard work, that's all."

We didn't have much time to sit around and yap. I strapped on the suspenders for my rubber overalls, put on my jacket, cinched tight the hood, and slipped on the sand-coated gloves. Then Wade and I lifted off the hatch covers and laid them on the net. The salmon were packed tight against each other in an ooze of slime, and I wasn't real crazy about diving in. Dad stood above me smiling, hands jammed deep into his pockets, a toothpick between his teeth, talking with some guy from the tender with white hair and black-rimmed glasses. Dad said something I couldn't hear and both of them laughed.

I guess this is why Dad is a fisherman, I said to myself. Then I plopped down into the hold, my legs sinking deep into the pile of fish, the cold slime creeping up my overalls, the smell reminding me of all the work that needed to be done before we could relax.

Chapter 6

That night I woke up in the dark and heard the rain against the bow deck above our heads. Water streamed down a crevice in the hatch and dripped onto my bunk. It dampened my pillow and my mattress and some drops landed on my face. I reached up groggily and pulled down the hatch cover and clamped it tight. But still the water seeped in. I turned on my side, all the way against the curve of the hull, until I smelled the chipping, peeling paint. I probably could have touched it with my tongue. Then I pulled the edges of the sleeping bag over my head, and pretended I was somewhere else.

In the morning the rain still came down, louder now, and steadier. Everything ached inside me. The muscles in my lower back had wound up like a rubber band, and my fingers felt as if they'd been welded into claws. Dried blood ringed the fingernail of my thumb, where the friction of the net had worn away the skin. I clenched and unclenched my fists, and then I touched my knotted calves. It hurt my shoulder to reach down that far.

Someone should come and give me a massage, I thought. Someone female. Or I should sit in a hot tub all the way up to my neck, a pair of soft, smooth hands all over me at once, making the soreness go away. And maybe her lips on my shoulders, or on my lower back, or somewhere else. God you're a weanie. All worn out by two days of work. But it hurts. It really does. Sure it does. Try telling Dad. I bet he's not hurting. No way is he.

Then I heard his voice. He was already out on deck. Figures.

"Pete, you wanna get up here and give me a hand?"

"Give me a couple minutes."

When I tried to sit up, my back muscles tightened, and I turned sideways, my pillow urging my head back down, my mouth falling open, eyes closing against my will.

"Peter! What the hell's taking you?"

"I'm coming," I mumbled back.

"Well, hurry up! We gotta pick this anchor and get on our way."

Out on deck the rain was nastier than I'd imagined. The wind drove it horizontally against my face. I put up a forearm, like someone shielding their eyes from the sun. Of course you couldn't see the sun. You couldn't see much at all.

"Guide the cable while I run the winch."

I nodded without looking up.

"Thank Christ we weren't out there fishing in this," Dad said. "Or not fishing."

Sentences came slowly out of my throat. "The next opener. When is it?"

"Maybe the day after tomorrow. If we're lucky."

I didn't say anything.

"Come on, Pete, wake up. We're finally going to see what it's all about. Might be fishing four days a week for the rest of the season. Nothing wrong with that, is there?"

The cable rubbed hard against my palms, and dripping brown water chilled my fingers. The winch whined loudly from the pressure. Heavy rusted chain with links as big as my wrist replaced the cable, and finally the anchor lurched into its slot on the bow. It was coated in sandy mud, seaweed, and bits of clam shell. We needed the deck hose to blast away the debris. Then we lashed down the anchor with two thin yellow braided ropes.

"Let's get out of this mess," Dad said. "I'm cold."

Inside the wheelhouse Dad shook the rainwater from his hair like a wet dog, then flipped on the VHF. At first all we heard was static, but voices began to drift in from God knows where. They seemed to be muttering to themselves. "The best damn spot you gonna find," someone was saying. "Four kings, bright as hell, the first couple hours I had the hooks in the water." When the person laughed, he sounded as if he were choking on something. Then a Canadian was worrying about things being too rough for his yacht. He sounded British and I imagined him standing in the rain in white deck shoes and trousers, and a V-neck sweater, with "Captain" written in white lettering on the breast. Maybe a sailor's cap, too.

"Must be a pretty big yacht," Dad said, "to even give it a thought on a morning like this."

"Is this normal?"

"Up here it is."

"But it feels like February."

"Come on, we had nice weather for almost a week. What were you expecting?"

After a few minutes another skipper came on the air. He read a series of code numbers and identified his vessel as the *Delta Nellie*. "It's a seiner," Dad said. He turned up the volume a notch. "Listen."

Sometimes the man stopped in mid-sentence. "We come out here, thinking 'Jesus Christ, things are finally going to start to hit.'" A pause. Then a spurt of static. "It would be about time, you know." A deep breath. "After how crappy it's been the first few weeks." Another pause. "But then, goddammit, things ain't worth a piss."

"Not for us," I said.

"Hold on, Pete."

The voice became louder and clearer, then scratchy and distant. "I guess a few guys got 'em at Noyes yesterday. But everywhere else." A breath. "Piss poor just like before. Goddammit I've never seen it so bad!"

"Good thing we were at Noyes," I said.

"Quiet!"

Dad turned up the volume two more notches and craned his neck. The radio let out another squawk of static followed by a scattering of words. Then the voice returned, clearer than before.

"The rumor is they're going to shut us down solid. For the next two weeks." A longer pause. "Goddamn bastards."

I looked at Dad. He looked away.

We traveled for the next couple minutes without talking, the rain running down the windows in large drops. Dad flipped on the wipers, but they didn't do much good. "We going back to Petersburg?" I finally asked.

"No," Dad said. "To Craig."

"I've never heard of it."

"It's tiny. As tiny as a town gets."

"But wouldn't it make more sense to go back to where we were?"

Dad looked at his navigation chart, then at me. "You wanna steer for the next fourteen hours?"

I didn't answer, thinking whether it would be worth it to go back to Petersburg. It might be, if things worked out. Although it was hard to figure. It was always hard with girls.

"Craig'll be all right," Dad said. "It's just another town."

By the time we got there it was raining even harder. Purse seiners were jammed together, rafted four or five to a berth. Most of the boats were the wide steel types, the ones that always fished the ocean. Guys in yellow raingear moved slowly around the decks. From the boat I couldn't see much of the town. It made me think there wasn't a whole lot to see.

After we tied up I walked up the dock and onto the main road. The biggest building was something called The Craig Inn, with the emblem of a steer's horns painted pink against a white background. When I looked at the horns again I saw they might actually be a pair of female legs spread very wide, one of those inkblot tests that show what a pervert you really are. I found a pay phone, but with six people already there, waiting and grumbling. I didn't bother to get in line. I'd call Mom some other time, when I felt like it. Two of the men were Indians, with long hair and cowboy boots and flannel shirts beneath their parkas. At the other end of the road stood an old wooden cannery that needed a paint job, a couple more taverns, and a field of gnarly bushes with pink flowers on thorny stems.

I went back to the boat and tried to read. The sailing ship I was reading about was somewhere in the South Atlantic, where it was summer even though it was January. It didn't take long to fall asleep, not once I started getting warm beneath my sleeping bag.

When I woke up Dad was staring at me from inside the fo'c'sle door. He had on the kind of smile that takes a real effort to keep it there. If he relaxed even a little, the anger would start oozing out.

"Better get ready for some more vacation time," he said. "They've gone and closed the whole damned show."

Gordon stuffed his copy of *Harper's* magazine in the space between his mattress and the curved wall of the hull. "For how long?"

"A week, two weeks. We'll just have to see. That old guy on the radio was right: Noyes was the only place they caught a damn thing. The state's afraid the whole run's going to be a disaster, that not enough fish will get upriver and spawn."

"So what are we going to do?" I asked.

"Don't know yet. A lotta guys will be talking about running for Puget Sound."

Gordon clasped his hands behind his head. "It might be worth thinking about, Mike. We could fish the first opener down there, and then turn around and race back up here. It could turn out pretty good."

"Not for me," Dad said. "Once we got there we probably wouldn't feel like coming back."

"How 'bout Petersburg?" I suggested, trying to sound like it didn't really matter.

"I guess that's where we'll go," Dad said. "No use spending a week or two in a shithole like this."

Back in Petersburg the next evening I went to find Ceci. Neither she nor Ruth were in their room so I walked back through the cannery. The rain pounded against the corrugated tin roof, and the building smelled of ammonia. I passed a sign with red lettering that said "Caution: Employees Only" and through the door I saw a row of workers in rubber boots and aprons and gloves standing in front of a conveyor belt, clutching at the dog salmon as they scooted by. The room buzzed with machinery, and the dull lights gave everything a yellow tint. Cold mist escaped from beneath a door that led to a storage chamber. The workers were using long, narrow knives to lop off heads and dorsal fins and tails, the fish parts piling up in a steel disposal bin.

Ceci had her back to me, her short black hair curling out from beneath a cannery baseball cap. She was hunched over the conveyor belt, the knife held tight in her fist with the blade sticking up, as if the salmon that coasted by might try to swim away. Each time a fish came along she grabbed it by the tail, wrestled it off the belt, and diced off the fin. Then she got the fish back on its way and threw the fin in the garbage.

I said "Ceci!" but she didn't hear me over the machinery so I walked around to the other side of the belt. A surprised smile crossed her face but she couldn't say anything because another big dog salmon was sliding her way, its back arched sideways, its mouth frozen open, as if it had been trying to shout something right before it died.

"Hi," she said, real quickly, her eyes going back and forth between me and the fish. "I'll be off in twenty minutes. Come back then."

I waited for her in the main walkway of the cannery, in front of a row of fire extinguishers. On the wall were heavy canvas jackets and black helmets. The ammonia smell was stronger here. She came up behind me and squeezed my arm, just above the elbow. "Welcome to Hell," she said with a grin.

"Is it really that bad?"

She shook her head. "I just like to complain. How was fishing? Ruth told me you stopped by. How was the ocean?"

"We caught lots of fish. But they closed the season for at least another week."

Ceci looked down at her hands, pink and wrinkly from all the moisture. "Maybe they'll send us all home. Is your Dad pissed off?"

"I'm pissed, too," I told her, glancing at her dark-green eyes, the thin black brows above them, and the square jut of her chin. "Although mostly I'm glad to be back. Because I've been wanting to talk to you."

"Well, that's nice. At least I think it is."

"Can we go somewhere. And talk?"

She looked at me with her chin out, her hands on her hips. "I should warn you, I smell like fish. Even after I wash."

I said that I was used to the smell. Then we walked outside, the hoods drawn on our rain jackets. Ceci stomped through the puddles in her rubber boots, but I had to tiptoe around the edges. We stopped at a cafe that stayed open all night, filled now with old guys and a few old women sitting at countertop stools, drinking coffee from styrofoam cups and smoking, the haze drifting toward the ceiling. Ceci said she hated the smoke, and then she insisted that we order the chocolate milkshakes because they were so thick.

The waitress frowned when we told her what we wanted, and I remembered when I was here before, watching her huff and puff as she gouged out the hard ice cream with a metal scoop. But Ceci said that was her problem, not ours, and if they didn't like making the milkshakes, they shouldn't have put them on the menu.

When the milkshakes finally arrived Ceci took a big mouthful of hers, and wiped away the moustache that formed above her lip with a paper napkin. Then she looked out the big square window at the rainwater streaming down a gutter along the sidewalk.

"Ruth told me she sold you $20 worth of pot."

"Yeah," I replied. "She did."

"Don't you know that stuff gums up your lungs?"

I swirled my spoon around the edge of my milkshake. "It's only for emergencies."

"Like what? If your boat's going to sink?"

"No, you know, if things get real depressing."

Ceci folded over her napkin until it was a tiny square. "You remind me of my little brother. He can be a real headcase."

I wondered if that made me a headcase, too. I said, "Does your brother get high all the time?"

"More than he should. Makes me want to slap him."

"Do you?"

"He's too big for that. Besides, it's not his fault—he just doesn't know any better."

The waitress came back and tore off our bill, then set it on the table without a word. I watched her stride away, swinging her thick white arms.

"I'm not that young," I said.

"Neither is my brother."

"I'll be seventeen in December."

"And I'll be forty-three twenty-five years from now. What's the big hurry?"

"No hurry, I just wanted you to know."

"You *are* a headcase." She poked me in the shoulder and laughed. "But that's OK. You're a nice headcase."

It was all right for Ceci to think I was a headcase, as long as she kept smiling at me like that.

"Can we go back to your room and listen to The Cars?"

Ceci looked up at me, then glanced down. "If you really want to. But at least let me finish my shake."

A few minutes later we walked back along the main road, past the bar across the street with its red neon Rainier sign, a bunch of guys shooting pool inside. Then we passed the grocery store that sold fishing supplies, the bakery with the delicious maple bars, the drugstore that carried postcards of humpback whales, and the movie theater where I'd seen that lousy film.

Ceci let us in with a key, flipped on the overhead light, and locked the door behind us. She pulled off her boots, and I unlaced my Converses, soaked now from the rain. She hung our dripping jackets on nails in the wall, wiped her hands on a small white towel, and started the tape player. Ric Ocasek sang about a frozen fire, his one desire. Then came the drums. I sat down on the bed next to her, an arm across my lap, trying to cover the bulge. I put a hand on her knee and my arm around her shoulder, and I smelled something like coconut oil in her hair, the grainy pink cannery soap on her hands and arms. Without thinking any more

I pressed my mouth against hers. Her lips spread, and her tongue moved slowly in a circle. Then I sort of forgot about everything.

But after a minute Ceci drew back her head and looked at me with a serious expression. Then she started to laugh. "You know, you *are* pretty young," she said. "But you're nice." She kissed me on the lips. "I bet you've never been with a girl before."

"Can you tell?"

"No, I mean for real. You know."

"I can learn."

I had my hand on her boob. She peeled it off, drew the hand into her lap and held it there between her hands.

"I'm sure you can. But for now let's just talk."

"About what?"

"Anything you want."

After a moment I said, "What happened to your boyfriend?"

"Nothing happened. He just left."

"And you don't know why?"

"If I did, Peter, then maybe he'd still be here."

"You think he'll come back?"

"I don't know. And I don't care."

"Really?"

She lowered her eyes. "No, I care. But let's talk about something else."

"We could talk about Jim Morrison. Do you really think he's like a god?"

"No, you dummy, I was only kidding."

I glanced out the room's one tiny window at the rain running down. I thought about what Gordon had told me, about God being manifest in all things. I had to ask him what "manifest" meant.

"I try to believe in God, the main God. But sometimes I feel like he isn't up to the job. It's like he created this world, set it spinning in its orbit, and then it spun out of his control. But maybe," I added, "I'm really just talking about myself."

Ceci mulled this over. "All I know is that things happen and all you can do is hope they're for the best. Sometimes they are, even the bad things. So you're bummed out about your parents splitting up, but is that the worse thing in the world? You think I'd still want mine together, always screaming at each other?"

"But couldn't they have worked things out?"

"Peter," she said, as if I didn't know a thing, "parents don't work things out. Parents stay married until divorce does them part."

One song faded out, and then a new one began.

"Don't you miss your dad?"

"Sure I do." Now she was frowning. She tried to smile but the frown kept coming back. She ran her fingers between my shoulders. "But can't we talk about something nicer?"

"Let's not talk." I got my mouth against hers, but this time her lips stayed shut. Then she turned her head. "No, Peter. This isn't any good."

"What's wrong with it?"

"I don't think I want it."

"Then what do you want?"

"I don't know. I don't know what I want."

"Do you want me to leave?"

"Yes. I mean no." She sighed noisily. "Oh I don't know."

I turned away and we sat there not saying anything. But when I finally got up and reached for my jacket, she hugged me and kissed me on the lips, tongue and all. I couldn't figure it out. I hung around for another half-hour, just sitting there with my arm around her shoulder and talking. She said everything in the world was shitty, and that she hated it. The world didn't seem all that bad to me, though. At least not right now. Fact, I wished things always seemed only this bad.

Chapter 7

By the next morning the rain had let up, but the sky stayed heavy and gray. No one felt much like getting out of bed, and I probably could have slept until noon. But we had a lot to do. During the two days in the ocean the net had caught on a bolt on the stern and Dad had sworn loudly when he heard the popping sound of the mesh ripping open. Now he had us out on deck, running the net back through the power block, spreading it out and checking for holes. Dad liked patching the rips because it showed how fast he was with his hands. But it still took a long time, especially if you had to stand there and hold the net in place. It was like watching someone knit.

We were tied up close to the cannery and every ten minutes or so a jet of steam drifted our way. It smelled like crab that's been boiled too long, and it made my eyes water and my throat scratch. I thought maybe it was ammonia, but Dad kept telling us we didn't have a thing to worry about. "Besides," he said, "it doesn't smell that bad."

"It smells bad enough to me," Wade said, squinting at Dad from beneath the hood of his wrestling sweatshirt. Then he pinched his nose. Gordon shook his head.

"Hold your horses, big guy. It stinks, but it's harmless. Purely organic."

"It better be."

Dad shrugged. "If I drop dead you'll be the first to know. Now no more of this standing around. We gotta get this done today, one way or another."

"But we're going to be here another week or two," I said. "What's the big hurry?"

Dad glanced at me but kept on working, his needle of twine darting between the mesh as easily as a small fish, his knots spaced as if punched out by machine. "It's still better to do things right away," he said, "'cause we might be on our way a lot sooner than you think. It all depends on what the state decides."

George let out a yawn. "I don't know about you, but I'm already pretty tired of wasting away in Petersville. Frozen concoctions or not. God knows the last thing I need is to be sitting around getting fat."

"Once we start fishing you'll shed those pounds in no time," Dad said. "You're not so fat. Not yet, anyway."

"Not as fat as Debbie."

"No siree."

Dad finished patching the hole and then he ran the power block so that about five yards of net passed through. Wade and I spread the web, he taking the heavy lead-line and me the corks, bunching up the mesh with our fingers as we worked toward the middle. Gordon and George kept an eye out for holes.

"I was talking to Stan up at the Harbor Bar last night," George said, "and I had to admit, he was right—guys are starting to take off. You see the *Michelle* and the *Avatar*? Loading the net in the fish hold, gettin' ready to run for home."

"That's their business," Dad said, "not ours." He flipped his needle into the air, then caught it in his fist. "But it makes you wonder why they even came."

"At least they'll get a chance to fish," Wade said, rotating his shoulders and flexing the muscles in his neck. "I hate not fishing. I hate just sitting around."

"Maybe you should go find someone to wrestle," Dad said. "The skipper of the *Anna Rose*, he's about your size."

"I'm serious, Mr. Kristiansen. I can't stand all this time off."

Dad spread a new patch of net and examined the tear. "No need to panic. From what everyone tells me, up here you can't really hope to make much money until August."

"I agree," George said. "Entirely. But it seems kind of silly to be sitting on our butts when they're catching fish in our backyard."

"You just miss your woman," Gordon said.

"And you don't miss yours?"

Gordon looked surprised. "Who said I even had one?"

"Lucky you," George said, "no responsibilities."

"It's not that lucky."

I stood atop the coils of cork-line that had piled up on deck, balancing on one foot and leaning forward with arms out like wings. It was pretty challenging, and more fun than holding the net for Dad. I didn't notice him watching me. Not until I slipped and fell on my ass.

"What about you, Mike?" George said.

Dad glared at me. "I've got all kinds of responsibilities."

"No, I mean, don't you miss your wife?"

"I try not to think about it."

"I know it's none of my business. And it don't matter anyways. Because I don't want to go home myself. At least some of the time I don't."

George paused, tapping his needle against his palm. "God, I disgust myself—I'm getting softer all the time. But the baby's due in a week or two. Sure would be nice to be around for the big event. I know Debbie would appreciate it. And I've never seen a baby being born."

"I don't think they give the husband a front row seat," Dad said. "At least they didn't when I was in that position."

"It's different nowadays," George said. "The doctor says the husband ought to share in things as much as he can. Although I don't know if that's good or not."

"It's pretty scary, as I remember it." Dad pulled his knife from his hip pocket, folded it out, and cinched tight the knot in the web. Then he held the twine with his thumb against the blade and sliced through it with a jerk of his wrist.

"Or at least it was in Rita's case. It was like Peter was fighting as hard as he could not to come out. I guess you can't blame a kid, when you think about it. But they tried and they tried and the whole time I was pacing around the waiting room by myself, like I was going to put my fist through something."

"So what happened?" Wade asked.

"What always happens." Dad pointed at me with his knife. "He was born. But they finally had to cut him out with the blade. It seems stupid, looking back, but I was only nineteen, and it didn't seem stupid at all. I kept thinking about slicing up a salmon, to get at the roe."

I wound a piece of twine over and over my palm, pulling on it hard, until the flesh around it started turning white.

"Nowadays we take it all for granted," Gordon said. "But you go to the Third World, or hell, maybe in some of the worse neighborhoods in L.A., it's not a pretty sight. Women die all the time."

"For Chrissakes, would you watch what you say?" George spat into the water. "I gotta go through this in a week or two, only via long distance. You want to be giving me nightmares?"

"Not a thing to worry about it," Gordon said. "Bellingham ain't exactly L.A."

"But that was the thing," Dad said. "And I know I shouldn't be saying this. But there were complications. The whole what do you call it—Caesarean—took a lot longer than they figured. I'm no doctor, but Rita looked pretty damn pale when they finally let me in."

"How was Peter?" Gordon asked.

"He was fine." Dad folded up the knife and put it away. I yanked a little harder on the twine and felt it cut against my skin. "I guess it's not that unusual," Dad said. "I mean maybe you're right, that death is something we usually manage to ignore." He glanced at his boots. "Hell, I don't know. It sure seems that way when you're a fisherman."

"Maybe farther north, in the Aleutians," Gordon said. "But people don't die too much down here."

"They die often enough. Just last summer, there was that boat from Blaine, the *Jewel of the North*, it went down off Dall Island. Probably 'cause that stupid bastard Kovich had too many fish on board."

"What is this?" George said. "The Morbid Hour?"

"How come you never told me this before?" I asked, whipping the twine off my hand and wadding it into a ball.

"About the *Jewel of the North*?"

"About Mom."

Dad shrugged. "That you almost killed her? Why would I tell you that?"

The tips of my ears grew hot and red, and something bitter was rising in my throat. I turned and chucked the ball of twine over the side of the boat. Then I swung around to face Dad. "No wonder I didn't want to come out! Who the hell would, with a father like you?"

Gordon and George stared at me. Wade smirked. Dad's face stayed the same. "Sorry, Peter. I meant it as a joke. I guess it wasn't very funny. Besides, I thought you knew."

"It's not one of the things a guy normally hears."

"I know it isn't. And you're right—I shouldn't have brought it up." He shifted the lever to the hydraulics that made the power block spin. No one said anything now—George and Gordon pretended they hadn't been listening, and Wade just stood there with that stupid smirk. I told myself to relax, to not lose control. At least not any more than I already had.

I knew some things, but not about being born. What I knew went back farther than that. It was one of those things Mom told me after she'd drunk a lot of wine.

She said it happened right on the *Stavenger*, in the bunk my grandfather normally slept in. It was a warm night in August, maybe the warmest of the whole summer, so warm you could still smell the salmon that had been unloaded the evening before. Neither she nor Dad had ever done it before. Mom didn't know she was going to do it until right before she did. And as soon as it happened she knew something was wrong. She told Dad right away. She was awfully scared. But he just laughed and kissed her and told her not to worry.

Now Dad stopped the power block, and Wade and I spread the net. It was damp in this part and smelled like clothes that were washed but not dried and then left in a closet. That was mild compared to what came next.

"Jesus!" Wade said. "What the hell is that?"

We spread the web and found a rotting humpy caught in the mesh by its gills. Its eyes were almost gone and a pair of flies touched down on its skull, probing the mushy flesh with their forelegs. I buried my nose in the collar of my sweatshirt, thinking this is how everything ends up, if you don't bury it quick enough. Or even if you do. I'd seen cartoon-like bumper stickers with the caption, "Life stinks," but it wasn't life that smelled. Life smelled just fine.

"It's the hydrogen sulfide escaping," Gordon said. He peeled the mesh from beneath the humpy's gills, then dumped the fish into the harbor.

George was pointing toward the ramp that led to the main road. "Is that Stan the man coming our way?"

"'Fraid it is," Dad said. "I don't know if I'm ready for this."

Stan carried a white bakery box with a styrofoam cup on top. Coffee had leaked from a slit in the lid, and he slurped it up and wiped his mouth on the shoulder of his jacket. Then he peeled back the top of the box. Six of the donuts were glazed and three were filled with gloppy red jelly, but none of us felt much like eating. Stan said, "So when are they going to let us out to fish again?"

"Damned if I know," Dad said. "You got any idea?"

"Wish I did." Stan rubbed his red face and scratched his nose where the skin had begun to peel. "This season's been kind of a joke so far. What have we had, four days to whack away?"

"Three for us."

"Yeah, right. I see some of these guys fleeing for Puget Sound, but I say that's an unwise thing to do. 'Chickenshit' might be a better word. You won't see the *Navigator* putting its tail between its legs, yapping all the way home. At least not right away."

Dad looked at Stan, and Stan said, "I guess I should explain. See, I was thinking since they might not open things any time soon, I might venture on down to Ketchikan. Then, if the closure is really long, we're fourteen hours closer to Point Roberts, we could make the run in under three days if we absolutely had to. You know, defeat with dignity."

Dad rubbed his jaw. "Might not be a bad idea, now that I think about it. At least the running to Ketchikan part. I'm getting pretty tired of this place."

"Me too." Stan munched on a jelly donut and sipped his coffee. "A man comes up here to fish, not to sit on his ass."

"Right on," Wade said, balling up one fist.

I pretended not to hear him. "Aren't we closer up here to the good fishing spots?"

Stan said, "If this year were like normal, there'd be fish all over the place south of Ketchikan. Still will be, if you ask me."

"Sure better be," George said. "And soon."

"Ain't that the truth." Stan took another hurried bite of donut. "Listen, boys, I gotta be going. Got something wrong with my radar I want an electrician to look at before I run south. But I plan to leave first thing in the morning. Let me know if you want to tag along."

When Stan started back up the dock, Gordon said, "Sounds like a real good idea to me," and elbowed George in the ribs. "We'll have to go back to the... what was the name of that place?"

Dad frowned. "You guys better hold off on making plans. I'm not so sure I want to get sucked in that direction."

I thought of the stripper in Ketchikan who smiled at us while she was fiddling with her nipples. But even that seemed kind of stupid, when all you could do was watch.

"Why don't we stay right here?"

Wade smirked. "What's the big deal to you, Peter?"

"What you want doesn't have a damn thing to do with what we decide," Dad said. "But we're not doing ourselves any favors right here."

George nodded. "Running to K-town might make sense."

"Then maybe we ought to quit talking about it." Dad turned and looked across the water, one foot on the bulwark railing and his chin against his fist.

Another wave of anger rose in my chest.

"I still need to think it through a little more," Dad said. "But I can't think of a good reason not to."

I said "fuck!" and kicked the pile of corks. Taking off on a moment's notice, that was part of being a fisherman, Dad would have told me, had I bothered to ask. But I didn't want to hear about it. At least not right away.

That evening I went to see Ceci again. I wanted to pick up where I'd left off. And forget everything else. It seemed simple enough. You take things to a certain base and each time you go a base farther. That was how everyone told me you did it. But it wasn't so easy. Even when I told her I might never see her again.

"That only works in the movies," Ceci said. "Not with me."

We lay on her bed with the lights out and a dark-green blanket pulled over us. Jim Morrison sang about how into this world we're born like riders on the storm. You could hear the rain come down at the beginning. "Then what does work?"

"That you'll love me forever." Ceci laughed. "Or something like that." She had on a white t-shirt with Mickey Mouse on the front, and I was pretty sure she wasn't wearing a bra. But she wouldn't let me find out.

"OK," I said, nestling my head against her chest, as if I planned to sleep there. "I'll love you forever."

"I was only joking."

"So was I. But what's the big deal? I won't tell anyone. And I'm not asking for much."

"That's not the point." She drew back her head, her hands on my shoulders. Then she placed two fingers against my lips. "The point is that I don't want you to. I hardly know you." She sighed and turned her head. "You're getting pretty bold for just a kid."

"You're not so old yourself."

"Older than you. You've got your whole life to do things you shouldn't."

Her breath felt warm against my face, with a peppermint smell. Her whole body felt warm. I wondered if Mom was telling the truth when she said she didn't know until right before she did it. Girls were funny that way. Although it was hard to think of Mom as a girl. And this was a bad time to be thinking about Mom at all.

"We couldn't, anyway," Ceci whispered, "because Ruth is coming back."

"The hell with Ruth, we'll keep the door locked."

"That wouldn't be very nice.

"I thought you didn't like her," I said. "Because she's so sarcastic."

"Actually, I like sarcastic people. They know what the world is really like."

"So what *is* the world really like?"

"The world is a fine and splendid place." She looked at me and laughed. "How should I know what it's like?"

"Because you've lived in it so long."

"Don't get smart with me."

"Hey, I thought you liked sarcastic people."

"Oh stop it."

I grabbed her by the shoulder and we leaned back on the bed. Then I threw my leg over her and started to kiss her, one arm wrapped tight around the small of her back. I was kissing a lot harder than she was, rubbing up and down against her thigh. But then she told me to stop. I'd been sort of expecting it. Fact, I felt kind of relieved. Although I knew I wouldn't, later on. She sat up and ran a hand through her hair, then tucked in her shirt. "Come on," she said, "I'll walk you to the boat."

She walked with her arms folded, her chin against her chest. It was chilly outside and she didn't have on a jacket. I was pretty cold, too. But at the edge of the harbor she locked her fingers inside of mine and squeezed my hand.

"I'm sorry if I treated you meanly tonight. That's because I shouldn't be getting mixed up with anyone at all right now. If I did I'd probably get all mixed up myself."

She gave my hand a tug. "But if you do come back, be sure to stop by, OK? Don't pretend I don't exist."

I nodded, and she kissed me on the cheek. Then we said good-bye. I watched her go along the dock toward the bunkhouse, her shape getting smaller, finally disappearing against the dark walls of the cannery. I thought about what it might be like if I saw her again. But I tried to think about other things. I decided to go call Mom. It'll be a big relief, I told myself, for her to finally hear from me. God you're a jerk, not calling all these weeks. Maybe she thinks we're all dead. I walked to the pay phones and pushed the zero button. The operator sounded young and foxy, and that made me think about Ceci again. I told her our number and listened as she dialed the call. I waited for Mom to answer. She has to be home, I told myself, now that I'm finally calling. But I kept waiting. The operator asked, "Do you want to try again later?" and I said no, I want to talk to her right now. But the operator said I'm sorry, you can't, she's not home, and I said the hell I can't, and hung up. It took the whole way back to the boat for me to cool down.

I climbed over the bulwarks and slid open the door to the galley. Dad lay on his bunk reading a thick paperback called *Submarine Down*. His shoes were off and his mackinaw hung from a hook on the wall. Out of the radio came piano music, the kind that makes old people fall asleep in their chairs. Dad asked if anything was wrong, and I told him that I tried to call Mom. He wondered what the big deal was, and I couldn't really say, when I thought about it. Except that it was awfully late for her to be out of the house. But Dad just shrugged and told me not to lose any sleep over it.

I said, "Maybe she's with Mr. Reynolds right now." When Dad didn't say anything, I said, "Doesn't that make you mad?"

"Why should it?"

"Because I thought maybe you wanted to get Mom back."

Dad inched back his head farther against his pillow. "Look, Peter, that's not really any of your business. For the record, yeah, of course I do. If we're both ready for it. But it's like I told George—I'm trying not to think about it. Because it's a little more important to see how we come out this summer."

I grabbed a stool from beneath the galley table and sat down alongside his bunk. I was thinking about last summer and the summer before, coming into port after fishing at Point Roberts, Mom picking us up at the harbor, the three of us driving home together, maybe stopping off for something to eat at the Burger

Barn near Interstate 5. It didn't matter that sometimes we ended up in a fight.

"I sure wish you hadn't sold the *Stavenger*."

"Jesus. It's a little late for that now."

"But why did you?"

"So I could buy this boat."

"No," I said. "For real."

"Because you can't be afraid of change. That's why."

He looked down at his book again, but I said, "Maybe if you hadn't sold it, if we were still fishing back home, you and Mom wouldn't have split up."

Dad folded over the corner of a page, shut the book, and stuck it on the shelf above his bunk. "Peter, you forget: your mother and I separated in December, and I didn't buy the *Ambition* until April. I didn't even think about buying it until January."

"But did you have to leave her with Mr. Reynolds?"

"Your mother's a big girl now. She can take care of herself." Then Dad turned so he was facing the wall.

"What would you do if you found them together again? In our house?"

"Come on, give me a break," Dad said to the wall. "You been having more weird dreams?"

"Maybe I just want to go home," I said more quietly.

Dad turned and stared at me again. He looked toward the ceiling, muttered something, and rubbed his temples with his hand. "Then do whatever you want. Because I'm tired, Pete, I'm tired of the whole thing. You wanna take off, I'll write you a check, you can fly home from Ketchikan the day after tomorrow."

I shook my head. "That's *not* what I mean."

"I don't know what you mean. But first of all, quit assuming your mother is some poor damsel in distress. If she hadn't wanted to see this Reynolds fellow, she wouldn't have." Dad stared at me, his eyes bloodshot and with little wrinkles around the corners I'd never noticed before. "Peter, do you understand why your mother and I married in the first place?"

"'Cause you knocked her up."

"Yes. If you want to be blunt about it."

"Couldn't you have been more careful?"

"You're lucky we weren't. Do you really want to know what happened?"

"You already said quite a lot about when I was born."

"I'll be less specific this time. But I can give you the general idea. Your mother was pregnant, pregnant and nineteen. A wonderful situation. Your grandfather, Dr. Hotshot Morini, had long since left town."

"She didn't want to have me, did she?"

Dad ran his fingers through his hair and lowered his head. "It's a lot more complicated than that. Let's face it. Your mother and I weren't exactly *Good Housekeeping*'s Parents of the Year. I was wild as hell. Drank like a madman, just about got myself killed out on Chuckanut Drive."

"And Mom wanted to go to college."

"Sure she did, but people want a lot of things they can't have. I wanted to fish year round, San Francisco Bay in the winter, the Bering Sea in the spring."

"Did you think about not having…"

"What kind of a question is that?"

"Well, did you?"

"Your Mom's Catholic. And I felt a guy had to live with his mistakes."

"That's a great way of putting it," I said, and I tried to stop thinking about it. It was not the kind of thing that was easy to forget.

"Oh Pete, don't take it wrong." Dad smiled and tapped his fist against my shoulder. "As soon as you were finally born, as soon as I saw you… there wasn't a single doubt."

I waited for him to go on. But he just looked at me with those tired, wrinkly eyes. "Hell," he finally said. "You know what I mean."

"I guess I do."

"Good. You all set to head to Ketchikan?"

"What time are we leaving?"

"Five a.m. But I'll let you sleep in this time. As late as you want."

"I think I'll go get started."

Chapter 8

Three days later we left Ketchikan for good. But we headed west, not south, toward Cape Chacon and the ocean. I went back to sleep after breakfast, when the islands around town still protected us from the wind. But I woke up as soon as we were out in the open, feeling as if I were lifting free of my mattress, floating above it. Then I slammed back down against the railing in my bunk. The fo'c'sle was like a space capsule, tumbling end over end, falling toward earth. It will land safely if you let it, I told myself. As long as you relax. But then came the bile, deep down my throat. I barely had time to slip on my boots.

I hit my head on the overhang leading into the engine room. The diesel fumes made things worse. So did the freight-train roar of the engine. The floor rose and fell but my stomach stayed in the same place. Now I headed up the ladder and into the galley, then out on deck, into the wet, cool air.

"You all right?" Gordon called from inside.

Just thinking about the cherry-scented smoke from his pipe made me sicker. I dropped to my knees and wrapped my arms around the bulwarks. I hung my head over the edge and waited for it to happen. But nothing did. I tried but it wouldn't come. The dizziness grew stronger, and I sat back on the fish hold covers with my arms around my legs. Seawater seeped through the seat of my jeans, wetting my boxer shorts, dampening my skin. I gazed toward the wide gray throat of Dixon Entrance, then closed my eyes and stuck my head between my knees.

Gordon put his hand on my shoulder. "Up top, my man." He pointed to the flying bridge, toward Dad and George. They had their rain jackets on. It wasn't raining, but the waves kept crashing against the bow, dousing them with spray. "It's better up there," Gordon said. "Fresher air."

I nodded, headed up the ladder, and sat down on the bench next to George. Then I laid my head against the railing. "You look awful," Dad said. "You take some of Gordon's pills?"

"I will. In a minute."

"You know, the boat's buckin' things pretty good," Dad told me. "Even better than I expected."

I lifted my head. "You think maybe we should try out those stabilizer poles?"

George said, "Better hold off on that. Once we get around Cape Chacon, this southwesterly will hit us broadside. Then we'll really see what kind of boat she is."

"I can't wait."

"Hang in there," Dad said. "You'll be OK."

After a while I got used to the chop. Of course the Dramamine helped. It made me want to go back to bed. But I was afraid. The rocking and rolling might lull you to sleep, but it would jostle your stomach fluids pretty good. And then you'd have to pay the price when the nap was over. So I stayed on the flying bridge, trying to think about something else. It wasn't easy. I tried to imagine something without motion, or taste or smell. Sleeping was the only thing that came to mind.

When I opened my eyes, I saw Cape Chacon jutting into the ocean, a lump of rock barely rising through the water. The waves crested above it in white tongues of foam. A small red lighthouse stood farther inland, its beacon going round, sending its signal across the dull sky as suddenly as a flash cube. Closer to shore another purse seiner bobbed in the chop, sinking partly beneath the surface, then surging above it, so you could see the red copper-paint on its hull.

George nudged Dad with his elbow. "Looks like a nice spot for a shipwreck, doesn't it?"

"Why do you think we're way the hell out here?" Dad said, glancing at his chart, pinned to the bench-top by a donut-sized ring of iron. Then he studied the compass and the fathometer, and swung the boat even farther to the port. You could see the foamy white strip where the tide from the two bodies of water met, and in a moment we were in it, leaning way over to one side. But Dad seemed in control, more or less. He cranked the wheel the other way and after a moment the boat leveled out.

We headed northwest, rolling from side to side. In the evening we reached Noyes Island and dropped the anchor on the inside of Cape Ulitka, to protect us from the southwest wind. But the wind got worse during the night. Its roaring-furnace sound woke me up. Something large and wooden whacked against our hull. Dad stomped his foot on the wheelhouse floor, and I got out of the fo'c'sle in a hurry. Out on deck I saw another boat only a few feet from our bow, with men in cotton long johns dangling bumper balls over the side. George said, "They let their fuckin' anchor drag!"

Gordon stepped carefully across the deck in bare feet, his arms folded and his elbows cupped in his hands. "No surprise, with this wind. We'll be lucky if any of us are fishing tomorrow."

Or not lucky, I thought, watching the other boat drift toward us, silent as a ghost ship. The two men in long johns glanced at their skipper, then at us, then at their skipper again.

"Get a bumper down!" Dad shouted from atop the cabin.

I stumbled onto the bow and grabbed a tire with a rope looped around it. Walking against the wind, I hung it over the edge. The rubber screeched as the other boat rubbed against it, followed by the groan of wood against wood. I wrapped the rope more tightly around my right hand and with my left pushed off against the other boat's bow.

"Watch your fingers!" Dad warned.

But then the boat rumbled to a start and backed slowly away. I yanked the tire back on deck, only to slosh its water all over my pants. The bristles on the rope left pink marks in my hands. "Check the anchor cable," Dad said. "Make sure we're OK."

Gordon glanced over his shoulder, his arms still folded, his V-neck undershirt flapping in the wind. "Looks OK to me."

Dad said, "Then I guess we're all right."

"You gonna go back to sleep?" I asked him.

"What's the point? We gotta get up in a couple hours."

"You mean we're going to fish in this?"

"How the hell should I know? Now go to bed."

I stepped to the side of the boat and unzipped my fly, my piss driven sideways by the wind. I washed my hands and climbed down into the engine room and through the door to the fo'c'sle. It was hot, without enough air coming through, and smelled like sweaty clothes. Climbing into my bunk I stepped on Wade in the stall below me. He said, "Watch out, damn it!" and snapped on the light. Then he turned over and pitched face forward on his mattress. George moaned and draped his arm over his eyes, while Gordon lay down on his back with his hands behind his head, staring into the glare. "No way we'll fish," he said. "No chance in hell."

"Why not?" Wade rolled back on his side to face him. "We gotta make money somehow."

"I'm more interested in surviving until the start of the school year."

Wade snorted. "I don't got another job like you."

"It doesn't matter. A couple hundred dollars isn't worth the risk."

"Maybe not a hundred," Wade said. "But how 'bout a thousand?"

"You know how cold that water is? You know how long you'd last?"

"Come on, Gordon," George said groggily. "Whatever happened to all that crap about this being a great adventure?"

"There's adventure and then there's foolishness. And I think I know the difference."

"Sure you do," George replied with a yawn. "Adventure is something that seems dangerous but really isn't. Something that will make a great story in the faculty lunchroom."

"I know what it's like to be on a boat that sinks. None of you do. And I hope none of you find out."

"Drop it," George said. "So we can get some sleep. And turn out that goddamned light."

But in the dark I was afraid to sleep, because I knew as soon as I did, it would be time to get up. So I stayed awake for more than an hour, breathing the stale air and listening to the wind. Gordon is right, I thought. The money doesn't matter. Your money or your life? It sounds like an insurance commercial. I know what I'd choose. But what about Dad? Deliver us, Lord, from every evil, and grant us fish in our day. And nice weather. Deliver us. And if I die before I wake. And if. I won't die. Yes you will. But not for another sixty years. Now shut up and *sleep*. Don't think, sleep. Yes. Sleep.

Just as I'd feared, in what felt like minutes, Dad was waking us up, saying he had started the engine. We picked up the anchor, the sky getting lighter as we slipped around Cape Ulitka. The wind wasn't as bad as in the night, but still it blew hard, carrying with it tiny drops of rain. Dad and I stood at the wheel, Dad in his long green rain jacket, his hood drawn, looking through binoculars. He stood for a long time, the boat heaving up and down, and after a while he spread his feet for better balance. Then he yawned and sat. The binocular strap pulled his head down with it, and his eyes closed, his chin touching his chest.

I grabbed him by the shoulder. "Dad. Wake up!"

His head snapped up and he clenched the wheel. "I was just resting," he said, trying to smile, rubbing his eyes with his right hand. The circles beneath them looked darker than usual, and his face seemed paler, less fleshy.

"You get any sleep at all last night?"

"I couldn't. Not with this wind."

I leaned over the railing and closed my eyes, the rain stinging my face like bits of sand. "We gonna set in this?"

"You bet." Dad looked out toward the open ocean. "We gotta see if there's anything out here."

"What if there isn't?"

"Then we're fucked. But we gotta try."

"How long we got?"

Dad squinted at his watch. "Fifteen minutes. Can you go down and make me some coffee? And tell those other guys to get ready."

I climbed down the ladder, gripping the rungs with both hands, digging in with the soles of my boots, shifting my weight to meet the rising tilt of the deck. I slid open the door to the cabin, stepped inside, and closed it behind me. The warmth of the oil stove filled the galley, coating the windows in mist. A plate of raspberry Danish sat on the table, sugary icing dripping down the sides, smelling as if they were just baked. Wade held one and chewed it slowly, bracing himself with his other hand against the edge of the sink, his stool tottering on three legs. "Make sure that door's shut tight," he mumbled.

Gordon scraped from his bowl the last spoonful of granola while George poured steaming water from a tin coffee pot over a bag of tea. Then he squirted in honey from a plastic bottle shaped like a bear. The bottle tumbled over as soon as he set it down. So did the cereal box. George stuck the honey in a rack beneath the table, and stirred the tea with the handle of his fork. Without looking up he said, "What's the word, Pete?"

"We're gonna try one in a few minutes."

Gordon tapped his spoon against the rim of his bowl, sighed, and wiped clear the window with a peach-colored dish towel. The view changed with the swell, from light-gray sky, to waves with swirling white peaks, back to sky again. "I'm not so sure that's a wise thing to do."

"Dad said we have to try." More quietly I added, "He thinks it will be OK."

"Well, I don't know if I agree with him. I don't know if the skiff can handle it."

"I wouldn't worry about it, Gordo," George said, pressing his big butt against the wall for balance. "That little baby's tougher than you think."

Gordon flipped his bowl into the sink. "You're not the one who's going to be inside it."

"It's not like we're going to be having a picnic on deck," George said.

Wade wiped his mouth with the dish towel. "Maybe after this we'll go home."

"It doesn't matter, we still gotta fish today," George replied. "So we may as well get ready."

Wade grinned. "We could mutiny."

"Save it, Wade."

"I don't mind fishing in this stuff, so long as we make big bucks."

"While you're on this boat, you do what Mike wants," George said. "Understand?"

"Sure I do."

"Good." George grabbed his jacket. "Let's get the skiff hooked up right away."

I slid open the door and headed out onto the stern. Gordon buttoned up his rain jacket and followed me. The wind blew harder now, straight in from the ocean, and everything pitched up and down. Twice I fell to my knees. But finally I got the end of the net hooked up and then I fed the lines to Gordon. He tied things off and fired up the engine of the skiff. Dad maneuvered the boat around in a half-circle so the net would lie parallel to the beach. The skiff kept getting thumped around by the waves, Gordon inside with his arms folded, his hood drawn. A big one broke over the side and doused him, making him shiver and shake his head.

"Are we ready?" Dad yelled.

"We're all set," George called back.

"What about you, Gordon?"

Gordon raised his arm but didn't look up.

"Then we may as well let her go."

The skiff end of the net peeled into the water, corks swiveling off their pile, rings and lead-line weights banging against the steel stern roller. Gordon got smaller and smaller as we left him behind. Then he spun the skiff around so he was heading forward, taking the waves head on. Spray shot over his bow, and he tucked his chin tightly against his chest.

On deck, the boom rocked side to side, jerking at the rigging. It was tricky as hell keeping your balance. The wind raced toward us in sudden gusts, rippling the water. The boat kept leaning way to the starboard, and I expected to start feeling sick. Two boats jogged nearby, not dumping their net, just watching us to see what happened. A smaller wooden seiner called the *Arlene* raced back toward Cape Ulitka, its mast sweeping in a wide arc, as if it might scrape the ocean's surface, or topple over and sink. Farther down the beach two wide steel boats had cut loose their skiffs, starting the set. But they were a lot bigger than us.

George grabbed my shoulder and pointed to the cork-line. "This I can promise you: we're gonna have a hell of a time getting it back on board."

The wind made it hard to hear. "Then why did we let it go in the first place?" I shouted back.

George put his arm around me and pulled me toward him. "You gotta trust your father, Peter. I can't explain it, it's like a sixth sense, I just know to believe in him, to do what he thinks is best."

"But what if it isn't best?"

"Come on, Pete," Wade said, sitting on the bulwarks and leaning way backwards like a crewman on a sailboat. "It's not that bad. It's kind of fun." He let out a whoop and waved his arm in the air cowboy-style.

"*Jesus Christ, Wade!*" It was Dad, on top of the cabin. "*Get away from the fucking edge!*"

Wade glared back at him. "What's the big deal? I wasn't hurtin' anything."

"The hell you weren't! You wanna fuck us up good?"

Wade didn't say anything. Dad went back to the wheel, and I stepped inside to make him his coffee. Granola had spilled all over the table and drips of honey stuck to the formica. Plastic cups rolled back and forth. Dad's book and some papers had fallen off the shelf above his bunk, and the pillowcase that held his dirty socks and underwear had spilled onto the floor. I took off my rain jacket and laid it over a stool near the stove. Then I warmed my hands. Looking out the window I saw the skiff. Fishing wouldn't be so bad, I said to myself, if you didn't have to go outside.

I dumped a tablespoon of instant coffee into a mug. To be safe, I spooned in another. I grabbed the tin pot and held the mug still with my other hand, but the mug slid down and the hot water splashed onto the table, some of it leaping onto my knuckles. I shook the hand and ran cold water on it, and then I tried again. This time the water came right to the edge. The coffee crystals bubbled on the surface, and I stirred them with a spoon. It didn't smell much like coffee. More like something you'd make in a chemistry class.

I tried to squeeze the mug with both hands, to keep it from spilling. But the surface was too hot. I carried it by the handle and started up the ladder. A big swell came and some of the coffee sloshed over the side, barely missing my fingers. I got on top the cabin and walked unsteadily across it, the boat leaning sharply toward the net. Dad had his arms around the railing, his eyes on the skiff.

I handed him the cup, and he thanked me and took it by the handle without looking. "How's Gordon doing?" I asked.

"He'll be OK. I think." Dad sipped the coffee. "What's in this stuff? Drano?"

"I thought you'd want it a little stronger."

"God knows I can use a jolt of caffeine." He stared back at the skiff. A large wave headed its way, lifting it up and tilting it to one side. "Ooh!" Dad said. "That was a big one."

"Is Gordon all right?"

"He's fine. But I think I've seen enough."

Dad held the microphone to his mouth. "Let's seal her shut," he said.

Gordon stood and signaled with his arm, but the swell forced him to sit back down. Then he turned the skiff toward us. He looked tiny so far away. I was glad it was him out there, not me. But George was right. Things wouldn't be very fun on deck. At least we wouldn't be alone, though. If something happened, it would probably happen to all of us at once.

Down below, I stuck my boots through the legs of my rubber overalls, balancing on one foot and then the other. Next I hooked in the shoulder straps. Then I put on the jacket, buttoned it up, and cinched tight the hood. It would be hard to swim in raingear, I thought. George had told me that if your boots filled with water, they'd pull you straight to the bottom.

The skiff pounded against the trough as it drew shut the circle of net. Gordon was almost alongside us, his beard soaked, his eyes half-closed, his teeth clenched. He flung his rope to Wade, and then he got ready to cut behind the stern, beneath the line that led to the other end of the seine. But he was having a hell of a time. Every time the boat rose in the swell, the weight of the net pulled the line down, slamming it shut like a mousetrap. Gordon didn't seem crazy about trying to slip under it. Finally he positioned himself on the crest of a wave and gunned the engine, shooting beneath the line just before it snapped down.

Now he circled in to throw me his tow-off rope. The skiff rose and fell in rapid jerks, sometimes lifting clear above us, as if it were about to crunch down on deck. Gordon crouched in the cockpit, his arm cocked back, the yellow line coiled and ready to cast. His eyes were enormous. He let fly the coil but the waves pulled him in the other direction. The line flew toward me and I leaned way over the edge with my knees locked against the bulwarks. But the rope fell short of my outstretched hand.

"Damnit, Peter!" Dad said. "Catch the fuckin' thing!"

Gordon hauled the line back in, coiled it furiously, got himself parallel to us, and heaved it toward me again. This time I clutched it in both hands and hooked it up. Then Wade and I started to bring the net on board. My legs went rubbery as I piled the corks. My stomach felt empty, and I remembered what Gordon had said. But I didn't have time to think. The wind made the seine billow like a sail. Wade struggled to keep it under control, his arms moving more and more quickly. The mesh got hooked up on bolts and pulley blocks and metal corners, and we tried like hell to pluck it free. But we couldn't keep up. My pulse drummed in my ears and I wheezed for air. Then Wade was inside the net, thrashing his arms, fighting to get out. The black web wrapped around him in a thickening cocoon.

"Help me!"

Dad shut off the power block and George and I peeled Wade free. It was like freeing a big fish you couldn't sell, trying to save it before it suffocated. Wade let out a deep breath. The power block began to roll again and he climbed back on the pile.

"You OK?" I said.

"I'm fine!"

"This wind. It makes it almost impossible."

"Just keep piling," George said. "Don't say a word."

Then the rings were out of the water, sealing shut the bottom of the net. George joined us on the pile as it rose higher and higher. Clinging to the cork-line, I stared over the edge. The net seemed to rock closer with every wave. As the circle of corks got smaller, the pile became harder and harder to surmount. It was like a steep hill. The water looked dark green.

The boat jerked hard to the starboard, and I slipped from the pile, down onto the stern, right to the edge. I let out a yell and reached back for something to grasp. My fingers clutched at the web and I dug in as deeply as I could. I stared down into the water. The wind lifted the spray off the edge of the waves and blew it against my face. The mesh cut into my fingers. Someone pounced on me and pinned my legs with his chest and grabbed me by the back of my suspenders. It was Wade, dragging me to the middle of the stern.

"Back on the pile!" Dad yelled. "Hurry, hurry, hurry!"

The wind shrieked worse than ever, but I didn't hear it now, not as a separate sound. I blocked everything out, the whine of the power block, the clang of the lead line and rings, even Dad's words of command. The boom swung crazily back and forth. I imagined it snapping off, falling toward us. But I blocked that out, too. I didn't want to climb back on the corks. It didn't matter, I didn't have a choice. None of us did. So I grabbed the cork-line and hoisted myself on top. The net was just a tiny circle now. If we had anything inside, we'd see it swimming around. But I didn't see a thing. I didn't care. I'd stopped thinking. I wished I were asleep. The net came up on deck. It was mostly empty. It didn't matter. Nothing matters. The set's over, that's what matters. That matters a lot. You bet it matters.

We spilled it as quickly as we could. All I saw were jellyfish, and maybe twenty or thirty salmon. We stood still, catching our breath. George's big chest heaved in and out. Seawater dripped from Dad's eyebrows. A red string of jellyfish clung to Wade's cheek.

The skiff engine roared above the wind. Gordon headed toward our stern. He climbed into the bow of the skiff and made a funnel around his mouth with his hands. He was shouting something I couldn't quite make out.

"Should we hook him up?" I said to Dad.

Dad shook his head. "Don't try. It's too nasty." He braced himself against the davit and pointed toward Cape Ulitka, where big breakers crashed against boulders along the shore. "Have him follow us inside."

Dad hustled atop the cabin, while George signaled to Gordon and pointed toward the cape. Gordon nodded and gunned the engine.

Now we headed that way, Wade grinning stupidly, me doing the same, Gordon's eyes still huge, the wide aluminum bow of the skiff pounding against the waves, its engine whining with all its force, following us to shelter.

Chapter 9

By the time I got up the next morning the boat was bouncing hard in the chop, and I banged my shoulder against the wall as I passed through the galley. George had his back to me, peeling potatoes. Wade was studying the pictures in *Sports Illustrated*. He looked up, nodded, and looked back down. I headed out onto the deck to piss over the side. The day was overcast as usual, but windier. I braced myself against the aluminum davit and tried to figure out where we were. The wind shaved off the peaks of the waves. It blew my piss back on deck. We rolled hard to the starboard, and seawater rushed through the base of the bulwarks, soaking my deck slippers and socks, and my jeans almost to the knees. Wade stared out the galley door, grinning and pointing, because my dong still hung out. I zipped up my fly, thought about giving him the finger, but instead climbed the ladder to the flying bridge.

Dad sat at the wheel alone, a blue skullcap covering his ears. It was strange being with him again, after the night before. I thought of lots of things that I wasn't able to say. And now was not the best time to try.

"How long till we get to Ketchikan?"

"Got a good haul in front of us, Peter. I hope you weren't in any hurry."

I looked at the navigational chart upside down, with Petersburg at the bottom and Ketchikan at top. "Dad," I said, "doesn't it seem funny, going in the wrong direction?"

He had one hand on the wheel, the other balled in a fist beneath his chin. "What's that, Pete?"

"I said it seems weird running south like this."

"Probably would have done it sooner or later, anyway. We just gotta hope that pretty soon things start heading in the right direction."

I glanced at the dashboard, cluttered with half-empty Swiss Miss packets, a spoon, two ceramic mugs, and a couple of cereal bowls with bits of corn flakes glued to their sides.

"But I got some good news already," Dad said. "We heard on the radio that they might open things on Sunday after all. At least according to Stan."

A wisp of spray wetted the Plexiglas visor and sprinkled my face. I wiped it away with the back of my hand.

"You don't seem excited," Dad said. "You sure you want to go?"

"'Course I do. This next opener, think we'll fish the ocean?"

Dad shook his head. "The way it's blowing out there, it's probably nasty as hell."

"I'd probably get sick."

"You didn't last time."

"Last time it was calm."

"It doesn't matter, we're going to take care of that now. Stan said I ought to get a pair of those aluminum stabilizer poles. You lower them from your mast so they stick out like wings. Then from the wings you drag a couple of weights through the water. It keeps you from getting jerked around so much in the heavy swell."

We dropped into a deep trough, and both of us ducked and grabbed the railing. Dad waited until we flattened out. "They'll cost me a bit—maybe a thousand bucks. But hell, you gotta spend money to make money."

"It's not like we've made much yet."

"We will. One way or another." He looked down at the compass, examined the chart, and scrawled something in the log book.

"What if we don't? Will you have to sell this boat, too?"

"We will. One way or another." Dad turned his head toward shore, away from me. "That's the new rule around here, Peter. No more worrying. We'll worry ourselves sick before we know it."

"If you had to sell"—and now I felt kind of dizzy—"what would you do?"

"That's why we better start catching some fish," Dad said with a shrug.

But we hardly caught anything that week. On Sunday we fished south of town in a place clogged with boats, and we had to take turns. Dad hated taking turns. He said from now on we would fish the ocean. "Because at least out there a guy can still work hard."

The next morning we unloaded in Ketchikan, Salmon Capital of the World. But not this year. At least not yet. Maybe not at all. I thought about what Robert Frank had said about the run being bad this year and whether he was pleased with himself, the way things were turning out. But it was still too early to tell. Way too early. At least that's what everyone kept saying.

I walked to the main part of town, near a big white cruise ship. Old people in white slacks or white skirts with tennis shoes, and cameras hanging from their necks, wandered around pretending the damp air didn't bother them. I found a row of pay phones and I got hold of the operator. I waited for Mom to answer. It was early in the morning, so there wasn't a reason in the world she shouldn't have been home. Instead I got Mr. Reynolds.

"How you doing, sport? You knocking 'em dead up there?"

I imagined his open sport shirt and dark blue jacket with the wide lapels, his silver moustache carefully trimmed, Brut splashed all over his hairy flab. He told me Mom was in the shower.

"We figured we'd take the whole day off, just enjoy ourselves," he said. "It's wonderful weather here—in fact, I'll take the Porsche for a spin later on, crank open the sun roof. You know, I got it up to ninety-two on the interstate the other day. Some of the people I passed, you should have seen the looks they gave me!"

I was watching a ferry pulling out of its berth, picking up speed and turning south. I finally said, "Are you there—all the time?"

Mr. Reynolds hesitated. "Not really," he said. "Just sometimes. Now and then, you might say." Then, after another long pause, "So how have you been? We read in the *Herald* that the fishing hasn't been very good. Wait, hold it, sport, I think your mother is coming down the hall. The lovely lady is on her way."

"Jesus," I whispered. Then I waited. It seemed like a couple minutes.

"Peter? You know you've worried me sick?"

"I was hoping you weren't going to see him anymore."

"That's really none of your business."

"Dad's going to be pissed," I said, although I wasn't so sure.

"If your father's so worried," Mom said, "he can call me himself."

"Good! 'Cause I don't feel like talking anymore."

A light rain was falling, and I looked out toward the harbor at the tourists with their umbrellas drawn.

"Don't hang up," Mom said cheerfully. "We haven't had a chance to visit. How are things?"

"They suck."

"Don't talk that way, tell me the truth."

"It rains all the time, and we've barely had a chance to fish. Some guys already took off for Bellingham. But we won't. Dad's dead set against it."

"Well, be careful, and don't do anything stupid. Tell your father to call me." I asked her why, but she said, just have him call me, and she said it was none of my business. She asked me more questions about the fishing and the places I'd been, but I didn't feel like answering much. Then we said goodbye, and I walked back to the boat.

Dad stood inside the wheelhouse, his hands jammed into the pockets of his mackinaw, listening to the VHF. I told him what Mom had said about his calling her, and his head jerked up, but then he shrugged and said he'd call her when things were more settled. When I told him about Mr. Reynolds being there, he stared at the red digits of the VHF for a long time. "That's too bad. Why don't we talk about something different?"

I looked out the window at the rain hitting the water. "Did Stan do better than us?"

"Worse, I think. The place they were fishing, they probably had to wait hours for a set."

"You think maybe he'll take off for Bellingham?"

"I doubt it. Be too much of a blow to his ego." Dad glanced at his watch. "You know, I talked to that fellow about the stabilizer poles. He's going to put 'em on tomorrow. After that we'll be ready to go out again and fish."

"You think they'll let us?"

"They will within a week or two."

"By then it will almost be August," I reminded him. "If we left right now we'd have lots of time to reach Point Roberts."

Dad scratched his neck and looked out the window. "The guys from Bellingham, they're fishing down there today. It does kind of make me wonder how'll they do. But we'll find out soon enough."

The next morning, a few patches of blue appeared between the broken white clouds and I thought we might even see the sun. But then everything turned gray again. A man with a leather tool-belt around his waist climbed way up our mast, drawing out a tape measure that Dad held firm on deck. In the skiff Gordon worked on the engine, his hair held back in a bandana and his forearms splotched with grease. George scrubbed the galley table with a washrag, while Wade and I stood behind the cabin, trying to keep warm. "You guys look like you need something to do," Dad said. "You want to run up to town and buy me a couple of oil filters?"

Wade said, "Why can't Peter go by himself?"

"Because I told you to go with him."

Wade mumbled something while I stepped inside the galley and pulled on a rain jacket over my sweater. Then we trudged up the dock, onto the main road. The parts store was a long way off, probably more than a mile, but I didn't want to tell Wade because I didn't want to hear him complain. After about fifteen minutes of walking, he stopped and put his hands on his hips and scowled. "Where in hell is this place?"

"Right next to that little grocery. We're almost there."

Wade turned and looked over the railing at the edge of the harbor toward a small cluster of purse seiners. "Jesus, Pete, how long we gonna stay in this fuckin' town?"

"I think we'll go to the ocean pretty soon. If the weather's all right."

"That'd be cool. Although it would be a lot easier on one of those big steel boats. How come your dad didn't buy one of them?"

"Because they probably cost a million dollars."

Wade snickered. "Aw, come on, Pete, that shouldn't be a problem. Your dad seems pretty used to owing people money."

"You're lucky that he is," I said, "or you might not be here."

"Is that lucky?" He leaned over the wooden railing at the edge of the harbor and spat. "There's lots of places I'd rather be."

Down below us a pair of seagulls fought over something dead in the water, but one gave up and flew away with a frantic squawk. Everything smelled like diesel oil and garbage. Wade was looking hard at one of the boats, leaning farther and farther over the railing and pointing. "Isn't that the *Navigator* down there?"

"I think so." I recognized the white hull and mast with the American flag near the top. The crew stood on deck, running the net through the power block. "They must be checking for holes."

"Jesus, Pete, have a clue. They're not patching. They're piling it into the fish hold. The lucky bastards. They're getting ready to leave. Come on, let's take a look."

I followed behind Wade, walking quickly to keep up, staring at the thick cords of muscle in his neck. When we got close I saw two of Stan's crewmen squatting in the hold, ramming the net into the sides. Stan had on jeans and unlaced high-top basketball shoes, the tongues sticking out from his big ankles. He paced back and forth with his arms folded, his pale freckled cheeks hanging slack, dragging down the corners of his mouth.

"Hi, Pete," he said slowly, his eyes still on his crew. "I guess it looks like we're going home." He rubbed his hand along the left side of his face and managed to smile. "Well, we are. I may regret it, who the hell knows, but in this business you gotta decide what to do and stick to it."

"My dad's going to be surprised" was the best that I could reply.

Stan shook his head. "Jesus, you bet he will. But if things hit in the Sound, I want to be there. Not up here wishing I was there."

"Maybe we'll head down with you," Wade said. "'Cause I'm getting sick of this whole goddamned state."

"You shouldn't. Not if you've never fished up here. For you guys it should still be an adventure."

Wade stuck his hands inside the gut pocket of his sweatshirt. "It's not an adventure for you anymore?"

"Hell, I haven't spent a summer at home in six or seven years. So I got a right to go home. Because it's not fun anymore. Not when I'm worrying about my wife and kids all the time. That's why you kids are lucky. You don't have kids, you're just kids yourselves."

Stan turned to watch the wet black net pour into the hold, the chubby crewman named Scottie guiding it in. Then to me, "But make sure that your dad comes over right away. I'd at least like to say goodbye."

So we walked to the parts store, bought the oil filters, and returned to the boat. Dad was using a power drill to bore a hole in the bulwarks for the brace to hold one of the stabilizer poles. Smoke smelling of sawdust swirled out of the hole, and the roar made us want to cover our ears. Finally he shut the thing off, set it down, and peeled off his goggles.

We told him the news.

"Then he's even more of a jackass than I thought. To leave right now, that's just plain foolhardy."

He slipped the goggles back on, shook his head, and restarted the drill.

"I'm not so sure, Mike," George shouted. "You never know, he might come out just fine."

Dad kept drilling.

"Yeah," Wade said. "Maybe *we'll* look like the stupid ones."

This time Dad shut off the drill and let it bang against the deck. "For Christ's sake, Wade. Why don't you leave those decisions to me."

"I didn't mean anything by it."

In the skiff, Gordon was cranking on something with a pipe wrench. "Still better to keep your mouth shut." Then to Dad, "You hear how they did down there?"

"All I heard was that a couple of guys got 'em at Lummi."

"Then those Puget Sound sockeye are on their way through."

"Maybe. But that's a real chancy thing, especially when you only get a couple of days to work."

"But what if we get closed down again up here? And they keep catching fish?"

Dad shrugged. "We'll talk about that if it happens. Why speculate?"

"Mike's got a point," George said. "It's not even August. This year, we're a Southeast boat, no ifs or buts."

"That's right," Dad said. "And we're not going to waste any more time talking about it."

"But it's important," Wade said.

"Dammit, Wade, don't tell me what's important!"

Wade hung his head and put his hands on his hips. "Geez, sorry. Can't I even say what I think?"

Five minutes later Dad and I started the long walk back to the *Navigator*. By the time we got there, the skiff was suspended above the stern, and the crew was using the winch to hoist it on board. Then they lowered it down, its keel banging hard against the deck, the men moving quickly to secure its big aluminum bow with chains and steel binders and bristly brown ropes.

"So I guess you got my message," Stan said, rubbing his bare cheek again, looking toward the deck. "As you can see, what is done is done—we're just about on our way."

"Think you might turn around?" Dad asked.

Stan laughed. "That's what I did five or six years ago—raced down to Point Roberts, went into Blaine after the opening, said hello to the wife, then raced back up here. But that was a hell of a long time ago, Mike. Longer than I care to remember. Don't think I could do it today."

Dad said, "Me neither."

Stan glanced over his shoulder toward his crew and shouted something about the skiff. Then to Dad, "You going to put on the stabilizer poles?"

"It's being done right now."

"So from now on, you're a coast boat."

"I guess so. But it wasn't like I had much choice. Not after the way things went down. The fuckin' jellyfish were horrible, too. That was enough for me."

Stan looked down at his unlaced shoes. "Just remember, Mike, fall comes early up here. Earlier than you'd believe."

"Well, I'll be damned if I let a little cold weather bother me. Not if we're catching fish."

"That's the spirit, Michael. Knock 'em dead."

"We'll try. Be sure to say hello to Beth and the kids."

"Sure thing." Stan reached for Dad's hand and shook it hard. Then he turned to his crew.

"You guys ready to blow out of here?"

"Ready as I'm gonna be," Scottie called back.

"Then I guess we might as well cut it loose."

Dad and I climbed back onto the dock. Stan waved from the upper wheelhouse and we waved back. A puff of soot lurched from the smokestack. The crew slipped the lines and Stan threw the engine into reverse, nudging the boat from its berth. "No use standing around," Dad said. "Let's get back to work."

But we stood and watched the *Navigator* slide out of the harbor and into the channel that led to Dixon Entrance, the boat shrinking against the low green hills.

"They'll be home before Friday night," I said.

"We'll go home sometime, too," Dad said.

"When?"

"When we're ready."

Chapter 10

We heard the wind beyond the cape, and we saw the foamy swirl of the waves, but we were just spectators now. Where we dropped anchor was safe and calm. The rain had stopped, and the sky arched overhead like a concrete dome. The tide moved across the sandy beach with barely a ripple. Farther ashore you could see the brambly bushes dotted with pink blossoms, and the dark green canopy of the forest.

Dad sat alone on a stool in the wheelhouse with his head cocked, listening to the VHF. A ropy vein twisted from beneath the collar of his shirt, stretching tight along his neck, disappearing in his beard. The radio whined with static, sometimes spitting out fragments of speech. Above us the flashing digits of the fathometer skipped from low to high, and then dipped low again, as if we had drifted over an undersea mountain. I figured something must be screwed up. Or that what we saw was actually a record of Dad's rising and falling hopes, a graph of his disappointment.

"Something wrong with that thing?"

"I guess it's got a mind of its own," Dad said, attempting a smile. Then he pointed toward the radio. "They say the weather's not so bad farther south. So maybe things will lighten up here in a couple hours, too."

"Then what?"

"Then we'll go out and try her again."

Out the rear door of the cabin I could see the heap of net. In good weather, it lay smooth and even. Now it looked as if it had tumbled off a flatbed truck.

"You sure?"

"Sure I'm sure."

"We didn't catch much."

"That's 'cause the wind was blowing so hard. Flattened out the net, probably lifted up the lead line, too. Makes it real easy for the salmon to escape."

"You think there's some out there?"

"Someone's got to be catching something," Dad replied, staring out the side window toward the cape. Purse seiners rotated slowly on their anchor cables, like hands sweeping away minutes on gigantic clocks.

Behind me in the galley Wade lay on the bench by the door flat on his back, his knees raised, hiding the rest of him from view. "I bet the other guys won't be crazy about trying another one," I told Dad. "Especially Gordon."

"Gordon's not the skipper."

"But he's fished up here for quite a few years."

"Then he should know what it's like."

Dad wrapped the leather binocular strap around his left index finger. He unwound it slowly, as if it were adhesive tape. "We took a risk that last time, and it didn't pay off," he said with a shrug. Then he looped the binoculars over his neck and held them to his eyes. "But it showed me something, Pete. It showed me we can handle it as a crew."

I looked down at the strands of seaweed clinging to my boots. "It wasn't easy."

"I know it wasn't. But it could've been a lot worse."

"I almost fell overboard."

"You gotta be more careful."

"I was almost *blown* overboard."

"I admit it," Dad said, "there were circumstances beyond our control. But you guys impressed me. Wade especially. You see the way he swooped on top of you and pinned you to the deck?"

"All I saw was the water."

But Dad went on as if he hadn't heard me. "All of you—Gordon, too—did a damn good job. Makes me think we'd be OK in just about any weather."

"That's a pretty lousy reward," I said, "for doing a damn good job."

"If we start catching fish, it will be a pretty good reward." Then, before I could reply, "Because the guys who make money up here are going to be the ones who keep the net in the water, who don't let up."

I gripped the wooden railing along the dashboard, as if to brace myself against an imaginary swell. Then I stepped close to Dad. I smelled coffee on his breath, and the wet fabric of his jacket.

"But we're smaller than everyone else! Didn't you see the way we got bounced around?"

Someone came on the radio and we both stopped and lifted our heads. But the speaker faded out before we could make sense of what he was saying. Dad stood up, put a hand on my shoulder and lowered his voice. "Look, Peter, if you felt a bit frightened, don't worry about it, I was a little nervous myself. I'd think something was wrong if you didn't feel that way. But a lot of times things aren't as dangerous as they seem. Especially now that we got the stabilizer poles."

I shivered inside my damp clothes. "You really think they'll do much good?"

"They won't hurt us none—that much I'm sure of."

From the galley I smelled bacon and frying potatoes, and then George brought Dad his breakfast. Dad thanked him and started in on the cantaloupe slices. I joined Wade and Gordon around the galley table. The galley was quiet, and warm, and I might have dozed off if I hadn't been so hungry. George pulled a pan from the oven, and set the bacon on paper towels to soak up the grease. He took our plates and dished up the potatoes and scrambled eggs. We still didn't say much—mostly yawns and grunts and sometimes a "this is good," or a "damn, that's good." It was nice, not hearing anyone talk. But then Wade set down his plastic tumbler of milk, wiped his mouth with a paper towel, and said, "You know, it was kind of cool out there, in a way. Especially when those big gusts of wind came up!"

"Real cool," Gordon said dryly.

"I bet we'd still be out there, if there were fish."

"I think we're gonna be out there anyway," I said.

George lifted a second pan from the oven with a flower-spotted potholder. "The wind's backed off quite a bit. So maybe we will."

"There better be a good reason," Gordon said.

"Making money," Wade replied, his cheeks crammed with potatoes. "That's a good reason."

Gordon rolled his eyes. "Last set was great for that. If you like risking your balls for twenty scrawny humpies."

Wade started to say something but Dad stepped into the galley carrying his plate. He held it under the faucet and ran water over it, blasting away the ketchup and the spongy yellow chunks of egg. Then he refilled his coffee.

"As soon as you guys are finished, we'll head back out and take another look," he said.

Gordon stared at the mess on his plate. Wade grinned. George leaned against the railing of the sink and ran a finger along his sideburn.

Dad said, "Is that going to be a problem?" When no one replied, he looked down at his coffee. Gordon stared at George. I looked that way, too.

"You sure you don't want to wait a little longer, Mike?" George finally said. "Might be calmer an hour from now."

"I'd like to, but we can't. One guy just got a couple hundred out there, according to the radio. Some sockeye, too."

"So you think we ought to try it?"

Dad said, "I think we have to," and turned his back and walked to the wheelhouse. Gordon closed his eyes and rubbed them with his hands. George scooped up the last of the potatoes and eggs from their pans onto his plate, and sat down at the table. "May as well enjoy the meal while you can."

"Because it may be our last," Gordon said.

"Jesus, Gordon!" Wade said. "Do you always have to be so goddamned negative?"

"I'm not negative, I'm just chicken."

"Well, I'm not. But I am sick and tired of not making money. So let's get out there and get to work, or else screw the whole thing. Because I *hate* sitting around!"

"Sometimes when you're nineteen you think you can live forever," George said, chewing on a strip of bacon as slowly as a cow. "But I got news for you, partner. You die, you're dead—and that's the end of the show."

Wade chewed his cantaloupe slice down to the rind. Then he looked at George.

"You sound real smart, you know that? You ever think about writing a book?"

Gordon said, "He could make you the main character and call it *The Idiot*."

"Go to hell!"

George yawned. "Come on, guys, we got better things to do than sit around and yap. Let's just see what happens. Mike might make us all really happy before this day is done."

But as soon as we got around Cape Ulitka, the wind picked up. It pushed us wherever it wanted. We never came close to getting the net in the water. Dad was more concerned about getting the boat back inside the cape. The next morning was just as bad. We stayed on anchor the entire day. Gordon and I played six games of cribbage, and he won every time. "Next time we'll play for money," he warned. Dad sat in the wheelhouse listening to reports on the weather. I'd heard of psychics who could control the events of nature just by thinking about them, and maybe Dad had the same idea.

Dad decided we should go back to Craig. I wanted to go to Petersburg, of course, but Dad reminded me that we were a coast boat now, so we might as well stay near the ocean. I wasn't so sure. The boats we tied up alongside had wide steel bows, and names like *Cape Ominous*, and *Ocean Pounder*. Dad said we'd just have to work that much harder, to make up for whatever else we lacked. Gordon said the main thing we lacked was brains. He laughed at his own remark.

On the third day in town the sky cleared, for the first time in about ten days, and I woke in the fo'c'sle alone, with the sun beaming through the bow hatch, right into my eyes. I got up quickly, washed my face and combed my hair. Then I headed back into the engine room and grabbed my stash of weed from the locker where I'd hid it behind a big gray toolbox filled with pipe wrenches. I folded up the zip-locked bag and stuck it in the thigh pocket of my jeans.

I said goodbye to Dad, who sat at the galley table adding something on a calculator, and I walked out around the little peninsula beyond the main part of town. I traveled along a gravel road, past tiny houses without front yards. A little kid with brown skin and black hair squatted between a rusting tricycle and a half-inflated rubber ball, wailing like a police siren. He wasn't wearing any clothes. A girl maybe a few years younger than me in a plain white dress smudged with handprints stood over him, glaring, as if she were his mother. She picked him up by the armpits and cradled him against her, brushing the dirt from his buns and stroking his oversized head. His pudgy fingers clung to her shoulders, making her stoop. She turned and her dark eyes passed over me. I looked the other way and walked a little faster.

From another house a large black dog yapped twice and pranced toward me, his bubble-gum pink tongue wet with slobber, flanked by pointy teeth. He wagged his tail and nuzzled his snout against my groin, as if searching for my dope. I walked slowly away from him, looking straight ahead, wondering if maybe he had rabies, or ticks. He loped alongside me, sniffing my butt. I stopped, turned, and said, "Go away!" At first the dog didn't believe me, but I glared at him, and kicked the dry dirt, and at last he shuffled off with his tail drooping and his head down.

After I went around another bend, all the houses disappeared, except for two trailers set on cinder blocks and overlooking the water. Farther down, the rusted hulk of a car lay upside down, its rotting wheel cores jutting into the air like the stubby legs of a turtle. But I left that all behind. I'd had enough of Dad, the crew, the boat—and of worrying about Mom. From now on, I decided, I'd let Dad do the worrying. You had to figure he still cared about Mom, even if he didn't admit it. Dad was reluctant to admit a lot of things. But I wasn't going to think about it. I wasn't going to think about anything. Not even the barefoot girl and the little brown kid. I turned off the road, down a short trail through the grass, and then over large, smooth rocks and onto the beach. The tide was in. I straddled a bleached log wider than a telephone pole, near a clump of stringy seaweed. I peeled off my t-shirt, slipped off my shoes and socks, rolled up my jeans, and let the wet sand squirm between my toes.

I pulled out the baggie, and the papers, measured out the weed and started to roll the joint. I dropped it once and had to start over. It was as if I had never done this before. My heart sped up. I wondered what it would feel like. Like it always does, I said to myself. But maybe a little better this time, different. I cupped my hand over the match and turned my back to the breeze. The paper curled around the edges and the tip of the joint glowed red. The smoke tickled my nostrils. I sucked hard and held it in for what seemed like minutes. It was like standing on the bottom of a swimming pool, testing your lungs. Then I exhaled. Something rushed through my head and made me shiver. I coughed and wheezed and wiped my watering eyes. Before long the joint was too stubby to hold without getting burned.

Then everything went numb: my fingers, my toes, even my balls. The sand felt better now, warm and gritty against the bottoms of my feet. Everything felt better. I wondered why I'd waited so long. I lay in the sand on the other side of the log, away from the tide. I listened to it sneak in and out, like a vacuum cleaner sliding beneath a table. It never stops, I thought. The tide comes in, goes out, forever. We might die and maybe the Russians will blow up half the world, but the tide will keep coming in.

I closed my eyes for a long time and almost fell asleep. But the sun warned me not to. I pressed my chest with the fingernail of my thumb, leaving a white mark against the reddening skin. I sat up, yawned, and slipped on my shirt. I was starting to get hungry. I put my shoes back on, and headed toward the boat. Back on the road the dog yapped again and trotted toward me, tongue out, tail flapping. He seemed to be walking sideways, his head raised, as if he were smiling. I crouched down and rubbed the fur behind his ears. He whimpered contentedly. I picked up a stick from the edge of the road and flung it, and he raced after it, his nails skidding in the dirt. He returned the stick, now slick with his slobber, and I threw it again. Then I kept walking.

I still wasn't ready to go back to the boat. I didn't feel like talking to Dad. So I stopped at the only restaurant I knew, a little place with swivel stools and tables made of slabs cross-cut from huge trees. When I stepped inside all the men with beards and baseball caps stopped eating and looked at me. At least it seemed that way. Hanging on the wall was a big saw with long, uneven teeth and handles at either end. The teeth looked like spiky cones of ice dripping from a cave. Nearby another wooden slab was painted with smiling figures of lumberjacks. I wondered what they found so amusing. I sat on a stool at the counter and watched the other people eat. Everything smelled of hamburger grease and melting cheese.

The waitress had her back turned, her faded jeans tucked inside her cowboy boots and a thin brown belt cinched tight around her waist. She was leaning against the window that led to the kitchen and talking with the cook.

"So finally I told him, 'I'll kick you out, I'll get someone who'll pay rent!' I'll be damned if he'll live off me!"

The cook stuck her head through the window, frowning. She was older than the waitress, stocky, with dark skin and hair held in a net. She said, "If a man can't pay his way, he don't deserve to be a man."

"That's what I always told him," the waitress replied, shaking her head. "But Rick thinks I'm just bluffing. He says, 'if you're not careful I'll start playing hardball,' and I say, 'well, I can play hardball, too.' And I will, you can bet on it."

"Excuse me," I said. "Can I order?"

The waitress turned and stared at me. She had a gap between her front teeth. It made me think of a guy I knew in middle school who bragged about how far he could spit.

"Just hold on a second," she said.

"I'm pretty hungry."

She sipped from a glass of cola, lit a cigarette, and fingered the necklace of shells that hung at her throat. "The world's not going away in the next five minutes, now, is it?"

"I'll settle for a chocolate milkshake."

"Hold on, I'll be there when I can."

So I waited. But then Wade, George, and Gordon walked in and sat down around one of the tree-trunk tables. I hoped they wouldn't see me. I was afraid they'd smell the pot on my clothes. But it was impossible to hide, sitting here at the counter. Everyone was staring again.

George called out, "Peter! C'mer!"

I could hardly feel anything below my thighs. I kept looking at the floor, to make sure my feet were touching. I wiped away the stupid smile but it came back each time on its own. I glanced around at the men in their baseball caps.

Wade was smiling, too, but for a different reason.

"It's great to see you, Pete," he said, slapping me on the shoulder, as if it had been months. "Because we were all talking, we think maybe it's time to go home."

I sat down with them and rubbed my forehead with both hands. All three of them looked strange. Wade's ears stuck out like a monkey's, and George's face appeared round as a tomato. Gordon's beard came to an elf-like point.

"Now wait a minute," George said. "Don't go giving Peter the wrong idea."

"About what?" I asked kind of sleepily.

Gordon looked up, frowning. "It's just idle chit-chat, that's all. Because we're pretty frustrated."

"We all think we should take off for Bellingham," Wade said.

"No we don't," George said.

My head snapped back and forth, as if I were one step behind the action in a ping-pong game.

"And why don't you keep your fuckin' mouth shut?" George said to Wade. Then to me, "All we're saying is that it'll be interesting to hear how the guys in the Sound do in the next week or so. If they do good, I'm sure Mike will think twice about hanging around."

I looked away, toward the waitress. Her nose had a pretty slope to it, slanting up at the bottom like the lip of a slide. Her t-shirt was nice and tight.

"Maybe he will," I said, not really thinking.

George stared at me real closely. "You look sunburnt as hell, Pete. Not to mention sleepy. You been gettin' enough rest?"

"He's probably stoned," Wade said.

"Yeah, right," I replied, wondering how my voice sounded.

"Anyways," George said, "Mike's always been a reasonable guy to work for. And I don't expect him to be any different. I'm just starting to wonder if these damn humpies are ever gonna show."

The waitress set down her cola and rubbed out her cigarette. "Hey, look at that," Gordon whispered to George.

Then she was at our table, taller than I'd imagined, hands on her hips, head tilted to one side. She wasn't all that young. Close up you could see the strands of gray in the dark clump of hair behind her head. George ordered a cheeseburger with fries and coffee. Gordon looked at the waitress, then pointed at George. "His wife is having a baby. Isn't that great?"

"Thrilling." The waitress was scrawling on her order pad.

"I told him that if it was a girl he ought to name it after you."

She looked first at me and then at Wade and asked who was next, but Gordon said, "Don't you think that's a good idea?"

"Jesus," the waitress said.

"No. I'm serious. Now all I need is to know your name."

The waitress stared at him. "Don't you think I take enough shit from fishermen?"

"Come on, Gordo," George said. "I'm hungry. Would you give her your fuckin' order?"

I looked around and said, "What the hell were you guys just talking about?" but no one paid any attention. The waitress was facing George. She still didn't look very interested. "He serious? About you expecting a kid?"

But before George could answer, Gordon said, "We're hoping that when the baby comes, the salmon will come, too."

"Oh, I'm sure they will. If you believe in miracles. You gonna give me your order or not?"

"Well, excuse us," Gordon said. Then he asked for a grilled-cheese sandwich. I wanted a double cheeseburger with fries and a chocolate milkshake. Wade ordered the same. The waitress turned toward the kitchen, her boots clicking against the floor. Gordon watched her and then got up to go to the john and George said that sounded like a hell of an idea and followed him.

"You sure you're not stoned?" Wade whispered, jamming an elbow in my ribs.

"Would I tell you if I was?"

"I bet your Dad would kill you."

"That's between him and me."

Wade smirked. "Just as long as he doesn't kill the rest of us."

"Now you're sounding like Gordon."

"We gotta get out of here one way or another." Then he tipped his head in the direction of the waitress. "Did you see her blow off Gordon? Wasn't that great?" He started to say something else when the waitress returned with our food. I took a big bite of my cheeseburger and chewed it slowly, letting all the juice pool in my mouth.

"So what were you guys just saying?" I asked.

"That's between me and the other guys," Wade said.

"The hell it is. Just tell me what's going on." My voice rose on its own.

"Jesus, Pete, you want everyone in this place to be staring at us? I just told you what I know. We all want to go home."

"It didn't sound like it."

"I'll let you know more," Wade replied, "as soon as I know myself."

"You better."

"Sure thing. Although you might not like what you hear."

I spooned down about half the milkshake, finished the cheeseburger and fries, left four dollars on the table, then told George and Gordon I'd see them later, and headed out the door. I still didn't want to go back to the boat. I didn't feel stoned anymore. Wade had ruined it. There was only one thing to do. Ceci would hate me. Dad wouldn't be real pleased, either. Not to mention Mom. But no one will know, I told myself. Only me. So maybe it *is* a problem. But hell, I decided, everyone has problems. And there's no point worrying about them. At least not while you're enjoying whatever it is you're not supposed to do.

The dog came with me this time. I called him Earl. I sat on the log and stroked his fur. I rolled another joint, smoked half of it, offered the rest to the dog, then tucked it back inside the zip-locked bag. A dog doesn't need to get stoned, it occurred to me. Dogs are always that way, grinning and wagging their tails.

"That's OK, you're a good dog." Earl hung out his tongue and panted.

Then I looked over the water. The pot didn't help any this time. Fact, it made things worse. The sun was lower in the sky, its light reflecting off the bay. The salmon are still out there, I kept on telling myself. I know they are. But what if they aren't? I grabbed the dog behind his ears and turned his head toward mine. "Then what do you do?" But Earl just whimpered. I hung my head and thought some more. Then I prayed. I couldn't remember how at first. I clasped my hands together and tried to think pure thoughts. It was hard, being stoned. I sniffed the salty air and waited, as if God might return my call. But God's got more important things to worry about, I decided, like wars and hurricanes and little kids without any food.

Earl scratched behind his head with his left hind leg. I flung a stone into the bay and watched it splash, the rings spreading from the center. I waited until the water was calm. Dad needs all the help he can get, I decided. And so do I.

Two days later we left for Noyes Island, where we fished for the two days after that. The wind blew from the southwest, light and warm, and the sun shone through broken clouds. The waves swept in at an easy pace, and we had no problems dumping the net, or piling it back on board. Dad had worried about the skiff engine overheating, but Gordon checked it every half-hour, sometimes pouring in fresh water from a plastic Clorox jug, other times letting it blow out the tip of the towbit like a steaming geyser of piss. We made twenty-nine sets in thirty-nine hours, and everything went according to plan.

Except the humpies still didn't show. At least not how we wanted. Even Dad admitted we didn't have much time. But it wasn't like he was giving up, not by a long shot. Not Dad. Not yet, anyway.

Chapter 11

Back in Craig the next morning, two more Seattle boats were loading their nets into their holds and getting ready to run for home. Dad crouched near the davit, coating a steel pulley block in rust-protection paint the color of brick. I sat next to him, filling a needle with twine. When I pointed to the boats, Dad shrugged and said all that meant was less competition when the salmon finally arrived.

"Don't you mean *if* they arrive?"

"All depends on how you look at it, Peter."

It was a Tuesday, bright and almost as warm as a summer day in Bellingham. For a moment I imagined riding my bike with my shirt off along the boulevard overlooking Bellingham Bay. Instead I saw the bare hills beyond Craig's harbor, dotted with the stubble left behind by the loggers. "You're doing pretty good," I said, "if you can look at it like that."

Dad laid the brush over the rim of a coffee can full of paint thinner. "Come on, Pete, it's not like we haven't made anything these last couple days. I think we did pretty good, when you figure what little was out there."

We had unloaded our fish the evening before, about a thousand humpies, and a couple hundred sockeye, silvers and dogs. Now we scrubbed the algae from the hull with rectangular-headed brooms, touched up the paint job, and used the hydraulic hose to blast away jellyfish stains from the sides of the boat.

From inside the galley George said "Damnit!" and stumbled out rubbing the back of his head, muttering something about how he couldn't find the cheese grater.

"I didn't realize it was gone," Dad said. "Should I call the police?"

George grimaced and folded his arms across his gut. He stared at Dad in a way I'd never seen before, and Dad stared back a little surprised, maybe even nervous.

"Well, I just about knocked myself out trying to find it," George said. He studied the rest of us one by one. "I sure wish whoever did dishes around here would leave a goddamned clue where they put things. I'm not a magician, you know."

Dad managed a weak smile. "Just got to be patient. It'll show up."

"Oh, yeah, around fucking Christmas time!" George butted his forehead with the heel of his hand. "I'm getting damned tired of being patient. We don't even know when they're going to let us fish again."

"Sunday seems like a pretty sure thing," Dad replied. "My guess is Monday, too."

"Then what?"

"Then I guess we'll just have to wait and see." Dad dipped his brush into the solvent and rubbed it against the bottom of the can, turning the liquid cloudy and brown. He pulled out the brush and pressed it against a paint-splotched board, then squeezed the bristles with a rag. The solvent's prickly vapors cut through the windless air, making me hold my breath.

"One thing that was good, though," Dad went on, "was that the humpies we did catch, they looked nice and bright, like maybe the run's just starting to come together. If they were dark and mushy I'd be right alongside these other guys."

Gordon was bent over the bulwarks, scrubbing the hull with a broom. Now he turned and sat on the railing, the broom across his legs. "Jesus, Mike, you're starting to sound like the state biologists. You know what they're saying now? That maybe the Japanese are intercepting the fish somewhere off our coast."

"It's possible," Dad replied.

"Which would make it all the more reasonable to take off."

"That depends," Dad said, "on whether you trust your instincts or not."

George said, "I don't know what to trust," then grabbed his t-shirt from the bench inside the galley and slipped it on. "You guys'll have to do without me. I gotta make another phone call."

"Maybe you'll get some good news," Dad said.

Gordon grinned. "Because if the baby comes—"

"Drop the bullshit," George said, and climbed over the bulwarks onto the dock. "I'll see you guys in a few minutes. If I don't strangle the sonofabitch in front of me with the telephone cord. You'd think these bastards might notice once in a while that eight people are waiting to use the goddamned phone."

Gordon raised his broom above his head as if it were a golf club, then swung through an imaginary ball in George's direction as George trudged up the ramp that led to the main road. "The expectant father is getting a bit edgy these days. Not that I can blame him."

Dad nodded. "I think we're all getting that way. Sometimes I feel like I'm the one who's expecting."

"Something better happen pretty damn quick," said Wade, his voice muffled and his body draped over the stern, so all you could see were the soles of his boots and the hump of his butt.

Gordon said, "Or maybe we'll have to abort the whole thing."

Dad rubbed his fingers hard against his temples. "Why don't we forget about it for now?"

My needle was full and I tossed it into the box at the base of the cabin. I didn't feel like wasting a nice day like this, not after all that rain. Dad said that if you really cared about something you did the little things, too. So maybe I didn't care enough. To me, a lot of the time up here seemed wasted, now that we weren't in Petersburg. Sometimes I felt I was wasting the whole summer, although I couldn't exactly say why. It wasn't like I had a gang of friends who were writing me letters, begging me to get my ass back to Bellingham. And it had been a couple years since I'd played baseball, even though I kept promising myself I'd make a comeback. Maybe what I really missed was the hope that something exciting might happen—something that might spill over into the school year and make me happier than I'd been before.

I grabbed a bottle of Windex and a roll of paper towels from the galley and went from window to window, spraying and wiping, until the surface glistened and I could see my reflection. My hair was greasy, and it had been months since I'd been to a barber. Blackheads lined the ridges of my nose. I took one of the wetted towels and wiped it across my face, scrubbing hard against the soiled skin. Then I sat down. No one could see me, sitting like this against the far side of the cabin. Loafing was nice sometimes, so long as you didn't get caught.

George was coming back down the dock now, still frowning, a hand cupped under his jaw.

Dad said, "So what's the word?"

George sighed, then stroked his chin. "The word is no word about the baby. The other word is bad, maybe you don't even want to hear it, but here it is: Stan the man nailed 'em at Point Roberts the other day. So did everyone else."

Dad sat cross-legged, studying a wooden pulley block. "How much he catch?"

"Two thousand sockeye."

"Good for Stan," Dad murmured, still not looking up.

Gordon dropped his broom, its handle clacking against the deck. Wade lifted himself off the stern roller and sat on his haunches. I thought about Bellingham Bay again, the wind making little white dashes against its blue surface, the steam from the Georgia-Pacific plant rising in a billowy cloud. But it made me nervous the way everyone else was looking at Dad.

"That's big bucks!" Wade said.

Gordon nodded. "Let's just say that I'd settle for it."

"The amazing thing," George said, "is that some guys did a lot better. The *Harvester*, Debbie told me, had five or six thousand."

Dad picked up a hammer and tapped its claw-head against his palm. I could see the muscles tensing in Wade's neck. "Let's see," Gordon said, staring into the sky, "five thousand sockeye, six pounds a piece, that's thirty thousand pounds. At a dollar-eighty a pound... let me think... that's a $54,000 market—all in one day. Jesus, Mike, that's close to twice what we've made all season."

"You don't need to help me with the math." Dad grabbed the pulley block and squeezed it between his knees. He held a flathead screwdriver in his left hand and aligned it with the shaft in the center of the block, then cocked back his other arm, his fist wrapped around the hammer's wooden handle.

"So Stan's move paid off," Wade said. "He did the right thing."

Dad glared, the hammer above his head. "*You'd* do the right thing by shutting your trap."

"But he did! He made money and we haven't."

"Careful, Wade," Gordon said. Then, to George, "Did Debbie say when the next opener is?"

"Probably Monday."

"So there still must be a hell of a lot of fish left. And enough time to make the run back down."

Dad let the hammer slide out of his hand, its stainless-steel head banging against the deck. He stood up, adjusted his cap, and thrust his hands into his hip pockets.

"Forget it, guys, because I know what you're thinking. But we've come too far for that now. The only place we're going soon is back to Noyes Island."

I said, "What if we could make all that money down there?"

"There's a world of difference between 'could' and 'would.'"

"And there's an even bigger difference between fishing and not fishing," George said. "The way it looks now, Mike, I got to get down there even if I have to charter a sea-plane."

Dad took off his cap and rubbed his brow, his hair clinging in sweaty tangles to his forehead. "It's your money, George. I guess you can do whatever you want—if it doesn't interfere with the days we fish. But don't forget, that baby's gonna be born with or without your help."

Wade glanced at George and said, "Maybe I'll go with you."

Dad said, "You want to lose your fuckin' job?"

Wade looked down at the deck. "It's crossed my mind."

"Well, you better not let it cross too often." Dad picked up the hammer. "Now as for you, George, don't decide anything too quick."

Gordon said, "You think maybe we've waited long enough? Those sockeye in the Sound aren't going to hang around forever."

"I think maybe we should stop talking about it. Because I'm getting tired of the whole goddamned thing."

"Sorry, Mike," George said. "But I can't do much of anything until this baby thing is over."

Dad frowned. "I know. But there's not a hell of a lot I can do, either. I know a lot of guys who weren't anywhere near their wives when they gave birth."

He bent over his work with his head down, his neck sunburned and blistery, his fists streaked with grease. He thrust the screwdriver at the shaft, trying to knock it free. But it wouldn't come. He swung the hammer hard against the head of the screwdriver but missed and struck his thumb. He cried out and squeezed the thumb with his other hand, his shoulders lifting and falling.

"What are you all staring at?" He looked all around at us. "Don't you guys got anything better to do?"

The next evening I found Dad sitting by himself in the galley, tallying up figures on a big yellow legal pad. Only now he was grinning.

"So what do you know, Pete? We might not go broke after all."

"How you figure?"

"I'll tell you if you'll wake up and listen."

I was still sleepy from my nap, which had ended only a couple minutes before. I'd smoked some more weed at the beach earlier that day, which wasn't such a hot idea—all it did was depress me.

Afterwards I went back to my bunk and tried to read, but the only thing I managed to do was fall asleep.

I shook my head now, and banged it with the heel of my hand. It was past 8 p.m., and I wondered why no one had woken me for dinner. But nothing was on the stove, and I didn't see anyone else.

"You see," Dad went on, "even as poor as this last opener was, if we can just do that five, six more times, and I make a little money back home in the fall season, then keeping up on the payments might not be such a problem. Our expenses are pretty low— George has done a good job keeping the grocery costs down, and the bill for fuel's not bad at all, given that we're in the middle of an oil crisis. All we need is to just keep fishing."

"But we could do that back home, couldn't we?"

"Remember what a disappointment last season was?"

I was thinking of Bellingham again, the Douglas firs along the boulevard, the way Mount Baker towered over everything else. Summer seemed to take a long time to get going in Washington, sometimes it was still cold and wet on the Fourth of July. But by now the weather was usually excellent. It was the time of year that Mom liked to barbecue salmon out on our deck, then serve it with a big pitcher of iced tea, and watermelon for dessert. Afterwards we'd sit and watch the sun set over the bay.

"But it might make Mom happy if we came home," I said.

Dad looked at me as if he'd never considered this before.

"It would make a lot of people happy. George's wife especially. But you don't make money making people happy. You make people happy by making them money. At least that's what my dad used to say."

He stuck the legal pad in the drawer below his bunk, slid the drawer shut, and grabbed his cap from a hook on the wall. "You want to go get some dinner?"

I nodded, and Dad suggested the same place where I'd run into George and Gordon and Wade the week before, the place where I'd thought everyone was staring at me.

This time the restaurant was empty, except for a couple of Indians smoking and drinking coffee, and a large white woman with three grimy kids, one with a runny nose that needed to be wiped. I saw the same waitress through the window that led to the kitchen, cleaning off the grill with a rag. She looked pretty busy. But this time she came right over.

Dad had been staring at his menu, a single laminated sheet with a dried splotch the color of Heinz 57 that made it hard to read the dinner prices. At first he frowned, irritated, maybe, that he didn't have more time to decide what he wanted. But now he stuck the menu behind the metal napkin dispenser against the wall, looking at the waitress the whole time. His gaze went down and then back up, from the large strong hands at her waist past the taut flesh of her throat to those eyes that seemed to find everything around her both annoying and amusing.

"Can I help you fellows?"

Dad said, "Sure you can," then glanced around as if he couldn't remember what to say next. "I guess you want me to order."

"That's normally the way we do it."

Dad smiled as if half his face was paralyzed. "Well, maybe I'll just have a cup of coffee to start with. Can you bring me one?"

"'Course I can." Then she looked at me. "Where's the rest of the guys?"

"Were you hoping they'd be here?"

"Hardly. A woman puts up with enough crap in a place like this. She don't need no more of it. Though I do need the tips."

"Hell," Dad said, "if it was my crew, the worse you treated them, the better." He smiled again, this time more normally.

The waitress smiled, too, showing her gap teeth. "So you must be the skipper. And I suppose you're nervous as hell about these goddamned fish and whether they're ever going to come."

"Actually, I've decided there's not a lot I can do about it."

A lot of the time I wished Dad would worry more, just so I'd know I wasn't alone. But the waitress said, "That's the right way to look at it. Sure wish more of the guys in this town would think like that."

"So you live here?" Dad asked. "Year round?"

The waitress looked at Dad the way you might study a stranger on your porch before opening the door. "Matter of fact I do."

"All alone?" Dad smiled crookedly again.

She looked at him a while longer. "There's a friend of mine, a fisherman. Though I wouldn't say we're especially close friends right now. If you know what I mean."

By the way Dad looked back at her, I knew that he did.

The waitress said, "Hold on a minute," turned away and slipped inside the kitchen. I stared at the menu. I couldn't believe how much things cost on the dinner menu—eleven bucks for the deep-fried shrimp. I whispered to Dad that maybe we should go someplace else. But Dad said, "Why the hell would I want to do that?"

"Because of the prices."

"To hell with the prices. I like it here. I sort of like this waitress, too."

"I don't think she'll mind. It probably happens to her all the time."

Dad shook his head and then his lips formed an O, as if he were about to whistle. "You got a lot to learn, Pete."

I grabbed a napkin from the dispenser, stretched it between my hands, then tore it in two, twisting the halves into wick-like snakes. "What're you gonna do? Pick her up?"

"If an attractive lady wants to visit with me, I'll let her visit all she wants. You got any objection to that?"

"You're as bad as Mom!"

"I didn't know Mom was bad."

"You know what I mean. You want to pick up some *waitress*."

Dad looked around. Then he clutched my wrist, and whispered, "Would you prefer that I held out for some lumberjack? Jesus, Pete, this is Alaska. And who the hell said I was trying to pick her up? We're just having a friendly chat. Maybe she wants someone to talk to."

"She's got the whole goddamned town to talk to." I shook free my arm and leaned over the table on my elbows, my butt barely touching my seat. "Besides, she just told us she's got a boyfriend."

"So I guess you've got nothing to worry about."

The waitress returned then with the coffee, and I ordered the Salisbury steak. Dad asked for the fried chicken with mashed potatoes. The waitress asked if we'd like anything else and said that her name was Christine. Dad said that was a nice name and told her his own. She said Mike was a nice name, too. Then she said she got off work around 9:30. Dad commented that that was only a half-hour from now.

After she brought our food Dad ate very quickly. He shoveled in the mashed potatoes and the long pale green beans, and then he tore through the chicken, stripping the bones of everything, even the stringy pink tendons.

The waitress returned as soon as he'd finished. She was staring at his plate. "Lord, there's hardly even a skeleton left! You want to chew the bones a while, too?"

Dad wiped his mouth with his fist. Then he grinned. "Best damn meal I've ever had."

"I bet. Just like wifey makes for you."

"Actually," Dad said, "wife stopped cooking for me some time ago."

The waitress scooped up the empty plate. "That's pretty common with you fishermen, isn't it? So she didn't want to come fishing?"

"I never invited her."

"Shame on you. A husband should let his wife share in everything."

Dad grabbed a napkin and dabbed his moustache and the corners of his mouth. He looked at the waitress, then shook his head. "My wife doesn't even like *water*. She'd get seasick on a goddanged lake."

"Then you probably never gave her a chance." The waitress looked down at us, her big hand on her waist, her elbow jutting out like a wing. "No wonder she won't fix you dinner."

I kicked Dad beneath the table, and whispered, "You want to get out of here?" but he put up his hand and shook his head. "Better be careful," he said to the waitress, "or I'll bore you silly talking about my marriage. Now you wouldn't like that, would you?"

The waitress looked at Dad for a long time again.

"Oh I don't know. I could probably bore you with some pretty good problems of my own."

"Well, then, maybe I ought to hang around here, right up until you get off work. We can sit around boring each other till we're blue in the face."

The waitress said, "Not much else to do in this town."

I stirred what was left of the gravy on my plate with a spoon. Dad smiled and patted his thigh and said, "S'pose not. I'd be willing to wait."

I glared at Dad and stood up. "I'm outta here," I said.

"Sure, Pete. Don't you worry about me."

I stalked out the door. It was cold outside, and I knew I should have worn a jacket. All of a sudden I wanted to smoke pot again, just for the hell of it. That was Dad for you, always making me feel like smoking pot. But I knew it wouldn't help much—it hadn't the last few times. That was the trouble with pot. You'd feel wonderful for the first few minutes, but then you'd just get lonely—even sometimes if you'd smoked it with someone else. I'd get lonely and wonder why.

I decided to go back to the boat anyway, just to read. That seemed like a better way to relax. After all, the book I was reading was about a different boat, not the one I was on.

I walked back down the dock, shivering. All the lights on the boat were out. From the dock it looked deserted. That was fine with me. I didn't feel like talking to Gordon or George or Wade. Especially Wade.

I climbed from the dock onto the bulwark railing, and balanced there for a second before leaping, my feet slapping hard against the fish-hold covers. The padlock was off and the door was halfway open. I heard voices in the dark, like evil spirits. Or maybe robbers. But what would they steal? Coffee mugs? I stuck my head inside. I saw Wade grinning, George scratching behind his ear. Gordon sat in the corner shuffling a pack of cards. They made a crisp, clicking sound. "Something going on here?" I asked.

Gordon smiled. His beret hung down almost all the way over his eyes. The ashes from his pipe had spilled onto the table, and the room smelled of his cherry tobacco smoke.

"Just a friendly card game, Peter. I'm teaching these guys how to play cribbage."

"In the dark?"

"I guess we didn't notice the sun going down."

"Shit, Gordon," George said, "why don't we tell him the truth?"

"What is the truth?" Gordon asked pleasantly. "I don't think we've determined that."

"Yeah we have," Wade said. "You bet we have."

George slid over on the bench. "Take a seat, Peter. I guess this is going to take some time."

I sat down.

"We've talked about it a lot the last couple days, Gordon and Wade and me," George said, "and we don't see any way out of it. Especially now, with them nailing 'em back home. It's ridiculous to stay up here, cooped in a little shithole like this, praying that the humpies are still going to come crashing in. Because they're not. The whole fuckin' run is a failure, and the sooner your Dad admits it, the better."

I reached above the galley table and snapped on the single bare bulb. Its glare made everyone shield their eyes. George sighed and wiped the bridge of his nose with the back of his hand. "So what do you think we should do?" I asked.

Wade said, "Blow the hell outta here, like I've said all along!"

George glared at Wade but then he closed his eyes and nodded. "Yeah, Pete. That's it."

"My Dad will never go for it."

"I know he just thinks I'm saying it because of Debbie, and yeah, that's a lot of it, I admit. But not all of it, not the main reason. Being up here—I never thought I'd say this about your father—but it's bad business, it doesn't make one damn bit of sense."

"And it's dangerous as hell," Gordon said, flicking the jack of spades face up on the table, its one eye leering at us. "It's bad luck, Peter, to be on a boat that sinks."

"Gordon's right," George said. "And I'm tired of trying to convince your father that he's wrong."

"But you said yourself, just last week, that maybe the humpies would still show."

George shook his head. "That was a week ago. What did we have these last two days? Fifteen hundred? That's crap and nothing but. A week into August, we should be getting six or eight thousand."

"So you think there's no way they'll come?"

George rubbed his cheek. "That's too final sounding. But I'm sure as hell not counting on it."

Wade and Gordon nodded. I looked away, scooped up a paper towel, and wadded it in my fist. "But if my Dad wants to stay," I reminded them, "there's not a heck of a lot any of us can do."

"I'm afraid there is," George said, lowering his eyes. I looked at him but he couldn't see me. Gordon flipped two more black cards onto the table, the five of spades and the ten of clubs, and then he looked down, too. Wade shrugged and grinned. I dropped the wadded paper towel, rubbed my slippery hands together and wondered where in hell Dad was. But I knew where, I knew exactly. Something that felt like a billiard ball formed in my throat.

"What?" I finally croaked.

George looked at me, then down at his cards, then up again. "We gotta tell him, that's what. That we've made up our minds on our own. That either we pack the net in the hold tomorrow, and leave for Puget Sound, or we all quit, right on the spot."

Across the harbor a boat engine rumbled, getting louder as it came our way. Out the window I saw its mast light high above the cabin, the rest of the vessel almost invisible.

"It would help us a lot, Peter," Gordon said, "if you would support us on this. We're not saying that you speak out against your dad. That would be a bad thing for everyone. If you could just abstain from the discussion, that would make everything go a lot smoother."

"Abstain from what?" I asked.

Gordon tried, weakly, to smile. "Three out of four, that would be pretty hard for your Dad to refuse. He wouldn't even know that you knew about our decision."

I scrunched the balled-up paper towel tighter in my fist. "What if I don't?"

"What's the point not to?" Wade said, his smart-ass grin replaced by something like a pout. "Don't you want to get back to Bellingham and make some money?"

"Sure I do."

"Then why don't you get your ass in line?"

I looked down at the scattered cards.

"Look," George said, "We're doing it for a good reason. I don't know, maybe it's the thing with your mother, but he scares me, Peter. There's too much at stake here to let this go on."

"But he's not ready!" I squeezed the towel even harder and pounded my fist against the table. Then I waited, looking from face to face. "Don't any of you see that? He's not ready yet to face my mom!"

"Then he's got some growing up to do," Gordon said.

"That's not the issue," George said. "The issue is where we can catch the most fish."

"No it isn't. Not for Dad. Not for you, either. You want to see your wife, and Dad doesn't want to see my mom. That's the issue. That's the only thing that seems to matter."

Wade was grinning again. "Tell me this, Pete," he said, drumming his knuckles against the table. "Why do you have to be such a dick about everything?"

"And why don't you stick your fist up your asshole?"

I flung the scrunched-up paper towel sideways and struck him between the eyes.

That was when things shifted into slow motion. I saw Wade's hands reach out and clutch my collarbone, his eyes getting bigger the closer they came to my face. I saw his nostrils open wide like a bull's and heard the tremble in his voice as he swore. It seemed forever before I finally jerked my left shoulder free and cocked back my arm. I aimed at the right side of his face. I didn't want to break his nose, I didn't want to make him bleed. And I definitely didn't want him to strike back, although I definitely wanted to hit him. I wanted to hit him hard. But I didn't get the chance.

Gordon grabbed me from behind, and George bear-hugged Wade. Wade struggled hard against him, his elbows flying. "You're a fucking asshole," I finally said. Wade stopped and looked back at me with that bitter smile and said, "So are you."

George said, almost quietly, "Both of you, knock that shit off," and squeezed Wade even tighter. But Gordon wasn't as strong as George. When he started to relax I drove an elbow into his ribs, forcing him backwards. Then I slipped out through the open galley door.

My foot caught on the needle box and I almost fell. But I kept moving. I swung my legs over the top of the bulwark railing, and landed on the dock below. Then I ran, my lungs getting louder and louder until finally I was far enough from the boat to rest. I wiped the hair from my eyes, and whatever it was dripping from my nose. Mostly I was glad I hadn't started crying.

I made it back to the restaurant as quick as I could. But Dad's table was empty now, not even a tip. I searched for the waitress. She was gone, too. I sat down and covered my face. Whoever was working now must have noticed, because she left me alone. I kept grabbing the napkins, then tearing them up. For a moment I wished I had the dope. But then I said the hell with that. And I couldn't go back. Not yet, anyway. I couldn't go anywhere. Not in the dark. So I just sat there. I cursed Dad for not being around, and I tried to imagine where he was, what he was doing. It wasn't very difficult. The longer I sat the angrier I got, the more I felt like something was pressing down inside of me, something else struggling to get out.

Chapter 12

I couldn't go back to the boat. But I couldn't hang out in the restaurant forever, either. I wished I had my down jacket; then I would head for the beach and huddle against the big bleached logs. But I'd freeze my ass in just a flannel shirt. I thought of sneaking on board, grabbing the jacket, then slipping back out before anyone saw me. Fat chance of that. I'd probably run into Wade. Then we'd pick up right where we'd left off, only this time with nobody around to break things up. So I waited. I drank two cups of coffee, with lots of cream, as slowly as I could. I listened to the tick-tick-tick of my watch. I read all the articles in a week-old copy of the *Ketchikan Daily News*. The biologists in Juneau were worrying about whether the salmon would arrive. Thanks for the update.

I tried to imagine where Dad might be. Somewhere with the waitress, that was clear enough. Not that I could do a hell of a lot about it. I gathered the shreds of napkin scattered across my table, dumped them in a trash can and walked back to the boat. It was almost midnight now. The galley lights were out. I crept on deck as quietly as I could, slipped alongside the cabin, and peered in the porthole that looked in on Dad's bunk. It was empty, the brown navy blankets tucked neatly at the sides. A pale light rose from the fo'c'sle hatch. I heard voices, but couldn't make out sentences. I climbed back onto the dock, walked quickly the other way, then mounted the ramp that led to the main road.

The night got colder after that, and the lights around town blinked out one by one. The pay phones were close by, and I considered calling home. Dad would love me for that. Mom, too. Although maybe it would serve her right, the part about the waitress. Farther down the road a guitar twanged in a country western song, and someone shouted, someone else laughed. I wondered if maybe Dad and the waitress were there at that bar. But Dad wasn't the dancing type. At least not nowadays. He danced a lot, Mom told me, back when they were teenagers, when everyone had those blockhead haircuts, before Elvis got fat and died. But that was a long time ago, she always added. I folded my arms tighter against my chest and stared into the sky.

Then I looked at the glowing dial of my watch. It was almost 1 a.m. Fuck it, I said. Fuck him. Maybe the rest of the guys had the right idea. At least it would get us out of Craig. I walked toward the boat, but after about thirty feet I turned back. I waited another twenty minutes. That's when I saw someone coming down the road with his hands in the pockets of his mackinaw. He was whistling.

I peered through the dark, just to make sure. It was him all right. I waved, and waited for him to get closer. He didn't seem in any hurry.

"Jesus, Pete, whatcha doin'? Standing guard?"

The billiard ball was still in my throat. "Do you know how long I've been here?" I whispered.

Dad grinned sleepily. "Don't make it sound like such a big deal." He nudged me in the shoulder. "Why didn't you just wait in the galley? In fact, why'd you bother to wait at all?"

I shivered hard. "Do you know what's been going on?"

Dad smiled again, then shook his head. "Listen, it's not quite like you probably think. You see, this thing with this woman and me, all that happened—"

"That's not what I mean."

"Aw hell, nothing happened that's worth telling you about, because it's none of your business. And it's nothing that needs to cause you any worry. Now let's get back to the boat and get some sleep."

"But we *can't* go back!"

Dad looked at me strangely and laughed. "Why, Pete? We been taken over by a band of wild Indians?"

I shook my head again and started to explain. I talked so fast I couldn't tell if I was making sense. Dad still had that strange grin, but now it seemed a lot more difficult to keep it there. The wind came off the water and he shivered and folded his arms. "Who wants to go home? Wade and Gordon?"

"George, too," I said.

"You sure you didn't misunderstand?"

"No, I didn't! Now won't you please listen?"

He grabbed me by the shoulders, hard. I smelled beer on his breath, stale and sweet. "What exactly did they say?"

The longer I went on, the smaller Dad's eyes became, the more intense his gaze. But in the end he just looked tired. He stood there for a moment slowly nodding. Then he squeezed my arm just above the elbow and said, "Come on, Pete, we better get on back to the boat now. When you got a fire on board, you gotta figure out a way to put it out."

We walked back quickly and I followed him inside. He flicked on the galley light, shook his head, and hurried down the ladder into the engine room. I followed him down into the dark, the air sticky from the heat of the engine, the swampy smell of bilge rising from the floorboards.

"Assholes," Dad mumbled kind of sadly, touching my shoulder and nodding toward the fo'c'sle. "You know, Peter, a guy's better off not trusting anyone, it gets you farther in life." Then he flung open the fo'c'sle door and snapped on the light. "What's this bullshit I hear?" he yelled into the room.

George was awake now, squinting through a tangle of hair that swept across his face. Gordon had turned over in his bunk so his back was turned to the light. Wade hadn't moved.

Dad grabbed George by the shoulder, jerked Gordon's arm, and butted Wade's chest with the heel of his hand. George moaned and Wade said, "Leave me alone!" Gordon covered his eyes with his forearm.

Dad was shouting now, his voice getting louder. "What the fuck is this I'm hearing? We are not going back! Get that through your thick skulls!" George crossed his arms in front of his face and tucked his chin against his shoulder. "Jesus, Mike? Can't we wait until the light of day?"

"Not this time we can't!"

Dad's fists banged against the sides of the bunks. Then he took two long strides back toward the ladder. I didn't have time to get out of the way. My knees hit against the rim of a plastic diesel-oil canister, and I landed flat on my butt. I reached out and stuck my hand against a sprocket coated in lubricating grease. Dad grabbed me by the armpits. "You OK?"

"I'm fine," I replied, then climbed the ladder with Dad behind me, made it into the galley and plopped down on a bench. With a paper towel I wiped the black grease from my hands. Then I studied the oil stains on the knee caps of my jeans. Dad stared out the big square window above the sink, his weight on his toes, his fists clenching the countertop railing.

"What now?" I said.

"You got any suggestions?"

Before I could answer, Gordon entered and slipped in behind the table, protecting his eyes from the glare of the light. Wade followed him, in jeans and bare feet and no shirt, his folded arms framing his pectoral muscles. He grabbed a seat on the bench across from me, watching me the whole time. George arrived last, his eyes almost closed, his wavy brown hair matted to one side.

"You know, Peter may have got the wrong idea about what we told him," George said. "We weren't necessarily insisting—"

"I don't care what you were insisting!"

Dad moved toward the unlit stove, poured cold coffee from the pot, sniffed it, and shook his head. "All I know is what I hear, and what I hear don't sound very good. Not when you guys are ready to take the boat down south by yourselves. What the hell do you expect me to think?"

George shook his head. "But don't you remember what we talked about? When it's time, it's time."

"Time for what? For giving up?"

Gordon had been sitting sideways, his long legs bunched up and his arms wrapped around them. Now he sat and leaned forward on his elbows. "You know you sound like a high school football coach?"

"Who asked you?" Dad said. "You want to quit, quit. Don't think you're irreplaceable, because you're not. I should've known, relying on some guy who's already got money coming in."

Then he turned toward Wade.

"And as for you, your father will be pissed. He's a good man, better than you, but nothing I can do about that. I got half a notion to fire your ass right now."

"What the hell did I do?"

"You know goddamned well what you did!"

Gordon said, "Don't you think you're overreacting?"

"*No!*" Dad flung the mug toward the sink, its handle cracking against the metal basin, the coffee leaping against the galley window. Then he glared at Gordon again. "How the hell would *you* react? Should I be happy that my whole crew is sticking it to me from behind?"

"Jesus, Mike," Gordon said, "would you prefer that we hung around up here until the leaves turn color? We're just asking you to see things the way they really are."

Dad took a deep breath. "Sorry, but I already see them as they are. It may be different from how you see 'em, but it's real enough for me. So if I gotta fire all three of you, get three new ones right on the spot, then that's what I gotta do."

Gordon slapped his hand over his eyes. "But this is ludicrous! It's worse than ludicrous! It's stupid!"

"Not to me it isn't."

"Me, neither," I said, my voice not as shaky as I had expected. It's one thing to get pissed off at your dad but another to tell him he's failed, it occurred to me now. And he hadn't failed. At least not yet. Not that I was ruling out the possibility of him failing later. It just wasn't the kind of thing I could start looking forward to.

Wade muttered something and shook his head. George said, "Isn't it time we talked about a compromise?"

Dad leaned against the stove, his legs crossed at the ankles, and reached into the sink to examine the jagged stump of the mug handle. "I don't like compromises. 'Cause I always end up getting screwed."

"But tomorrow's the 12th of August," George said. "Maybe down south the sockeye will hang around for two more weeks. So we got this Sunday and maybe Monday up here, we could fish it and still run for the Sound after that. Either we start catching humpies or we know for sure they ain't gonna come."

"Why even screw around?" Wade said.

"Shut up, Wade!" Then George looked at Dad. "So whatcha think, Mike?"

Dad grabbed a new mug from the cupboard, poured coffee into it, took one gulp, spat it out, and dumped the rest into the sink. "Tell you what. I'm pretty confident those humpies will be here this next week, that's where I still say you guys are wrong. But if you're not, and I am, then what the fuck—I'll go along with whatever you want."

George smiled. Wade frowned. Dad said, "So does that make the rest of you happy?"

"What do you consider a good opener?" Gordon asked.

Dad was staring at the ceiling. I thought about what must be going on inside, his mind turning over the numbers and sorting them into columns, adding everything up. "How about three thousand humpies a day? If we catch less, we go home, first thing Tuesday."

"Sounds good to me," I said.

"God, it figures," Wade said. "You always do exactly what your dad wants?"

George said to Wade, "One thing we don't need is more of your crap." Then to Dad, "This makes sense, at least we're finally talking. You got my backing."

"What the hell?" Gordon said. "Makes it all kind of dramatic."

"Real fucking dramatic," Dad said. "So why don't we all get ourselves some sleep." He sat on his bunk and began to unlace his shoes. "Just remember, I got a little more invested in this than you guys do, a little more on the line."

Gordon shook his head. He looked skinny in the narrow shaft of light, even skinnier than when we left Bellingham. "Don't you think everyone's life here is worth about the same?"

"I'm not talking about that. I'm just reminding you, I can't go running home before I've given it my best shot."

"On Sunday you'll get our best," George said. He turned toward Wade. "We can promise him that. Can't we?"

"Yeah," Wade said. "I guess." He climbed down the ladder into the engine room. Gordon followed him, then George.

Dad sat and pulled off his jeans and unbuttoned his flannel shirt, rolling up the jeans and placing them in the bunk above him, stuffing the shirt in his pillow of dirty clothes. Next he peeled off his socks. Then he told me to shut off the light above the stove.

I snapped out the bulb and tried to make my way down the darkened hallway. Dad looked pale in his cotton underwear, his legs white against the dull brown blanket. "You feeling OK?" I asked.

"Let's just say it may take some time for me to fall asleep. But things could be a lot worse, couldn't they?"

"Were you serious about going home if we don't catch enough fish?"

"Think I'd lie about a thing like that?"

"But then you'd have to face Mom."

"Aw, hell, Pete, that's the least of my worries right now—at least for the time being. Either way, I'll call her after this next opening. And don't you worry about this thing with that waitress. 'Cause it wasn't like anything really happened. Just turned out we had a lot in common, that's all."

"You gonna see her again?"

"I don't know." He closed his eyes and smiled. "And you don't need to worry about it. So why don't you go get yourself some rest? Because you might not get much at all, once we get back out on the coast."

So I went to bed and tried to sleep, but the caffeine was still shuffling around, fast enough to keep me awake. Although I felt kind of peaceful, otherwise. Either we'd start making money or we'd be on our way home. It was better than praying for the humpies to arrive. Gordon was right the time he said he didn't need the money himself. And I didn't, either. At least not a lot of it. But Dad did. Dad needed money for a lot of reasons. And you had to keep that in mind.

We left Craig two days later. We cruised around the back side of Noyes Island, and dropped anchor in Steamboat Bay. The rain began before we slept, and by the time we got ready to fish the sky had the grainy look of a black-and-white photograph. The air was damp, cold like usual, and all of us had a tough time getting out of bed. Except Dad. He paced around the deck, hands in his rain jacket, the blue skullcap pulled over his ears. We'd heard good things the day before, how the humpies had started to jump like crazy. And Fish and Game had given us two days to work. But we hadn't seen a thing ourselves. Wade said it was just another lousy rumor, that we'd be running home the day after next. Gordon said so, too.

Dad studied the open ocean. "Whatever happens now, there's not a hell of a lot we can do about it. We just got to go out there and see if things fall in our favor."

But in the first set we had maybe twenty fish, the one after that only twelve, and Wade muttered some more about going home. I had to admit that it sounded pretty good. I imagined sitting in the living room watching TV, the heat turned way up, Mom in the kitchen baking a ham with pineapple and a sugary glaze. And afterwards spreading myself out on my own big bed, pulling that green knitted blanket all the way up to my neck, resting my head on a pair of thick pillows.

The third set we caught about fifty humpies, and Dad said, "I guess we'll find out pretty soon." The set after that was a waste of time, nothing but a load of red jellyfish. Wade kept talking about what a nice trip home it might be, how the weather would get better the farther south we got, how they didn't even have red jellyfish in Puget Sound, how maybe we'd have our shirts off by the time we hit Point Roberts. He was acting pretty chummy, considering everything. You could never tell with a guy like Wade.

But pretty soon we stopped talking about going home. We brought a big bag over the side, maybe four hundred humpies, slick and fresh and flapping all over the place, and Dad gave a little pump of his fist as the humpies slithered into the hold. "So what do you know, Mike?" George said, slapping his big hands together. "What the hell do you know?"

"I know it's better than we've been doing," Dad replied.

Wade and I toted the wooden covers back over the hatch. Wade was smiling now. It was like we were old friends. "Jesus!" he said. "There's some big bucks to be made!"

After that we worked steadily, and the humpies piled up. We weren't seeing them jump, but it didn't matter. All we had to do was set the net to take in a big wad. By noon we had pulled in three good sets in a row, and by early evening we had our three thousand, easy. It was even better the day after that. We set the net in the water and then we hoisted the fish on board. Fishing didn't get much simpler than this. We kept at it until 9 p.m. Then we headed back into Steamboat Bay and unloaded our fish and sat around and drank beer and ate baked chicken and mashed potatoes and chocolate cake for dessert and tried to figure out how much money we'd made.

Dad had made everybody happy—at least for now. And no one mentioned that night in Craig.

Chapter 13

The next morning the boat was lurching all over the place, and I had to get dressed in a hurry. Out on deck the ocean had that familiar gray color to it, the waves exploding against a small rocky island with only a scattering of trees. We swung hard one way, and then back the other, and the water flooded the deck with a sound like the whoosh of a toilet. I grasped the towbit, fumbled with my fly, and, being careful, pissed on the hatch covers instead of over the bulwarks. Then I headed for the wheelhouse.

Dad sat on his tall green stool, its legs teetering with each swell. He held the wheel with one hand, a mug of coffee in the other, but the mug kept bouncing against his lips, the coffee running down the side. I asked him if he needed a napkin but he shook his head. When I asked where we were, he set the mug on the dashboard and pointed toward a dark cluster of trees.

"See up that way?" he said. "That's Warren Island."

"Is that supposed to ring a bell?"

"It means were going back to Petersburg."

"You're kidding," I said, and right away I felt a little more alert, and a lot more willing to hang around in Alaska.

Dad jerked his thumb toward the stern, where the skiff sat strapped to the deck in chains and ropes. "That baby's still got me worried, the way it's been getting so hot. I need to make sure the guys in Petersburg have a chance to take a look. Next time we fish, that could be the big one. God knows we don't want anything crapping out.

"Besides," he added, "it's not going to kill us to be out of Craig for a few days. Might even help crew morale a little bit."

"It would sure help my morale," I said.

My dong rested against my right thigh, pressed tight by my jeans, relieved of its morning pressure by my long piss. But now I felt a steady enlargement. I thought of Ceci's bare neck, its one black mole hard like the head of a nail against her pale skin. Then I ran my fist up my thigh and nudged myself back into place.

"Won't hurt George any, either," I heard Dad say.

I shook my head and tried to concentrate. It was tough with everything shifting around. "Is he still thinking about flying home?"

"It would be pretty hard," Dad said, "since they may send us back out any day now. And you know George isn't going to risk missing the big bucks. Debbie wouldn't want him to."

I watched the ocean's surface heave and twist, the spray drumming against the windows, leaving BB-size drops. I thought of how Debbie had looked the morning we left Bellingham, like an enormous duck in blue rubber thongs.

"You know, Pete," Dad said, "I gotta admit this whole thing with the crew the other night, maybe it put a little better frame on the big picture. I wouldn't tell them this, no way in hell I would, but they made some pretty good points. Even Gordon. Nothing's worth risking your life."

I said, "You're not going to get an argument from me," but it sounded as if someone else was speaking. I was recalling how Ceci's jeans lay flat against her crotch with just the slightest indentation.

"And I'll tell you something else," Dad went on, "I'm even looking forward to talking to your mother. Because I think by now maybe she'll have changed her tune just a bit."

I chased away my dirty thoughts, and felt disgusted for having had them. But then I imagined Mom and Mr. Reynolds, the room smelling of shoe leather, and Brut cologne, and whatever that stuff was he rubbed in his hair. "As long as she isn't still seeing Mr. Reynolds," I said.

Dad nodded slowly, both hands on the wheel, his shoulders rolling with the heave of the boat. "That's a good point. But now that it looks like we're finally going to start catching some fish, maybe this Mr. Reynolds won't seem like such a big deal."

"How you figure?"

"Well, you see, Pete, that was a lot of the problem. Your mother, she didn't believe I could cut it anymore as a fisherman."

Dad's coffee mug teetered and almost spilled, but I grabbed it and held it in place. "You sure? To me it never seemed like Mom really cared how you did."

"She used to. Of course there were other things. But a woman like her, she likes a man who can earn his share, that's probably why she was drawn to this hotshot real-estate guy."

We slanted hard to the port and Dad turned the wheel the other way, until things flattened out. "Remember," he said, "her own dad's a doctor, for Christ's sake. And since we hadn't done so well in the Sound the last couple years—who knows what went through her mind?"

"So you're saying if we catch lots of fish, you and Mom will get back together?"

"It's a lot more involved than that. But it sure wouldn't hurt. Not one darn bit."

I gripped the railing again, and tried to gauge the force of the swells. After a few minutes it didn't seem so bad, so I told Dad I was going back down to get some sleep. He said I might as well, since the tide was going to be pushing against us all the way to Petersburg.

I went down the ladder into the engine room, climbed into my bunk, and discovered no one else around. I checked again and slipped inside my sleeping bag. The swell was gentler now, without the jolt to it. I lay back and relaxed. We could really use one of those solid-stick air fresheners down here, I said to myself. Although after a while I forgot about the smell, of sweat or dirty clothes or whatever it was. My dong started thumping again, this time straight up, against my zipper. I unbuttoned my jeans and let the zipper slide down. Then I peeled back my boxer shorts, and took it in my hand. I told myself not to do it, not now. I'd gone a couple weeks, ever since we left Petersburg. Except once when I was stoned. But that didn't count. Now I stroked it, faster and faster, and I thought, Do it. Every chance you get. But something told me to stop. It wasn't easy. I pinned my hands behind my back. Save it for the real thing, I kept saying to myself. Save it *for the real thing*.

We reached Petersburg late that night, and the next morning I headed for Ceci's bunkhouse. The clouds had finally cleared and the sun had risen over the harbor, making the old wooden yachts and small fishing boats look as if they had just been painted. I tried to think of what I should say. Maybe not a thing, I decided. Maybe she'll hug me and French-kiss me before I have a chance. I banged hard on the door. I hoped Ruth wasn't there. I wondered if Ceci was still asleep. She'll be pissed if I wake her, I thought. But no one was around. I whispered "Goddamnit," and walked back through the cannery, hoping to surprise her again. A stout Indian woman in rubber boots and an apron was spraying down a conveyor belt with a hose attachment shaped like a gun, and a Japanese man was carting off a load of silver salmon. I didn't see anyone else.

The next day was cold and damp, the sky dark like a fading bruise. I had on my raingear, just to keep warm. We finished patching the net and Dad instructed us to bring it back through the power block onto the stern. I piled the corks in a neat figure-eight, and Wade stood next to me, bunching up the web into long humped piles.

He nudged me with his elbow. "You know, it's probably sunny today in Bellingham. Don't you wish you were there?"

I looked down at my cork-pile. "I thought you were the one so gung-ho about making money."

"Oh, I am. But I just thought it might be different for you."

"Sorry, Wade, I got more important things to worry about."

"Like what? You got a girl up here?"

"As a matter of fact I do," I told him.

Wade laughed. "Sure, Pete. Even if you did, I bet you wouldn't know what to do about it."

"As if you would?"

Wade stood staring at me and I stared back. I still had to be careful with him. It was hard to figure when he'd really get pissed. The last of the web came through the power block, and Dad shut off the hydraulics. "I gotta go make a phone call," he said. "And I don't want you two strangling each other when I get back."

"Don't worry about me." I smiled like I didn't have a concern in the world. "Because I got someplace to go, too."

"I bet you do," Wade said. But I didn't look back. I walked up the ramp, onto the main road, and stopped at the public restrooms to wash my hands. I wiped my armpits with a brown paper towel. Then I pulled a packet of Certs from my pocket, chomped on a tablet, took one last look in the mirror, and headed for the bunkhouse.

This time I heard someone moving around as soon as I knocked. The door swung open, and Ceci stepped forward like she wanted to hug me. But then she stopped and shook her head.

"It's... you," she said. "Well, come on in. And sit down."

She was wearing jeans and a plaid flannel shirt, with a scuffed pair of brown hiking boots, splotched with mud. Her hair seemed a little longer, curling a bit off her neck, but the mole was still there, her neck soft and thin. Alongside her sat the orange backpack, crammed all the way to the top. I tried to think of something to say, but all I managed was, "You go hiking somewhere?"

"Well, it certainly looks that way," she replied, her hands on her hips, staring at the pack. "Now all I've got to do is figure out where to put all this stuff."

"So where'd you go?"

"C'mer, I'll show you." We stepped outside, and Ceci pointed far up an enormous hill on the other side of Wrangell Narrows. "Way up near the top."

"It must have been a pretty cold night," I replied, stepping back inside the room. The fo'c'sle had been very warm, and I had imagined Ceci alongside me, her arms around my neck.

"It was damn cold," she said with a little shiver.

"Who'd you go with? Ruth?"

"No, not Ruth." She spoke slowly and carefully. I wondered if she and Ruth had had a fight. Looking around I saw that Ruth's cot was empty, the blankets folded in squares, nothing else showing except the striped-gray mattress. The Jim Morrison poster was missing, four red tacks against the beige wall the only sign of where it had been. The portable stereo was gone, too.

"Did she take off?"

Ceci looked down at her boots. "She flew home to Seattle the day before yesterday. Not that I can blame her."

"Well, I'm glad you didn't go with her." And suddenly I felt a little tremor, thinking about how nice it would be not having to worry about being interrupted, just lying there on the bed in the cool air, without any clothes.

Ceci loosened the drawstring at the top of her pack, reached inside and pulled out a wool sweater, then two cans of Sterno fuel, a box of wooden matches, and a pale-green plastic parka. She set the Sterno cans and the matches on her nightstand, and tossed the parka and sweater into a corner of the room.

"Let's just say it crossed my mind," she said, reaching into the pack again, removing a pair of muddy white socks. "The way things have been up here, it makes me sick. Sometimes we don't work for days at a time. And when you're stuck in Petersburg, you run out of things to do *awfully* fast."

"But at least it must have been fun going hiking."

"It was OK." She put her hand to her mouth, pressing her index finger to one of her front teeth. "So how have things been with you?"

"A lot of weird stuff has happened."

"I can probably relate to that."

"You wouldn't believe some of this," I said, and I told her about almost getting blown overboard in the ocean, how the crew threatened to quit, how we were ready to go home, if Dad hadn't caught so many fish our last time out. "It sure is good to be back in Petersburg," I added with a big smile.

But Ceci was looking the other way again, toward the empty wall. "So what about you?" I finally asked. "What do you got to tell?"

"Oh, nothing, really. Nothing as exciting as that." She had both arms deep inside the pack now, and she removed a pair of jeans, then two metallic packets of freeze-dried food, then a slinky pair of navy blue long johns. "Maybe I'll tell you about it some other time. Because I don't really feel like getting into it right now. Not with all the other things on my mind."

She sat down and leaned forward to unlace her boots. "Don't you want to sit down?"

"Sure," I said, squeezing close to her on the bed. And then our hips touched. Right away I felt stiff as a screwdriver. She must be getting ready now, I thought, maybe next she'll start taking off her clothes. I never imagined it would happen so quickly. I wasn't even sure I was prepared.

She slipped out of the second of the two boots, and peeled off her wool socks. Her bare feet looked tender and pink, shriveled from moisture. I wondered if the flannel shirt would come off next, if she had on a bra. But she just sat there, staring at her toes. Then she leaned back on her bed against the wall.

"God, I'm tired."

"Do you want to lie down?" I tried to make my voice sound deep and full of confidence, like a doctor on TV.

"That sounds pretty good."

"Here." I grabbed her pillow. "I'll fluff it for you." I held it between my knees and patted it with both hands.

"I don't know if you're doing any good." Then she smiled, maybe for the first time. She must be nervous, I thought. Maybe as nervous as me. And maybe now she's finally starting to relax. "But thanks for trying," she said.

She lay down and squirmed around, her hips swiveling, her butt small and tight inside her jeans. I bet she has on a sexy pair of panties, I thought. Maybe lavender, with black trim and a glossy surface. Then she sat up and leaned against the wall, her neck against the pillow. She looked real young to me then, even younger than me, the way she frowned with her arms folded across her chest. I tried to think of something I could do.

"You OK?" I finally asked.

"I don't feel all that great."

"You think you might be sick?"

"It's nothing physical."

"Then maybe I can help." I reached out and grabbed her hand. It was cool and limp. But maybe that will change real quickly, I thought. So long as I can get her into the right mood. I moved down to kiss her, my lips pressed tight, ready to open at Ceci's permission. But her head jerked away like a cat when you touch it in the wrong place.

"Don't," she whispered.

"Why not?"

"I'll tell you some other time."

"You must really be feeling bad."

"It's not that."

"Then what is it?"

"You really want to know?"

Ceci sat up, wrapped her arms around her knees, and rested her chin against her knuckles.

"Then I guess I better tell you." She took a deep breath, narrowed her eyes, and aimed them at her feet. "You see," she said, "the person I went hiking with, the person I spent the night with, that was Kevin. My old boyfriend."

I heard the murmur of machinery in the cannery, farther off the rumble of a diesel engine, and then my muscles tensed at once. It was as if a third person had entered the room, maybe Kevin himself, and I was someplace I shouldn't be. And now I was going to get caught.

"So I guess he's still your boyfriend."

"Yeah," Ceci replied, her head still down. "I guess he is."

I stood up, turned my back, and stared at the four red tacks on the opposite wall. "How the hell did that happen?"

"I don't know how it happened, Peter; those things just do. You should know that, you're not *that* young, after all." She lowered her voice. "So don't get so upset."

She frowned at me, and I frowned back.

"And really, what difference does it make?" she went on. "I didn't even know if you'd ever be here again, or if you were, whether you'd even want to see me. You never sent me a letter, you know."

"But I thought about you a lot," I replied, my throat getting that choked-off feeling again. "I didn't write because I didn't know I'd ever be back, either. But if I knew you were going to go back with this... this Kevin—"

"Jesus, Peter, do you always have to sound like such a boy?"

"But I am a boy."

"I know you are, you're a good boy." Ceci laughed with a twittering sound. "Come here, let me tell you something."

Slowly I crossed the room. It was hard now, remembering why I'd come. She told to me sit down. Then she grabbed one of my hands. "Maybe now you'll think I'm a bitch, and I'm sorry if that's the case, because I don't think I am. But Kevin and I, that's gone on for a long time. And I guess it's going to go on for a while longer."

"You think I want to hear this?"

"What I'm saying, Peter"—and now her voice got all stern and serious sounding—"is, don't think you're missing out on anything, just because you've never had a chance to screw. I mean, Jesus, you're only sixteen or something like that, you'll learn sooner or later that it's not all it's cracked up to be. Far from it, if you really want to know."

"I find that a little hard to believe."

"Then maybe you haven't lived long enough. Or maybe if you're a boy you don't have to worry about it. Because there's too many times—way too many—when I've wondered what we've done and worried myself sick."

She stopped and breathed deeply a couple times, her hand massaging the blanket atop her bed. "And it almost doesn't matter that it finally comes, that everything's alright, because it's the waiting that makes everything not right." She squeezed my palm. "Do you see what I mean?"

I stood up and tried to make my voice sarcastic and mean. "Yeah, I guess. But then why'd you go back to the guy? Why didn't you tell him to get lost?"

"I don't know why. And that just makes it all the more crappy."

She wiped her eyes with the long johns, then draped them over her shoulders. "There must be some reason," she said. "He's a nice guy, at least some of the time. But if I told you why, I'd just be lying."

She put her head on her pillow. Then she looked up. More quietly, she said, "I'm sorry. Thanks for stopping by."

"Maybe I'll see you some other time," I said.

"Yeah, maybe," and then she let out a high-pitched snort, and flattened the pillow against her face. I grabbed my jacket, fumbled with the handle of the door, and stepped back into the cold. Gray clouds circled over my head, and I stared up at them, trying to control my lungs, wondering why this was always happening to me, this hot helpless feeling just before you start to cry.

Chapter 14

I didn't want Wade to see me like this. Dad, neither. But I got tired of wandering around, of being alone. And I was cold. The wind blew through the streets, scattering leaves and pine needles, dirtied ice-cream bar wrappers and scraps of newspaper. I walked down the main road, stepped inside one of the grocery stores, grabbed a cart and pushed it up and down the aisles, past the potatoes, the cuts of beef, the half gallons of milk. But I didn't buy anything, I didn't even take anything off the shelves. I figured I'd probably be arrested, if this went on too long. But at least I wouldn't have to go back to the boat.

My face was dry by now, my breath almost back to normal. You can't hide from things forever, I decided. Although it would be nice if you could. I walked back down the ramp, ready for whatever Wade might say. Maybe he's gone, I thought, off fishing for Dolly Vardens, or whatever the hell he does for fun. But I found him perched on the bulwarks, wearing his maroon wrestling sweatshirt with the cut-off sleeves, a can of Skoal resting in his cupped palms.

"You're back pretty quick," he said, twisting off the cap, letting the sour smell of the tobacco drift across the deck. "Must have been pretty exciting. Or pretty fast." He laughed, and reached in and squeezed a pinch, tweezer-like, between his thumb and forefinger. Then he peeled back his lower lip until you could see the tendon at the base of his lip. "By the way," he added, slipping in the wad, "I think your Dad's inside. He seemed kind of pissed about something."

"Did he say what about?"

"It better not have anything to do with fishing, that's all I got to say. Because Gordon just went up to the cannery to find out what's going on."

"Going on where?"

"About when we fish again, dipshit. What do you think's going on?"

"Why don't you talk more clearly?" I said. Then I slid open the galley door and stepped inside. Dad sat at the table, his head tilted forward, his hands clasped behind his neck. He looked up, stared at me, then dropped his head back down. "'Fraid I got some bad news, Peter."

"You too, huh?"

He stared at me again. "Why? You already talk to her?"

"Who?"

"Your mother."

"What happened?"

Dad rubbed his hands through his hair. "Well, Pete, I guess we can forget about Richard Reynolds."

I sat down on the other side of the table. "Why?" I asked, kind of smiling. "Is he dead?"

"I guess your mother isn't seeing him anymore."

"So what's the bad part?"

"I guess we can sort of forget about me, too."

"Huh?"

"It's silly, maybe she doesn't mean it, I don't know what she means." Then he added, as if it didn't really matter, "Your mother said she wants a divorce."

Out the rear door I heard Wade spit, the sound carrying through the heavy air like the distant pop of a gun. The wind came next, rustling the sheets of newspaper piled on the table, lifting the yellow grocery receipts scattered across Dad's bunk, making the cabin sigh and wheeze. I wanted to say something, something that would cancel out what Dad had just said. But all I managed was to ask, "Why?"

"She claims she wants to go to college. To improve herself, maybe even have a career of her own." He glanced out the window.

"But why does she need a divorce? The campus is only a mile or two from home."

"That's the thing, Peter, she's thinking about selling the house and moving to San Jose, so she can be near your grandpa. And if she lived there a year she'd be considered a resident, she'd barely have to pay a thing for tuition. Plus, she says that San Jose is a really happening place. I guess that's where a lot of the computers are being made."

"Is she serious?"

"She sounded pretty serious to me. And she wants you to call her right away. Fact, she wants you to think about moving to California, too."

"Well, I'm not going to."

Dad locked his fingers behind his neck and flared his elbows. "You might want to give it some thought, Peter. It's your future, after all."

"You sound like you're on *her* side."

"At least in California you wouldn't be making the same mistakes as me."

I stood up, went to the sink, and ran water into a plastic tumbler glass. "What have you done that's so bad?"

"Nothing more than letting things get out of my control," Dad replied, his head turned away from me. "But that's enough, if you think about it. I know it's hard for a kid your age to understand. It wasn't like your mother and I wanted this to happen—it's the last thing either of us ever wanted. You marry someone, you make a commitment, you think you got your whole life planned out. Even as young as I was, even as foolish as a lot of people said I was, I knew *that* much from the start: that with your Mom, and with you already on the way, I'd have to start planning out my life. But that's what's always been so hard—trying to plan for the things you can't predict. Especially after my own dad was dead and I was running the boat myself."

He looked at me as if I had interrupted him with a question.

"Sure I did good, I did damn good, but that didn't make things all that easier. It seems like the more money I made, the more of it went back into the boat, or into the house, or into thin air. Sometimes I didn't know where the hell it went. I just knew that no matter how much money I earned, it would never be enough. Do you see what I mean? I wanted to give your mother everything, everything in the world. When we first started going out, I used to tell her how I'd buy her a big yacht someday, all kinds of crap like that. Of course she never got the yacht, she never got any of the things I promised. And that included making her happy."

Dad sat there staring at the unwashed cups and plates until his eyes were almost closed. I took a sip of the water, but it tasted like the inside of the metal tank. I dumped the rest down the drain.

"What exactly did Mom say?" I finally asked.

"I've told you what she said. But I've given up trying to figure out what she meant. Fact, I've decided it's better not to try to figure those things out, it's better just to forget about 'em."

"Isn't that kind of a bad attitude?"

"At least it doesn't set you up to be disappointed."

I looked at him again, sitting there with his head slumped toward the sink, and I wanted to grab him by the shoulders and shake him and say I understood. But I didn't understand, I didn't understand any more than Dad did, probably a lot less. I thought I was going to cry again.

Instead I forced open the galley door and stepped out on deck. Wade was still sitting there, grinning and spitting, the tobacco hitting the water in globs. I headed back up the ramp. I was jogging, I think, my head down, almost everything else blocked out. A couple seagulls twisted up from a rocky ledge, shrieking, then floating away. I spoke to the operator very quickly, listened to her dial, and then heard Mom's voice on the other end.

"So I guess your Dad told you," she said, "about what's going on."

"As much as I needed to know."

"I'm sorry I didn't tell you earlier, dear, I really am—" and then her voice went silent, and all I could hear was the crackle of the static and the shrieks of the seagulls. I pictured Mom as she was before I left, barefoot in jeans and a red Danskin top, twirling around in our backyard to some awful disco music playing on a portable stereo. She was taking a dance course up at the college and admitted she was still learning the steps. What I remembered was how carefree she looked, and, considering everything, how young.

"But it's not like it's for certain—about me going to California. Did your father tell you that? I said I *might* go—if I can work it out with Grandpa. And even if I do, it won't be for at least another year."

"But if you're not so sure you want to go to California, why's it so important to get a divorce?"

"Because"—and now she sounded almost angry—"it's what I really want. Do you understand that, Peter? I've never done what I've wanted. I've always done what your father wanted, or before that, what my father and mother wanted. I'm not a young woman anymore. I haven't been for quite some time. And now it's time for me to do what I think is right."

I didn't listen to what she said after that. I thought instead about the day Dad told us he'd sold the *Stavenger*, way back last March. I'd been sitting in front of the TV a little stoned, watching Jerry Mathers, the Beaver, trying to wriggle his head out from between the rungs of a wrought-iron fence. Then Dad arrived, all excited about how much better things would be. But none of us believed it, I don't think. Including Dad.

Now I rested the receiver against my shoulder. After a moment I said, "I don't want to talk to you anymore right now. Is that OK?"

She said I could call her when I felt better, and then there was a long pause. "*Please* be careful up there," she said. The crackling was getting louder, and her voice grew faint. "I was talking to Beth Nordsen the other day, I saw her grocery shopping. Now that Stan's back home, she's been telling me all about how rough the weather gets in Alaska this time of year, like it doesn't matter— now that Stan's back home."

I didn't say anything.

"Because I *do* care what happens to you. You and your father both. You understand that, don't you?"

"I understand," I said, without really thinking about whether or not I did.

"Good," Mom said. "I love you, Peter."

A small pink pleasure boat pulled out of its berth, its twin outboard motors making a choking sound, white froth spewing from the propellers. It cleared the dock and headed into the open channel. Then we said goodbye.

I turned and looked back over the harbor. Everything was quiet except for the whistling sound of the steam from the cannery, and I wondered if maybe Ceci was inside. But I didn't want to think about Ceci. I didn't want to think about anything. I headed back along the waterfront toward the boat, thinking, Another fucked-up day in a fucked-up life with a couple of fucked-up parents. Then I stopped to watch a seagull float above the water. But it's *my* life, I said to myself, as if this were something I'd just figured out. And I can't exactly trade it in for a new one.

I was nearly to the boat now. Gordon and George and Wade stood on deck smiling. They were all bastards, I decided, to be happy at a time like this. I couldn't imagine what they found so amusing. Gordon slapped George on the shoulder, and Wade shook his hand. I wondered if they were laughing about Dad's divorce. But then Dad appeared from inside the galley, with a big grin, which seemed awfully weird, considering. He reached out and squeezed George's big fist, and slapped him on the back, too.

I climbed quietly on deck. It was still a while longer before I figured it out.

"It's a boy," George told me. "The whole thing—it's finally over." He stood there smiling, until the smile changed into a laugh.

Then he rubbed his eyes. "Can you believe it? A goddamned little boy."

Gordon said, "And that's not the only thing. Up at the cannery, I just found out, the test fishing in the ocean was great—better than we could have imagined. Last I heard they were bouncing off the beach at Noyes like popcorn off a skillet. Isn't it amazing? The baby's here and so are the salmon."

"Right on!" Wade said, punching the air with his fist.

"Yeah, Pete," Dad said, his voice a lot more quiet, his hands jammed into the pockets of his mackinaw. "It does look pretty good. They've given us two days, starting, believe it or not, tomorrow. *No one* expected that. So that means we gotta fly out of here if we're going to make Noyes Island. Not a spare moment to fuck around."

He shook his head. "I don't want to guarantee anything, you can't, ever, in this business. But unless those test reports are dead wrong—"

"Which is still possible," George said, his voice quiet now, like Dad's.

"You bet it is. But unless they are, we're going to be looking pretty damn good."

"'Bout time," I said, and I smiled, too. It felt good to smile, better than I had expected. But then I looked at Dad and saw behind his own smile those same sad, tired eyes. Even the best news in the world wouldn't have let him pretend that nothing else was wrong. But he was doing a pretty good job. He looked excited and sad and tired all at the same time.

Gordon glanced at Dad and nodded. "This is what we've been waiting for, Mike—this is what makes fishing what it is."

"We'll find out soon enough," Dad said. "Now let's get everything we need, groceries, ice, all that shit, quick as we can. Because the sooner we leave this place, the better."

Two hours later we pulled away from the fuel dock and left Petersburg behind, the houses and buildings sinking into the gray afternoon, Wrangell Narrows gaping open in front of us. Dad veered the *Ambition* slightly to the left, positioning us so we headed straight down the middle. Soon we had penetrated the channel's damp green banks, and Dad settled back against the bench on top the cabin, noting something in his log book. He told me to hold the wheel for a minute, smiled and closed his eyes.

"This could be a lot of fun," he said, tilting back his head, his arms relaxing at his side. "You know, a chance like this doesn't come along every day. Maybe once in a guy's life—if he's lucky."

When the channel narrowed he stood up and took back the wheel, gripping it in both fists, letting the fast-moving tide sweep us along.

Chapter 15

I climbed into my bunk as soon as it got dark, but Dad stayed on top the cabin most of the night, piloting the *Ambition* down Sumner Strait, back toward Noyes Island. It wasn't until three in the morning that Gordon and I took his place. Now the clouds behind us were reddening, the sky was going from black to a gloomy gray. The ocean dipped and surged, birds with long necks and black wings skimming its warped surface. I shivered inside my down jacket, buttoned the snap closest to my throat, felt the rise and fall in my gut. Gordon sent me down to make instant coffee, and I spied Dad asleep on his back with his clothes on, his mouth open, his mackinaw spread across his chest.

Back on top the cabin we drank from our mugs and listened to the thump-thump-thump of the engine and the hum of the VHF. Out in front of us three purse seiners crept like snails on a shifting surface of glass, their hulls and blocky cabins dark against the pale sky, their masts and booms poking out as if they were antennae. "Down that way is Noyes," Gordon said, peering through binoculars. "You can just barely see it, but that's it, I'm sure of it. What time you got?"

"Four-thirty. You think maybe I should wake my dad?"

"I think you better let him sleep. He needs it a lot more than we do."

I nodded, thinking about how Dad's eyes kept closing, his head drooping to one side, when we relieved him and George at the wheel. "It still seems pretty amazing, if it's true," I said. "All these salmon coming in at once—just so they can go up river and shoot their wads."

"Men have been known to work pretty hard, too, under similar circumstances," Gordon replied. Then he turned to the weather channel on the VHF. A women's voice told us the winds would be ten to fifteen knots westerly for the next twenty-four hours.

Dad appeared behind us as soon as she had finished, the hood of his sweatshirt over his head, his eyes not quite all the way open. "Where you got us, Gordon?" he asked, his voice still thick with sleep.

"Warren Island's behind us, we're maybe an hour from Noyes."

"Good. So we might as well wake the other ."

"But don't you want to get a little more rest?" I asked.

"I got almost two hours in."

"Couldn't you have gone to bed a little earlier?"

Dad shook his head. "The way we were bouncing around? You know I can't sleep in that crap."

Gordon told Dad about the weather. "Let's just hope it stays that way," Dad said. "It won't be much fun brailing the fish on board if the boat's pitching all over the place." He took the binoculars from Gordon and stared toward the island. "Listen, we're not going to have time to see where these little buggers are jumping, so as soon as we get across the line we'll try one, straight out from Ulitka. Wherever we can find a place to dump the net."

Gordon pointed toward the purse seiners in front of us, and four more that trailed behind. "I think we're going to have lots of company."

"Let's just be thankful," Dad said, "that a lot of those other Washington guys already threw in the towel."

Gordon nodded slowly, looking the other way.

"And one other thing. Make sure you keep checking the temperature on the skiff. Those guys in Petersburg, they thought they fixed it, but it wouldn't be the first time a mechanic's been wrong."

Gordon nodded again, and Dad yawned. "When you get a chance, Pete, make me some coffee, real strong. And then we may as well wake George and Wade. I want to have that net in the water soon as the clock strikes six. Maybe even a couple minutes before."

When we reached the island, dozens of boats were cutting back and forth along the shoreline, maneuvering for position. Three of them sat against the beach beyond Cape Ulitka, where the test boats had caught thousands of humpies two days before. It was five minutes to six now and Dad circled us farther out, until the shoreline looked fuzzy and gray, the waves hitting the rocks in silent, harmless explosions. Down on deck I zipped up my jacket, tucked my chin and turned my head away from the stiffening breeze. A humpy broke the surface, its silver body bending like a bow. It flopped back down and disappeared, but right away it leaped again.

"Right there!" George shouted. "And there! And there!" A fourth one jumped. "Sweet Christ, right there, too!" He climbed the ladder and yelled to Dad, who swung the boat to the left. It was still three minutes to six but that didn't matter now, because no one from Fish and Game was around to stop us. Dad said to cut loose the skiff, and soon the corks and web were tumbling into the water. We saw four more jumpers while the net was out. Then Gordon drew shut the circle of corks, and Wade and I climbed onto the stern and started bringing the web back on deck through the power block. George winched in the heavy white purse-line, sealing shut the bottom of the net, trapping the salmon inside.

The fish began to thrash as the ring of corks shrunk small and then the bag was full of them, panicking. I yelled to Dad that maybe we should use the brailer to scoop the humpies from the bag, but he said the whole thing wasn't that big, that we could bring it on deck all at once. So the bag came up, bigger than I'd ever seen, bigger than the big set at Hidden Falls, making the boat lurch to one side. I thought of how cold the water was, how long it would take Gordon to scoop us up, if something happened. If the skiff didn't flip over with us. But then the boat tipped farther to the starboard, forcing Dad to one knee, his arm braced against the bulwarks. With his other arm he motioned for Gordon to circle around and help. I stared over the side again, saw how close the water had come, figured I could probably touch it with my boot. Not that I would dare it, of course.

Now Dad and George strapped the double-block hook to the skiff, and Gordon towed against us, until the *Ambition* was almost flat, the big bag hanging above the bulwark railing, the rigging taut like a bowstring before you fire the arrow, the pulley blocks shaking, the winch whining, the engine groaning from the strain. The bag flopped down on deck with a loud splat, water and slime and globs of jellyfish leaping from the salmon's bodies and tails, burning against my fingers and lips and tongue, making our raingear glisten. Our legs splayed out as if we were hockey goalies, trying to keep the big blob in one place, trying to shake it and spill it into the hold.

"Must be a fuckin' thousand!" George said.

We spilled as many as we could, but a lot slipped onto the deck, squirming against our ankles, slithering toward the bow. Gordon brought the skiff in behind us, Wade and I hooked him up, and five minutes later we had the net back in a half-circle, the skiff bobbing in the swell. We opened the hatch and pitched in the salmon two at a time, their gills quivering before they went stiff. We worked until the deck was clear, sprayed it all over with the hydraulic hose, and rinsed our hands. Then I hurried up the ladder to join Dad. He was studying the skiff.

"You think George was right?" he asked. "Think we got a thousand?"

"Maybe more. You think it would have been simpler just to brail?"

"Next time we will." Dad ran his fingers through his beard. "You're right, that was taking a chance, letting the boat slide over like that."

"I thought my balls had leaped into my mouth, and that maybe I'd swallowed 'em."

"I bet you did." Dad grinned, then gazed back toward Gordon. "Looks like some guys got some monster bags right off the beach, I still see them brailing. But that's fine with me, 'cause they're waiting turns. I'll take a thousand any time if you get to keep working."

Ten minutes later, Gordon was closing the circle again, his engine straining, smoke pouring from the exhaust pipe, both his hands on the wheel, the earphones clasped over his head. All of a sudden a spurt of steaming water shot from the towbit, and Dad said "Damnit!" and rammed his fist against the cabin railing. "That shouldn't be happening anymore, that's what I paid those guys to fix!"

This time we brought in the net even faster, and I kept peering into the ring of corks, trying to spot something swimming around. At first I didn't see a thing. But then the ring was small and the fish bunched together in a swarm. We hoisted the bag on deck, spilled it, and right away got ready to go. But Dad told Gordon to wait. He climbed into the skiff and stared at the smoke rising from the engine. "Please don't crap out on us," he said to the engine. "Please not today, you son-of-a-bitch."

The skiff did as it was asked for much of the day. We brailed just before lunch, at least a dozen scoops, and we probably had fifteen hundred that set alone. By evening the sea had flattened out and the humpies were piled three-quarters up the sides of the fish hold.

"You know what we'll have to do if we run out of room, don't you?" George said, sitting at the edge of the hatch, the soles of his boots almost touching the dead fish. "We'll have to start loading them right on deck. All over, even up on the bow."

Wade was on his knees, gripping a silver salmon by its tail. He slipped the point of his knife into the fish's butt, sliced open the belly and yanked out the guts. "I've seen pictures of it—a whole fishing boat buried by salmon!"

"So what do you do when you run out of space?" I asked.

"Geez, Pete, what do you think?" He grabbed a spoon and ran it between the two flanks of meat, scooping out the dark purple bloodline. "You go to a tender and unload your fish."

Wade rinsed the silver in a bucket, scrubbed the blood from his knife and spoon, douched the deck, and tossed the fish into the tarpaulin bag of ice water at the rear of the hold. George grabbed the handle of one of the hatch covers, and motioned for Wade to help. "I hope you guys are looking forward to pitching tonight. Because you're going to be at it for a long, long time. But you gotta be quick. We gotta get some sleep, too."

I started to say, "I can't wait," but then I saw Dad, standing atop the cabin, gripping a cleat on the mast and pointing toward the beach. "Look!" he yelled. "Look at the fuckin' skiff!"

The cork-line had lost its horseshoe shape and now lay in a jagged crescent, the skiff drifting at the other end with its bow pointed toward the rocks. Gordon stood in the stern frantically waving his arms.

"Christ!" George said.

"We better get him back quick, before we get tangled around someone else," Dad shouted. "Especially with the goddamned sun going down."

He cut back the throttle and told George to turn on the hydraulics. The boat groaned, the hoses at the base of the cabin flexing stiffly in response. Then we began to bring the net on board. The skiff crept toward us, rising and falling in the swell, dragged along by the seine. The aluminum cover to the engine was pushed back, and you could see the yellow paint, the smoke rising, Gordon standing with his cap turned backward, wiping his face with a rag.

When the net was all the way in we hoisted the skiff against the stern. Gordon climbed out and shook his head. "Something inside, something rubber—I can smell it."

"But did you check it?" Dad said. "Did you check it every hour, like I told you?"

"Yeah, Mike," Gordon said slowly. "I did."

Dad hopped into the skiff, steadying one hand against the stern roller, almost losing his balance, then dropping into the pit of the aluminum hull. He put his hand to the engine block, whipping it back the instant it touched. "Jesus! We're lucky it's not on fire."

Gordon, George, and Dad worked on the engine for the next half hour, the skiff rising and falling the whole time, Wade and me handing over screwdrivers and wrenches and engine rags, the three of them muttering about gaskets and hose clamps and relief valves and heat exchangers, all in a language I didn't understand. The sky got darker, and more and more of the boats around us headed for the tenders in Steamboat Bay. I thought of the lines that must be forming, of how long we might have to wait. "Dad," I finally said, "don't you think we better get going?"

Dad stayed hunched over the engine, bracing his free arm against the fire-hose chafing that covered the side railing. But George said, "Peter's got a point. Maybe on the tender they've got someone who knows more about this shit than we do."

"Jesus," Dad said, leaning his butt against the side, wiping grease from his hands with a rag. "They better."

We reached Steamboat Bay an hour later, and now it was almost completely dark, no stars, just heavy clouds, a sliver of dull-yellow moon. Tendering vessels sat anchored all over the narrow channel, their big sodium lamps lighting up their decks as if they were miniature football stadiums. Guys in dark green raingear guided the brailer nets in and out, their loads dripping with pink slime. We found our tender, the *Adventurer*, but at least a half-dozen boats were already in front of us. Some of the boats sat low in the water, dragged down by the weight of their fish.

Dad called the skipper on the radio and told him what was wrong. The skipper said he probably had what we needed. "Thank God for that," Dad said as he hung up the microphone. "Now we'll just have to sit tight."

"Do you want to sleep for a while?" I asked.

Dad yawned and rubbed his eyes. "I can't, Pete. I have to stay here and make sure we don't drift and bang into someone."

"But couldn't we drop the anchor?"

"No, because I don't want to fuck around lifting it. The last thing we need now is to lose our place in line."

"Then I think *I'll* go down and sleep." I turned and headed down the rear ladder, through the galley, and into the engine room. I took off my boots and left them alongside two drums of oil, peeled off my sweatshirt and hung it on a nail. I climbed into my bunk and snapped out the light. But every time I almost fell asleep I thought I heard voices, someone calling for me to get my ass out on deck. It was hard to tell, over the throb of the engine. Then I started to itch. First on my wrists and forearms and the backs of my hands, and I figured it must be from the jellyfish. But it spread to my upper arms, my chest, my back, even my butt and legs. I lay there thrashing around, my fingers going everywhere.

After a few more minutes I got up, put on my boots and my sweatshirt, and climbed out onto the bow deck and then back on top the cabin. Dad and George sat at the wheel, Dad's head slumped to one side. Purse seiners were strapped to either side of the *Adventurer*, its big green crane centered over the hold of one of the boats and carting out a brailer of salmon. "Are we next?" I asked.

George pointed to a dark-blue steel boat drifting near us. "That guy is. We got probably another hour."

"What time it is now?"

"One a.m."

"So we've already been up for twenty-two hours."

Dad lifted his head. "You mean you didn't manage to get any sleep?"

"I couldn't. My whole body started itching." I scratched hard, underneath my left armpit, and along my ribs.

"Sounds like jellyfish poisoning," George said. "But you'll live. Rub some baking soda on it." He patted me on the shoulder. "Listen, when you finally get in there, you're going to have to work like hell, because Gordon will be busy with the skiff. But be sure to pace yourself. You don't want to be totally exhausted. Not with all those fish."

Dad raised his head again and smiled. "Pretty good, Pete, don't you think? Maybe we'll do even better tomorrow."

I said, "It looks like tomorrow's going to get here pretty soon." Then I walked stiffly back to the ladder, and headed down on deck and into the galley for the baking soda. Wade sat on the bench near the door, his feet sticking out ahead of him so you could see the black soles of his rubber boots, his arms folded, his head thrown back, snoring. Gordon was squeezed in around the galley table, his arms crossed and his face down in a magazine. Slowly he lifted his head. "We ready to pitch?"

"Not yet," I told him. "Maybe another hour."

"It's like I said, Pete. This is what fishing is all about."

"Not getting a chance to sleep?"

"Making good bucks *and* not getting a chance to sleep."

"How much you think we made?"

Gordon sat up and rubbed his head. Then he folded shut the magazine, a smudged copy of *Newsweek*, and stuck it behind the cutting board at the end of the table. "Eight thousand pinks, that's about 25,000 pounds, a $10,000 market, $800 for each of us. Not counting the silvers and the dogs. So maybe a thousand bucks apiece. Not too bad, huh?"

I tried to imagine what I would do with it, maybe buy a better stereo. Mom would tell me to put the money away for college, but that would take all the fun out of it. Maybe I'd buy a little sports car with a removable top. Or a hot new motorcycle.

Pitching those fish can't be the worse thing in the world, I decided. Not for a thousand bucks.

But that was before I climbed into the hold. It was after two in the morning now. All the other boats had dropped anchor, their crews asleep for what was left of the night. I kept banging my head or shoulders or elbows against the ceiling, while my body sank deeper and deeper into the pile. The brailer held about three hundred fish, and Wade and I pitched them two or even three at a time. But the net filled very slowly, the sweat getting worse and worse on my face. I wanted to flick away a big drop at the tip of my nose, but I couldn't, not with those slime-covered rubber gloves.

"So how you doing, Pete?" I heard Wade say between breaths. "You're not gonna crap out on me, are you?"

"I'll be fine." I grabbed two more humpies from behind their heads, and flung them into the brailer. "That's three hundred."

"Then let's send her up."

I yelled to George and he began to hoist the bag out of the hold, while Wade and I ducked beneath the overhang to shield ourselves from the slimy drip out of the net. My armpits started to itch again, and so did my chest. "Just think," Wade told me, smiling. "Probably only about twenty-five more brailers to go."

"Don't remind me."

"But don't you see? This is a test. To see what we're really made of."

"C'mon, Wade, give me a break."

"Just don't you crap out on me!"

"Damnit, I won't!"

But soon enough I wondered if I might. We got the second brailer out, then the third, the fourth, the fifth, the sixth, and the seventh, and slowly the level of the fish sank. It got a little easier to clutch and pitch them. But I was getting tired more quickly than the fish were disappearing, and all I wanted to do was sleep. And scratch my armpits, and the backs of my legs. I glanced at Wade and that cheered me up, because his sneer was gone, his eyes had that heavy look, and he was moving more slowly. A strand of purple fish-blood hung from his chin. "Come on, Pete," he said, but now in a thick voice. "We gotta keep going. We gotta go. 'Cause this will show everyone what we're really like."

We made it through brailer ten, eleven, twelve, and thirteen, my back muscles tight and getting tighter. I stared at George and Dad, just standing up there running the controls, without any raingear on, without even a touch of slime, and all of a sudden I hated them. Because they weren't down here with me and Wade. And where in the hell was Gordon? He probably got done with the skiff an hour ago, I thought, now he's sitting on his butt, smoking his pipe, reading another fucking magazine. We finished another brailer. Number fourteen, I said to myself. Or was the last one fourteen? I looked at Wade and he looked at me and turned up his palms and shrugged. "I guess we lost count. Oh well," he added almost happily, "what the hell?"

I gripped the aluminum ridge of the brailer net with both gloves and tried to ignore the smell. Then I moved closer to Wade. "What do you mean, 'what the hell'?"

"Pete, it doesn't matter."

"The hell it doesn't! I wanna know when the fuck we're getting outta here!"

"Soon as the fish are all out!"

"Come on, guys," Dad said quietly from up above. "Don't slow down, we gotta get this done, quick as you can."

"Fuck you!"

Dad didn't move. "Drop it, Pete. Just keep pitching."

About a half-hour later Gordon swung his legs over the fish hold and leaped into what was left of the salmon, the humpies scattering from the force of his boots. "How's it going?" he asked, steadying himself against the bin boards and sinking up to his knees.

"Just great," Wade replied.

"Good news, the skiff is fixed, we're ready to go again."

Wade glared, like only Wade could. "Just start pitching."

I was going a lot more slowly now. My feet were cold, pressed against the ice beneath the salmon. I wondered if you could get frostbite this way. Then I looked over at Wade. He was slumped against a pile of fish, squirming around, trying to make himself comfortable. It was as if the pile was an enormous beanbag chair. "Hey! Get up and help us!"

"I'll get up in a minute. I just need a little—" He yawned. "A little rest."

"No you don't! Get off your ass!"

"Leave me alone. I didn't do anything to you."

Gordon was pitching as fast as Wade and me combined now, sometimes three, even four fish between his gloves, his beard wet and his eyes alert. I tried to keep up, but it was impossible, because my muscles weren't doing what I told them to do. Then Gordon motioned to George, and the brailer rose from the fish hold, dripping slime as thick as spaghetti sauce. Looking down I saw the foot of my boot, with only a shallow layer of fish surrounding my ankle, flat against the shaft-alley cover. I glanced around the rest of the hold. There couldn't have been more than a thousand left. I grabbed Wade by the shoulder and pointed.

"Hot... damn," Wade replied, as if each word were a challenge to pronounce. But now we both started to pitch more quickly. Another brailer filled, and then another, and finally I was on my hands and knees, crawling along the hard ice, grabbing the fish one by one, some of them creased like waffles, most of them in a heavy syrup of blood. I scooted them up to Wade and Gordon, who flipped them into the hoop. "That's it," Gordon said. "We're done!"

The brailer was hoisted out of the hold, swaying slowly above us, and finally clearing the deck. Gordon patted us both on the shoulders of our rain jackets with his slimy gloves. Then he grabbed onto the railing at the top of the hold and hoisted himself out.

George passed me the hose and I began to spray the bin boards and the shaft alley and the concrete floor, blasting away the blood stains and the red jellyfish wedged against what remained of the ice. Wade and I scrubbed with bristly brushes, squirted in Joy detergent, and then rinsed everything again with the hose. From above deck I heard the suck of the hydraulic pump, and I watched the suds swirl down the drain. The detergent had a pleasant lemon scent. I climbed up top, my arms like wet noodles. Then I turned on my butt, stripped off my rain jacket, and wiped the sweat and slime from my face with the collar of my shirt.

Dad moved back and forth, checking his watch, muttering something about how he didn't see any point in dropping the anchor, there wasn't time. I felt the chill of the morning air, saw the pink light in the hills behind us, the pale clouds overhead. So much for going to bed, I said to myself. The only thing we could do now was head back out and start fishing.

"So how you feeling?" I asked Dad about a half hour later as we neared Cape Ulitka, the wind a little more brisk up here on top of the cabin, but feeling kind of good the way it rustled through my clothes. "You going to be OK?"

"I'm still alive, aren't I? What more could I ask?"

I gazed at the waves smashing against the rocks at the base of the cape. "How 'bout sleep? You've barely had any for the last two days."

Dad shook his head. "That's nothing. When things weren't going well with your mother, when we were fighting all the time, I used to go nights without sleep all the time." He chuckled. "Things weren't so great when you were little, either. Even if I managed to nod off, you'd be sure to wake me up. God, what a set of lungs you had! I guess loud things come in small packages."

I glanced at my boots, still shiny and wet. "I'm sorry about what I said to you when I was pitching."

"Don't worry, it's not the first time someone's told me that." Dad blinked and rubbed his fingers against his temples. "What about you? You feel OK?"

"I feel like I'm dreaming."

"Don't be dreaming when you're out on deck. I don't want anyone getting hurt, especially you."

"I think I'll be all right," I said, fighting off a yawn. "You think we'll do better than yesterday?"

"I'd be satisfied if we did as good, or even half as good. Although it wouldn't hurt to do even better. Because I've still got a ways to go, to make those payments. You know how much that fuckin' permit cost me? Fifty grand, for a lousy piece of paper."

"So we still gotta catch a lot more?"

Dad shook his head. "Not that many. A good day today, a couple good openings after that, and everything should work out fine."

Behind us the skiff rocked up and down, the tire lashed to its bow squeaking against the bigger boat's stern.

"But it won't really be fine, will it?"

"Whatcha mean, Pete?"

"You know... with Mom."

Dad frowned at me. "I already told you how I feel about that, so there's no point talking any more about it. Your mother's made a decision and now she has to live with it. And so do we. I'm not happy about it, of course I'm not. But it doesn't help to sit around and mope." He pointed toward Cape Ulitka. "Especially when we got more urgent things to worry about."

Five minutes later I went down the ladder at the rear of the cabin and into the galley. Wade looked just like he had when we waited to unload our fish, asleep on the side bench, his mouth open, his red hunting jacket across his chest. Gordon leaned forward on his elbows and stared out the window, while George fumbled with a pot of coffee on the stove. "You want some, Pete?" he asked, lifting the pot by its black handle. Then, looking more closely at me, "I think I'm going to make you, whether you want it or not."

I sat down on the bench next to Gordon and closed my eyes. The dreamy feeling came quickly this time. It seemed like yesterday morning was now a couple days ago, that our last set after dinner was really around noon. My head buzzed and trembled, as if inside it a reel of film had rattled off track. Something clinked beneath my nose, hot steam rising into my nostrils. "Keep having a cup every few hours," George said. "All day long."

"But what about Wade?" I asked.

George frowned. "He'll be OK. Even if I have to kick him in the ass." Wade's butt was a big target right now, slouching over the edge of the bench. George grabbed him by the shoulder and squeezed his arm, his fingernails pressing through Wade's shirt.

Wade sat up slowly, blinking and shaking his head. "We're going to try one pretty quick here," George told him. "So you better get out on deck."

"Don't worry about me," Wade said.

"The hell I won't. Now get off your ass."

Outside the wind was stiffer than the day before, the swells a little deeper, with more snap. The caffeine raced in my veins, and the cold air made me even more alert. The ocean had that same slate-gray color to it, with little white peaks and ridges. Gordon climbed into the skiff, and Wade and I tied in all the lines on the stern. I had to wait for Wade a couple times. Then we moved back to the main part of the deck.

The boat rolled harder once the net was in the water, and Gordon had trouble keeping the skiff straight. But I was too cold to worry. Inside the galley I warmed my hands, watching the salt shaker on the table tilt and finally topple over. George filled a stew pot with water and set it on the stove's hottest part. Some of the water sloshed over the edge, dancing and sizzling in a cloud of steam. Another swell hit us, and a stool teetered and then fell, banging against the linoleum floor. George reached to grab it, and he slipped, too.

Through the rear door I saw water flood in at the base of the bulwarks, sending a broom and the metal bucket sliding across the deck. Wade had his arm crooked around the towbit, the thighs of his jeans soaked by the spray. He was swearing.

I turned toward George. "I thought we were supposed to have nice weather!"

George sat back against the galley wall, clutching the table with both hands. "We were. But that doesn't mean we will."

Out on deck the wind blew steady and stiff. Dad told us to lower one of the stabilizer poles, just to be safe, and Wade and I tossed the heavy steel weights over the side. Far off our starboard the skiff rose and fell, each time disappearing beneath the trough, so all you could see was the hood of Gordon's parka, a green dot against the water. Gordon closed the circle ten minutes later, and we began bringing the net on board. I kept my legs spread wide, my head down, my chin almost against my chest. I concentrated on making a perfect figure-eight with the cork-line. I did all I could not to think about anything else.

After a while I looked up, thought I saw a jumper, and wondered if we'd get another big bag. But we didn't see a thing once the net shrunk small, and we'd caught less than a hundred fish. Dad said we'd try it again right away, that we'd keep whacking away until something happened. Unless the wind got really bad. But the wind stayed the same—stiff and steady, not really dangerous, just making our jobs a lot more difficult. The fishing stayed the same, too, and at about 10 a.m. Gordon said maybe the salmon had shot their wad. But Dad said they couldn't have, not the way they were jumping all over the place the day before.

Around noon Dad told us to relax for half an hour, because he wanted to run down the beach, closer to Cape Addington. George served tuna sandwiches on paper towels, with ridged potato chips and carrots sliced lengthwise. A fresh pot of coffee bubbled on the stove, held in place by side-stays clamped to the railing. The boat rocked suddenly to the port, and a little of the liquid slipped out of the snub-nosed snout, onto the hot steel surface. Gordon watched the puddle sizzle, until nothing was left. "So much for getting a deck-load—if this keeps up we'll be lucky to cover our shaft alley."

George lowered his sandwich back to his plate. "Now don't go getting all pessimistic again. Things might change around faster than you believe."

"You really think so?" Gordon said. "Or are you just saying it to make me feel better?"

"Damn right I'm serious. I want more money. For me and my boy. For Mike, too. Hell, for all you guys."

It wasn't easy to imagine George with a baby in his arms—his hands looked too big to safely hold one. But I figured it was probably pretty hard to imagine Dad with me before I was born, too.

Wade gulped from a plastic tumbler of milk, then wiped the moustache from his lip with the back of his fist. "I want all the money I can get," he said.

"You're not the only one," George replied. "'Cause I'll tell you guys..." He set down his sandwich again and waited. "My son Robbie ain't gonna be like me, he's not going to piss away all these years trying to scratch out a living chasing fish."

"You mean he's going be a brain surgeon?" Gordon said.

"He's going to be something, I'll tell you that. Something important."

Wade looked insulted. "But fishing *is* important."

"Oh sure it is," George replied. "But I say let someone else do it for a while. That is, if anyone's doing it twenty years from now.

Maybe the Russians or the Japanese, or maybe all of us combined, maybe we'll kill off the whole goddamned thing."

"Geez, George," Gordon said, "you're starting to sound like me. Although you're probably right about no one doing this forever."

I know *I* won't, I thought, chewing slowly on my sandwich. No matter what Dad says. Mom had a point about not always doing what other people want.

"But we're doing it right now," Gordon said, and then he stood up and dropped his plate in the sink. "So let's do it good. Let's do it—hell, let's do it for Robbie Richards."

George said, "You know you make me sick sometimes?"

Gordon said, "I know," and stepped outside. Dad slipped past him, stuck his head into the galley, and told us to get ready right away.

As soon as we set, we saw a couple jumpers, coming straight down the middle, and George said, "Damn! Maybe it's startin' all over again!"

He was right, it was. We had six hundred, as bright and feisty as the day before, and things got better after that. At two in the afternoon we brailed, taking a dozen scoops, and at three we brailed again. The swell was bigger than the day before, but we were better at brailing, we had more practice. Now it was four o'clock, and every time I looked I saw humpies jumping, sometimes two or three at once, their tails wriggling and their bodies arching before they splashed down. Dad circled around and lined us up with Cape Addington, farther out from where a horde of boats drifted close to its rocky spire.

We cut loose the skiff, and let the net tumble into the water.

That was when the wind picked up.

It raced from the south and west, so you could see it before it hit, rippling the ocean's surface, hurtling toward us with a whistling sound, rattling the rigging, making the hull groan, whipping my hair across my face, pushing back my head, forcing me to grasp at something to hold. I moved to the stern and dropped to one knee, watched the boom jerk back and forth, felt the boat roll one way, and then the other. Here we go, I thought. Here we really go.

Then I staggered to the rear of the cabin and quickly climbed the ladder, gripping the rungs with both fists. Dad had his hands wrapped around the railing of the flying bridge, his head tilted and his hair parted so you could see the thinning spot on top, the white of his scalp. He looked at me, then looked back toward the skiff. I shifted closer, my mouth near his ear.

"Where did *this* come from?"

"I heard about it a little while ago, on the radio," Dad replied in a low, quiet voice. "That it was coming up the coast."

"You think maybe we shouldn't have set?"

Dad reached over the side and held out his hand, palm-first. The wind pushed back his wrist and fingers. "It's not that bad," he said with a shrug. "We can fish it."

I grabbed the binoculars, scrunched up my head against the wind, and focused on Cape Addington. "Those guys over there, it looks like they're running for shelter."

Dad said, "Give me those," and gripped the binoculars with both fists, barely leaving me time to loop the strap off my head. Then he stared through them for a long time. "If they are," he finally said, "that's their mistake. Not ours."

"You sure?"

"You bet. Because there's goddamned jumpers all over the place. Look. Right there!" He pointed about fifty yards off the starboard, where two humpies leaped twice each. But I was still watching the other boats.

"And don't let those other guys get all concerned, because there's no reason for it." He grabbed his cap from near his feet, and slipped it on. "Not with this kind of chance to make money." Under his breath he muttered, "Jesus."

I watched two boats heading north along the shore, lifting and falling in the swell. "If you think so," I said quietly. I headed back down the ladder. Pretty soon the skiff had turned our way, and I could see Gordon clutching the wheel, his elbows tight at his side and his head scrunched up, like someone driving a bumper car and about to get slammed. The skiff rose in one direction, then slapped down, and a big wave crashed against the side. Gordon ducked, but he still got soaked.

I grabbed hold of the mast, letting my hips sway as the boat pitched to the port. The skiff was close now, and you could hear the rise and fall of its engine. Wade balanced one knee on the deck with his arms spread wide, as if he were a gymnast completing a tricky maneuver. George's arms were folded across his chest. "Just do your jobs, guys. If you feel like fucking up, don't. Not this set, anyways."

Wade nodded as he got to his feet. Gordon pulled the skiff alongside us, handed off his line, and cut behind the stern. Then we began bringing the net on board. Every minute or so Wade or I fell, and once I landed hard on both knees. But fish were jumping all around us, and I knew this could be a big one, bigger than before. The rings came up, closing off the bottom of the net, and Dad and George jammed in the big steel hook that held them in place. George joined us on the pile, stumbling twice before he got there, and Dad started the power block again, the web billowing stiffly in the wind, the black mesh wrapping around us. Sometimes it caught on the pulley-block hooks, forcing us to pluck and peel it off as quickly as we could. Jellyfish the size of silver dollars drummed on our heads, and the boat kept rocking, the seine forming an enormous hump. Now I really felt like I was dreaming, and not at all ready to wake up.

George yelled, "Watch out! Red!" and I wondered what he was so excited about. But as I turned, the wind lifted the net in front of my face and something huge and hot pushed against me, knocking my cap off and smearing my mouth, my nose, and my eyes.

I let go of the cork-line, and heard someone yell, "Peter! Don't!" but it was too late, I was on my knees now, then on my side, twisting like an animal stung by a snake, both eyes closed, my nostrils on fire, trying to spit, trying to spit the flaming poison from my mouth.

"Peter, get up! Get up!" But I covered my ears, then flopped over on my back.

"Damnit, Peter! We *need* you!"

For the first time I opened my eyes, saw Dad towering over me, his feet spread wide, one hand clutching the cork-line, pulling it down, his face twisted from the strain, his arm bulging.

"Come on! Get on your feet!" Then, more quietly, "It's only jellyfish. It hurts, sure it hurts, but it's not going to kill you. Now come on and get back to work."

My face burned and my mouth was filled with a hot, bitter taste. But I didn't have much choice. Slowly I got to my feet.

"We all set?" Dad said.

I nodded, and Dad shifted the hydraulics back on, making the boat tremble and the power block spin.

Wade nudged me with his elbow. "Hang in there, Peter. We got a lotta fuckin' fish this time."

Within a couple minutes the net was just a small pool, maybe ten or twelve feet long, five or six feet wide, and I knew Wade was right. The fish flapped and fought and splashed, and two of them leaped all the way over the cork-line. You had to admire the way they were struggling. If I were them, I thought, kind of sleepily, I might just give up, let whatever happens, happen. You can't fight everything in life.

"Get the brailer!" Dad yelled.

"We gonna hook up the skiff?" Wade shouted back.

"Too dangerous. We'll have to scoop 'em out ourselves."

The big bag rose so high with the swell that all the water drained out, the salmon drawn together. Wade used a plunger pole to push the cork-line away from the boat, widening the neck of the bag. George and I dragged along the brailer, scoop after scoop, for what seemed like hours. Finally the bag was small enough that we were able to use the winch and power block to hoist it on deck. Then we spilled the rest of the catch into the hold so that the fish piled up almost as high as the day before.

It seemed very late now, and the sky was getting dark. Maybe it was only the clouds, fat with rain. I felt kind of peaceful, the way we were rolling back and forth, the wind whistling above us. Maybe we're done for the day, I thought. Maybe the whole opener is over, and we've made another thousand bucks. And maybe I'll finally get some sleep.

But as soon as I closed my eyes, Dad shouted, "Get ready! We got time for one more."

"*What*?"

"You heard him, Pete," Wade said, kind of hesitantly. "So let's go."

Gordon bounded out of the skiff, stumbled on the net pile, then lunged at a line stretched taut across the deck. "You sure about this?"

Dad sighed. "What do *you* think?"

"I'm getting the shit kicked out of me in the skiff! That's what I think! And I don't want the goddamned thing to flip when I'm inside!"

"It's not going to," Dad said, "and we don't got time to argue." He pointed at the hatch covers. "You know we probably had about four thousand fuckin' fish that set alone, if that means anything to you."

Gordon held out his long thin fingers, as if he were admiring them. "Oh, it means a tremendous amount to me. It means more to me than anything else in the world."

I looked toward Cape Addington. Only a couple boats were working now, wide steel ones, a lot wider than us. George glanced in the same direction, but looked away. "Come on, Gordo," he said. "I think the wind's come down a little bit. And just think, one more haul like that last one, who knows, we might deck-load this baby yet."

"Yeah," Dad added more quietly, "we'll make it quick. No point in towing much, the way the fish are so bunched up."

Gordon shrugged, then shivered. "What the fuck. It's not like I really have a choice."

"No," Dad said. "You don't."

Gordon climbed slowly into the skiff, and Dad headed back up the ladder. He gunned the engine, ran the boat ahead a little ways, stared back at us silently, nodded, and made a quick chopping motion with his hand. Gordon zipped up his parka and gripped the wheel, spinning it as the net paid off the stern, turning the little boat in a half-circle. The first wave hit him head on, a big one, the biggest I'd seen all day, and the skiff reared back like a horse on its hind legs.

"Shit!" Gordon said. His bow slammed down, the spray splatting against him, and then the big wave hit us, our stern lifting out of the water, making my legs bend forward, my butt sag toward the deck. Wade dropped to one knee. George shook his head and shivered, his cap blown off, seawater dripping from his hair. The skiff was flattening out now, but Gordon was still bouncing around, struggling to get control. After a while we couldn't see him anymore, just the skiff, a dull silver lump rising and falling against the water.

George shook his head. "At least it's our last set. Thank the Lord God for that."

"Maybe it will be my last set, ever," I said.

"Why, Pete?" Wade asked, down on one knee again. "You gonna quit just when we start doing good?"

"I don't know what I'm going to do." I ran my right pinky beneath my left eye. "But my face feels like somebody dumped battery acid in it."

"Don't worry," Wade replied in a girly voice. "You're still pretty to me."

Another wave hit us on the stern, and I grasped the railing. I waited until we had flattened out. "You know," I said, looking right at Wade, "we still gotta pitch these bastards sometime tonight. It's not going to be very easy."

"I know that, Pete."

"Well, don't *crap* out on me. Like you did last night."

Wade got quickly to his feet. "I was pitching twice as fast as you!"

He took a step toward me, his throat tense, but I didn't move, I just kept grasping the railing. If he punches me, maybe I won't have to help bring in the net, I thought. But George stepped between us. "Come on, guys," he said, clutching the towbit. "You can fight all you want after we get this net on board. Because if you really want to know, you were both pretty goddamned slow."

"I didn't see *you* down there," Wade said.

"Me, neither," I added, and climbed back up the ladder. I started across the top of the cabin, but the wind felt a lot stronger up here, it forced me to crouch on all fours, the heels of my hands pressing hard against the sand-coated surface. I made it to the bench-top, and sat down next to Dad. His eyes looked small, smaller than I'd ever seen them, smaller even than the night he dragged the crew out of bed in Craig. His cap was gone, it must have blown overboard, and he kept raking his hand through his hair. Far away the skiff was getting tossed hard, its bow rearing up, then slamming down, the waves tall and white all around it.

"What's wrong?" I said.

"I shouldn't have let the net go."

"You shouldn't have what!"

"I shouldn't have let it go."

I stared at him. He grabbed the binoculars and trained them on the skiff. "I didn't realize it was blowin' so fuckin' hard. It's worse now. Worse than last set."

Something heavy and wet, like fresh dough, slid down my throat, deep into my gut, almost out the other end. "So how are we going to get it back on board?"

Dad's jaw seemed locked in place, even when he spoke. "We'll do it, Pete. Don't worry. We'll do it one way or another."

We were closer to Cape Addington now, its triangle of rock poking through a band of mist like something out of a fairy tale. I couldn't see any other boats. I looked all around me, and finally I spotted a couple running back toward Cape Ulitka, their nets on their sterns, their skiffs strapped behind them.

"Where the hell is everyone?"

Dad tried to smile. "I guess we're the lone wolf on this one, Peter."

"But if something happens—"

"I know, Pete. That's why we gotta make sure nothing does." He grabbed the microphone from its hook and said something into it. "I just told Gordon to close her up, he'll be swinging around in a couple minutes. Just do everything like we always do. And don't tell George and Wade what I said."

He tapped his knuckles against the seat of the bench. "But remember. Just in case something ... happens, the survival suits, all five of them, they're right in here."

"Jesus!"

Dad rested his hand on my shoulder. "Don't worry, I'm saying this just like they do on airplanes, just so you'll know what's goin' on. Understand?"

I nodded.

"How's your face feel?"

"It's OK."

"Good. Let's get this baby on board."

I climbed down the ladder, grabbed onto the davit, and stared over the bulwarks. The boat wasn't responding like before. The hull lay farther on its side with each swell, and jerked back with more snap. "The weather's gotten worse, hasn't it, Pete?" Wade said, the big yellow hood of his rain jacket pulled over his head, seawater dripping down his cheeks, his eyes sleepy and dull. "Just our fuckin' luck, huh?"

George stepped out on deck from the galley, a sopping red rag in his hand. "I hope you guys weren't too hungry," he said, flinging the rag back onto the table. "Because that pot roast I had in the oven, the oven door slid open, and—well, take a look for yourselves."

I stuck my head inside, smelled the delicious odor of cooking meat, then saw the pool of grease across the linoleum, the scattered chunks of carrots and celery and onion, and the watery pink blood from the roast.

"Oh, shit," Wade said. "I'm *starving*."

And then I was, too, thinking about Sunday dinner at home, imagining the thick brown gravy spilling over mashed potatoes, and the hot creamed corn, the cool glasses of milk, the puffy rolls baked brown on the bottom, the knives and forks and spoons gleaming against white cloth napkins, the porcelain pots with their swirly blue designs. I pictured Mom and Dad and me sitting down to eat, knowing we had the whole afternoon, that we could take all the time we wanted. And that we could relax with iced tea and sugar cookies for dessert.

Now I heard the skiff, the horrible rise and fall of its engine dragging me back on deck. Gordon was soaked, his long hair plastered to his face in thick black streaks, his head cocked, his eyes half-closed. He flipped one line to Wade, and then he maneuvered the skiff toward the stern, waited until the end of the net lifted up, gunned his engine and shot beneath it. He threw me his other line, and I caught it with one hand and fell to my knees. The boat was jerking hard now, but Dad moved quickly around deck, telling everyone what to do, his voice as steady as usual. If we can just get the net on board, I said to myself. I said it again and again, until the words no longer made sense. Ifwecanjustgetthenettonboard. But why think about it? It doesn't help. It doesn't help at all. The only thing that helps is what you do.

I grabbed the cork-line and began pulling it down from the block. It came easier than I expected, and a few minutes later the rings were up, we were almost done. For the first time I wondered if we'd catch any fish. I saw two jumpers, then two more, then two after that. And now the net began to boil with motion. Fish jumped and twisted and slithered against each other, beating the swelling surface into a froth. More of the seine came up on deck and what was left was just a dense, dark mass, heaving against us like a single animal.

"Oh my fuckin' God!" Wade said, both hands gripping the web, the veins bulging in his throat. Then, in almost a whisper, "Have you ever seen anything ... like *that*?"

"Get the brailer," Dad said. "Be careful but work fast. Let's get these bastards on board as quick as we can."

Wade and I grabbed the hoop net and we began to scoop, the sky getting darker overhead, us leaning over the bulwarks, staring into the black swarm of fish, me getting dizzier and dizzier, forgetting everything for a while, thinking this is so much better than pot, so much more bizarre. We let each scoop spill into the open hold, the level of the dying fish rising like a river, until finally they flowed over the hatch and flooded the deck.

"Just keep dumping 'em," Dad said. "We'll take as many as we can, wherever we can take 'em."

"Jesus," George whispered. "A fuckin' deck-load."

Dad nodded. "It's a deck-load all right."

I looked at all the fish and felt a chill, first in my fingers and wrists and arms, and then in my chest. "But how many can we take?" I shouted.

"Like I said," Dad yelled back, "as many as we can. Just keep dumping 'em, let me worry about that."

Out in the skiff Gordon was still getting tossed around, but he didn't seem afraid anymore, he was looking back at us over his shoulder, watching us work. Once he took one hand off the wheel, and pumped his fist in the air.

And the fish kept spilling on deck. They slid against the bulwarks, against the board in front of the net, against the door at the rear of the cabin. They splashed onto other fish and banged against our ankles, struggling forward as if the deck were a crowded stream and they were still determined to spawn. Dad stood back and gripped a cleat on the mast, smiling, almost laughing, even as he teetered with the swell.

We're rich! I thought.

All of a sudden Dad's face twisted into a frown, the color vanished from his flesh, and he came trudging through the flopping fish, scissoring his arms like a referee signaling an incomplete pass. "OK, guys, that's it! That's it! Let the rest go!"

"Let 'em go?" Wade said.

"Yes, goddamnit! Let 'em go!"

We cut loose the end of the net, at least a thousand humpies still shifting around, some darting away, some floating belly-up, dead. "Don't even bother to hook up Gordon!" Dad shouted. "We'll run to the north side of Addington, then we'll try." He turned and climbed the ladder, two rungs at a time. I heard the engine shift into gear, our bow swinging around, the waves hitting us sideways instead of from behind. I said to myself, This day is done, it's over—thank you, God, for that. But something was wrong.

The waves washed across the bulwarks, sending the fish whooshing back and forth. Timidly, I glanced over the side, and then I saw how low we sat, the water only a foot or two from the railing. Everything thickened inside me. I thought of something I'd heard about soldiers crapping their drawers. The boat rolled again, and now it was happening. Water crashed over the side, hitting me at the knees, knocking me down. I screamed. Behind me George groaned and then Dad was flinging the bright orange packets, like miniature duffle bags, down onto the deck, into the swirl of water and fish.

"Jesus Christ!" Wade yelled, and he kicked off his boots, tore off his rain jacket, snatched one of the bags and yanked out the thick orange rubber suit, the arms and legs unfolding from it like an inflatable toy.

"What the *hell*?" George said, sitting on his butt, rubbing his head. And then, "Oh, Jesus!" and he crawled through the fish on all fours and grasped for one of the bags. Wade already had his legs inside of his, and was slipping in his arms. The other three suits lay scattered across the deck, half-buried now. I lunged after one of them, falling face first into the salmon, a tail slapping across my eyes, the orange bag sliding from my reach.

I got ready to go after it again, but something occurred to me that I couldn't ignore. I turned and grabbed hold of the ladder, hoisting myself up rung by rung, and I crawled across the top of the cabin, everything tilted at a sickening angle. I clenched the railing behind the bench. Dad stood with his feet spread, one hand on the wheel, the other gripping the microphone. He held the microphone to his mouth and shouted into it, something about Cape Addington. Then, more quietly. "Yes, that's it." A pause. "OK. Gotchya." Another, longer pause. "We'll do our best."

"Where's *yours*?" I screamed.

"My what?" he shouted back.

"Your survival suit!"

"I don't need it right now."

"Are we sinking?"

Dad glanced at the deck, at the way water and fish sloshed back and forth. Then he stared ahead, toward the jagged spire of Cape Addington.

"Yeah, Pete," he said, almost quietly, "I think we are."

"Then put your suit on!"

"I can't! I can't steer with it on!"

"But you just said we were sinking!"

"I don't know! I don't know what the hell's goin' on!" His head dropped, as if he were studying something on the dashboard. He looked back toward land, his hands squeezing the wheel, his body shaking, his eyes dripping with spray. "Just do as I say, Peter, put on your own suit and hang on—you watch, we'll ride this bastard out yet! 'Cause no fuckin' ocean's takin' my boat and fish!"

Then came a shuddering groan, pushing us over, lifting us high, higher than you're meant to go, until everything in front of us turned sideways. Dad slid away from me on his back, his boots in the air, his forearms crossed above his face, and I felt myself falling, as far as you can fall.

I didn't feel cold. I didn't feel anything at all. I opened my eyes now, realized that my head was above water, that I floated with my boots on, that I wasn't yet dead. This last thought occurred slowly, like the sun creeping above a ridge of mountains. I tried to scream but got a mouthful of salty water, and what came out was a gurgling croak. I ducked my head and stripped off my rain jacket, pulled my knees to my chest and yanked free my boots. My arms pushed out from my chest in short, jerky motions, and my feet began to kick behind me. Out in front I saw nothing but ocean, the twisting white peaks of distant waves.

Then I turned and saw the *Ambition*. It was on its side, maybe thirty feet away, the cabin half beneath the surface, dead fish and paper plates and cardboard canisters of Quaker Oatmeal bobbing in a widening slick of oil. I got ready to swim for it, but I couldn't, the waves kept pulling me away. And it didn't matter, the boat was going down fast. The denim of my jeans clung heavily to my legs, the wet wool of my socks drooped from my feet, my long thermal undershirt tugged at my arms. I wondered if Dad was drowning, too.

About a hundred yards away two bright-orange things floated like enormous seals, the arms on one of them paddling wildly. George and Wade. They were too far away to do me any good. I hated them now, for having on those nice warm suits. I yelled, but my voice was useless against the roar of the wind. I felt very cold very suddenly, and then kind of warm, and I thought, Mom's going to be pissed if Dad and me die.

I closed my eyes again and let my whole body sink beneath the surface. I wondered if I'd ever touch bottom. When I came back up the boat had gone all the way under, nothing but the garbage and the dead fish and the bubbling surface of oil. I took a big mouthful of water, hated its taste, spat it out and closed my eyes again. Then I remembered something from a swimming class about floating on your back, and I arched my spine as best I could. But it all seemed pointless now. I felt very sleepy, and sad, because everything was so unfair. My arms moved more and more slowly, as if they didn't belong to me anymore, and I wondered how much longer. And whether it would hurt. An engine whined far away, and I wondered where it was going, why it was in such a hurry. It was hard to think about anything for very long. But now the screeching sound was right above me. Twirling in the water I saw something huge and gray, and my first thought was to dive out of the way. Breaking the surface again I saw a tall man with long wet hair, waving his arms and shouting.

Gordon.

A yellow rope sprung from his arm like magic, and landed about ten yards from my head. I swam face down with short, choppy strokes, and when I opened my eyes the rope was only a few feet away. I leaped after it the way a fish chases a lure, snatching it with both hands and twisting it around my wrists.

"Wrap it beneath your armpits! Tight!" Gordon yelled, and then he began pulling me toward him. The aluminum siding of the skiff was looming closer, but the swell kept dragging it in the other direction, and then it all began to seem like a bad, bad dream, the kind in which no matter how hard you run you can't get to where you're going. "Damnit, Peter!" I heard Gordon yell. "Quit fighting it! Just relax!"

I stopped thinking. I let the water take over. My head sunk beneath the surface again. I shut my eyes and mouth, and waited to come back up. I felt as if I waited forever. But then Gordon had me by the arms and was lifting me into the little boat. I didn't know where I was, except that it was somewhere where I could breathe. I rolled on my side, spat out a couple mouthfuls of seawater, turned onto my back, and stared into the sky. Slowly I got to my knees. And then I remembered again.

"Where is he?"

Gordon acted like he hadn't heard me.

"Have you seen him?"

"Yes, damnit," Gordon said. "Now just hang on."

We cut back to where the *Ambition* used to be, through the garbage and the oil and the fish, and I wrapped both arms around the side of the skiff. My breath was coming back to normal now, but my heart was still racing like crazy. I shifted around in a half-circle, trying to take in the entire ocean at once, knowing, believing, at least, that he was out there somewhere, waiting for us, waiting for as long as he had to.

"Right there!" Gordon said.

Beyond the edge of the slick I spotted him, grasping a wooden stool, bobbing and spitting, sometimes sinking but then coming back up, his boots and his jacket still on, his free arm jerking around like he didn't know how to swim.

Gordon gunned the engine even harder now, and when we got nearer he flung Dad the rope. Dad clutched at it and pulled hand over hand over hand, as if he were yanking the skiff to him. We moved alongside him, his body lifting in the swell, and we grabbed him by the arms and dragged him chest-first over the side. As soon as we let go, he slumped against the railing in the stern, sucking in air in throaty gasps.

"Keep an eye on him," Gordon said. Then he spun the wheel and the skiff heaved up and down against the swell, slowly pivoting until we pointed toward Wade and George. Gordon sped up the engine again, and now the skiff tilted from side to side, sometimes balancing for too long on the crest of a wave, sometimes pounding us hard against the trough. Dad was crouched on his hands and knees, braced against the side of the skiff, coughing up seawater. I climbed into the stern with him, and tried to steady his shoulders with my hands, but he twisted away from me, still coughing and spitting.

We got Wade on board, kicking and swearing, and then we picked up George. He rolled hard over the side, his ribs slamming against the floor of the skiff. "Jesus," he said with a groan, and for a moment he just lay there, his breath going in and out, faster and faster. Finally he climbed slowly to his knees and ripped the rubber hood from his head. Then he looked at Dad, clutching the side railing now with both arms. "So what the hell now?"

Gordon pointed just to the left of Cape Addington. "We'll try to run for that cove. If we can make it."

"We *better* make it!" Wade said, the survival suit pulled down to his waist, his elbows tucked against his ribs, his hands clutching his shoulders.

"Yeah, we better," Gordon replied. A big wave hit us, jerking us all back. "You're damn right we better."

I crouched in the stern, next to Dad. His eyes were closed, but his chest was going in and out, and he was shaking. I put one arm around him and turned him toward me. "You all right?" I said.

His eyes opened, closed, and opened again. "Yeah," he finally replied in a mumbling whisper. Then, sitting up, "Pete... The boat?"

I hesitated, thinking of the oil and the fish, the way the mast had jabbed through the water before everything disappeared. "I don't know about the boat. But everyone else. We're all here."

"Good," he replied after a long pause.

The waves were still hitting us hard, but we were getting used to it now, we weren't getting slammed around like before. Gordon had both hands on the wheel, spinning it first one way and then the other, trying to line us up with the half-hidden cove just to the left of Cape Addington. The beach was sandy in front of the cove, but everywhere else was fronted by rocks. "Better hang on tight, folks," Gordon said. "God knows what'll happen once we get a little closer."

Wade started to say something, but he never finished, and it didn't matter because all of a sudden all we could hear was the roar of something huge and round directly above us, its red-and-white underside lit up in its own light.

Coast Guard, I thought. Yes. Coast Guard.

"Awright!" Wade shouted. "*Aw*right!" Gordon spun the wheel again, this time back in, away from the beach. George climbed hesitantly to a crouch, then waved the bright orange arms of his survival suit. The helicopter was dipping toward us.

I squeezed Dad's arm and whispered, "Look."

Dad sat up again. "Good," he finally replied. He hung his head, choked up two spurts of water, coughed some more, and wiped something from his nose. Then he closed his eyes.

I turned and arched my back, struck by an arrow of fear. "You think he's all right?" I said to George. I trembled all over when I said it, and for the first time I realized how cold I still was, how wet. "Isn't there something I should do?"

George looked at me and shrugged. "Don't worry about it, Pete. He's just sleeping. That's all. Just let him sleep."

"You sure?"

"Yeah. I'm sure." He spat over the side. "A guy needs his sleep now and then, you know."

Dad shifted around in my arms, his eyes still closed, his neck twisting one way and then the other. I thought of this morning, and the morning before that, and all the mornings since we left Bellingham, Dad getting out of bed after an hour's sleep, the dark pouches beneath his eyes, the clumps of matted hair, the straggly strands of beard, the struggle to keep his head from falling, collapsing from all that weight. "Maybe you're right," I finally replied, trying to smile, turning back toward George. "Because it's about time he got some sleep."

"You're damn right it is. So just let him be."

I stared out over the ocean, the white peaks twisting, the little hills collapsing, then forming all over again, and I tried to pinpoint where the boat had gone down. But I couldn't see a thing. The helicopter moved closer, and Dad pressed his face to my shoulder, his wet hair on my throat. I stopped looking at the water and held him more tightly, one hand gripping his arm, the other moving in circles around his back. I tried to think of something to say, something to make him feel better, but I figured it was better not to say anything. I didn't want him adding up his losses.

So I just sat there, imagining we were already inside the helicopter, rising above everything else. I imagined climbing onto an airplane in Ketchikan with pretty stewardesses and heavy brown blankets and hot coffee, then going home. Although even now that wasn't an especially pleasant thought. It was hard to say how Dad would feel about anything, now that the boat was gone. But there was no time to worry about that. Sometimes it was better not to try to plan too far ahead.

I thought, for a moment, of the time when I was still in elementary school, a damp, cloudy Saturday morning in the fall, when Dad and I had hiked up the hills above Chuckanut Drive to watch the dog salmon spawn. The trails had been slick with mud, and the air had that funny sour smell that comes after a heavy rain. It was kind of frightening, in a way. The salmon's hides had turned brown or red or green, and, on the males, sharp teeth jutted from their enlarged beaks. Dad said that was because they'd stopped feeding weeks ago, and that by the time they got here they didn't have much time left. Farther upstream I found a male's bloated carcass, its eye sockets empty like craters. I stared at it for a long time.

"That's gross," I finally said.

Dad nodded, then broke off a tiny bare branch from an elm tree that hung over the water, and crouched down closer to the salmon. "It's too bad that's the way the whole thing has to end," he said, testing the soft dead flesh with the stick. "Especially when you think how beautiful they are when they first come in from the ocean. But what the heck, Pete? You think these fish would want to go through the whole goddang thing again?" He shrugged, then cast the stick into the creek. "I sure wouldn't."

Now he was quiet in my arms, but I could feel the pulse of his blood, the heave of his chest, the warmth of his body against mine.

Glossary of Terms

Boldt decision A controversial ruling by Judge George Boldt. In the early 1970s, local Native American tribes in Puget Sound began to petition for fishing rights that would allow them to manage the fishery as an equal partner with the State of Washington. With celebrities like Marlon Brando working on their behalf, the tribes' cause became more visible to the public. The key decision came in 1974, when Judge Boldt announced that the salmon runs would be split 50/50 between Native American and non–Native American fishermen. The result was that non–Native American fishermen, who were more numerous, began to see their allocation of salmon fall significantly, while the smaller number of Native American fishermen saw their share of the salmon grow.

brailing The method of using a large hoop net, or **brailer**, when there is no other way to get the fish on board from the net that has trapped the salmon. The brailer is a large netted mesh hoop, about three or four feet across, that has a release opening at the bottom. Once the bag of fish is positioned over the fish hold, a crew member gives the signal to let the brailer open, and the salmon tumble into the fish hold. This maneuver is repeated until the fish are all in the fish hold. This is exciting when it happens, and is also safer than gradually leveraging the huge net of salmon on board the boat.

corking To "cork" someone is to cut in front of another purse seiner and drop one's net where the other vessel was about to fish. The practice is frowned upon, and, at the time of this novel, was largely unpoliced. Sometimes, the boat that has been corked retaliates.

drum A large piece of machinery shaped like a spool of thread on its side, used to spool the **seine** on board the boat. Drums have long been banned in Alaska, because they make the purse-seining vessels less stable. Mike Kristiansen had to rejigger his vessel in order to fish in Alaska.

"fish" This is jargon denoting that in rough weather, purse seiners often drop weighted steel "fish" to help stabilize their boats. (Also see **wings**).

fish hold As the name suggests, this is where the dead fish are kept. Crew members must periodically check the hold for possible oil leaks. Older wooden vessels tend to have more problems with leaks.

hairpin Each time a purse seiner makes a **set**—that is, releases its net, corks, and web—the hairpin is inserted to close up the net. Otherwise, the salmon would all swim away.

humpies This is the most plentiful variety of salmon by far. The vast majority of the humpies (also known as pink salmon) end up in canneries. The so-called "money fish"—including silvers, dog salmon, and kings—pay a higher premium.

jumpers When salmon are migrating, they often leap out of the water for an instant.

opener In both Puget Sound and Southeastern Alaska, fishermen must abide by regulations imposed by the U.S. Fish and Wildlife Department in these respective regions. The **opener** denotes when and how long fishermen will be allowed to fish. This is a conservation step for managing the fishery in a sustainable fashion. In Alaska, an opener can last 36 hours, or even longer if the demand is warranted by how many fish have spawned. The goal is to avoid over-fishing and manage the resource in a prudent manner.

pick Slang for "anchor."

power block A mechanized pulley located near the top of the vessel's mast. The power block was a major innovation introduced in the middle of the twentieth century, used to ratchet up the net of fish toward the mast and then bring it back down onto the stern of the vessel. Rather than spooling the corks, web, and lead-weights on a drum, using the power block contributes to the vessel's stability—a key issue in Alaska waters.

purse seiner   A fishing vessel usually more than fifty feet long that is distinguished by the way the salmon are brought up onto the boat. To catch the salmon, the net is encircled in the water, trailed behind a **skiff**. Purse seiners encircle the fish and then close the net as if closing a cloth purse with a drawstring (called the "**purse line**"), and hoists the fish onto the deck.

seine   The name for the net, corks, and web used to catch fish from a purse seiner.

set   Each time the purse seiner releases its **seine**—that is, the net, corks, and web—into the water to catch salmon, and then brings the trapped salmon on board, is called a "set." When salmon are plentiful, a purse seiner might have more than ten sets in a day.

skiff   In this context, the skiff is an aluminum diesel-powered vessel that tows the net in a half-circle before closing up the oval of corks and starting the process of bringing the salmon on board the purse seiner.

survival suits   A major advance in fishing safety in the late twentieth century, these suits provide two things essential for survival in the north Pacific: warmth and flotation. These suits are typically in bright colors, to aid visibility for rescuers.

wings   In tandem with "fish," wings, made of aluminum or some other lightweight metal, provide more stability when fishing in open ocean.

1989

Mitch Evich is the author of a collection of autobiographical essays, *A Geography of Peril*, also published in collaboration with Village Books. His earlier novel, *The Clandestine Novelist* (iUniverse), is written in the form of a mock memoir. His short stories have appeared in the *new renaissance, Fenway Fiction*, and *Further Fenway Fiction*. Most recently the author of a blog, *The Diminishing Window*, about his experience with young-onset Alzheimer's disease, Evich continues to write short stories. A native of Bellingham, Washington, he has lived in the Boston area since 1985.

CPSIA information can be obtained
at www.ICGtesting.com
Printed in the USA
LVHW091522261020
669852LV00033B/1095